ALSO BY JEAN STAFFORD

FICTION

Boston Adventure

The Mountain Lion

The Collected Stories of Jean Stafford

NONFICTION

A Mother in History

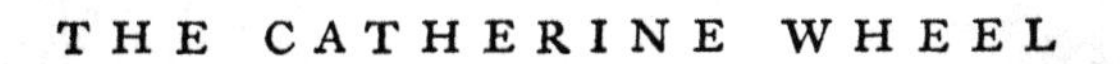

THE CATHERINE WHEEL

The Catherine Wheel

A NOVEL BY JEAN STAFFORD

FARRAR, STRAUS AND GIROUX • NEW YORK

Farrar, Straus and Giroux
175 Varick Street, New York 10014

Printed in the United States of America
Originally published in 1952 by Harcourt, Brace and Company
First Farrar, Straus and Giroux paperback edition, 2017

Library of Congress Control Number: 2017952221
Paperback ISBN: 978-0-374-53790-6

P1

To My Father and in Memory of My Mother

Man's life is a cheat and a disappointment;
All things are unreal,
Unreal or disappointing:
The Catherine wheel, the pantomime cat,
The prizes given at the children's party,
The prize awarded for the English Essay,
The scholar's degree, the statesman's decoration.
All things become less real, man passes
From unreality to unreality.

T. S. ELIOT, Murder in the Cathedral

Contents

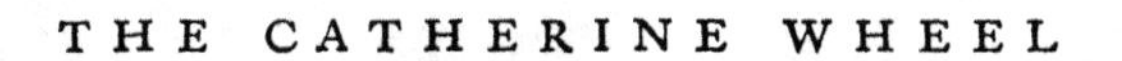
THE CATHERINE WHEEL

CHAPTER I

On the First Day of Summer

BETWEEN THE marriage elms at the foot of the broad lawn, there hung a scarlet canvas hammock where Andrew Shipley squandered the changeless afternoons of early June. Books lay in heaps beneath him on the grass, but he seldom read; he had lost the craft of losing himself and threads of adventure snarled in his mind; the simplest words looked strange. His kite was stuck in the top of a tree and black ants moved militantly over his pole and tackle box. He was waiting.

He waited, in the larger chambers of his being, for the world to right itself and to become as it had been in all the other summers here, at Congreve House in Hawthorne, far north, when he had gathered the full, free days like honey and had kept his hoard against the famine of the formal city winter when he was trammeled and smothered by school and a pedagogical governess and parents whom he barely knew and certainly did not understand.

From his Cousin Katharine Congreve's house at the top of the lawn where the long windows of the drawing room were open to admit the radiant northern air and light, there sometimes came to him the voices of his twin sisters, Honor and Harriet, who, while they embroidered, sang. Idly, he imagined Cousin Katharine crossing the room to seat herself at the easel on which her needlepoint was stretched, to resume weaving a carpet of *mille-fleurs* for the delicate feet of a unicorn and of the girl who embraced his arching neck. Now and again all three of them laughed and Andrew, lonely, tried to avert the stream of their intransigent happiness, stopped up his ears, spoke vicious words aloud; he rocked the hammock violently. But the laughter bubbled down like golden balls and then the song began again.

A gust of wind brought him the sound of the sewing-machine as the seamstress, Beulah Smithwick, making his sisters' summer wardrobes, briskly paddled the treadle. Then the neighborly telephone rang its four short, three long, one short, summoning some member of the household to receive an invitation or a carefree piece of news. Elsewhere, he knew, in Congreve House and in the orchards and gardens that blandished it, the others of the ménage were engrossed in their own styles of complacency. In the mid-afternoon, he saw Mary and Maureen, the doll-like maids, teetering a bit on their high heels, go down the graveled drive on their way to the village to shop and flirt, their limpid Irish voices dipping and ascending as if every word in the language were an endearment, their prim voile dresses not beginning to conceal the graces of their plump bosoms and their pretty legs.

He knew that Mrs. Shea, the pious cook, was telling her beads on the kitchen stoop, turning her rheumatic shoulders to the sun, her glass-green eyes half closed as, decade by decade, she further lost herself in the hope of heaven and the companionship of God. Maddox, the gardener, who was in love with flowers, would be crooning to the rosebuds and calling them by his mistress's nicknames, "Kate," "Kitty," "Kathy," as he ministered to them devotedly, hunting for snout-beetles amongst their crinkly leaves. Two self-conceited peacocks patrolled their pen on the eastern lawn and the Olympian white swans, Helen and Pollux, with their brood of cygnets, rode the oval pond among the lily pads. In the stable, the quiet horses laid their cheeks against each other and Beth, the coon-cat, rubbed her flanks along their legs and purred. Adam, Miss Congreve's coachman, who was lazy, would be stretched out on an army cot opposite the stalls, dozing dreamlessly or straining his eyes in the crepuscular light to read "Scattergood Baines."

And Andrew knew that across the lake behind his cousin's house, Victor Smithwick, the seamstress's son, his friend of former summers, his confidant and guide, his teacher and his audience, was equally absorbed as he sat, wide-eyed with idolatry, beside his ailing brother's bed. This brother, Charles, a sailor, whom Andrew had never seen but who was said to be six feet three and to have a cannon and a cairn of balls tattooed on his chest, was home on sick-leave, convalescent after some unusual disease, acquired romantically in Singapore. And Victor, who had always bragged of him and quoted his scenic postal cards as if they were tidings from on high (though half the time Charles only stated that Hawaii had no snakes or that the Yangtze was a filthy river), never left his side unless it was to sprint to the village on an errand whose purpose was to comfort or divert him. Sometimes, as he raced past Congreve House on his way to fetch paregoric or *The Saturday Evening Post*, he flung a non-committal salutation at the figure in the hammock, but he did not pause or even slacken his zealous pace and if Andrew called out, "When are you going to look at my new flies? Don't you want to see my crazy crawlers?" Victor replied, "Can't hear you," and vanished behind the lilac thicket.

It had been a joyous friendship, for it had sprung, full-grown, from leisure, and had not been predicated, as winter friendships were, on the extraneous considerations of school or dancing class or a mutual dentist. Andrew was poor at team sports, being small and, by reason of his smallness, timid, and he was therefore shy of half his school-fellows whose seasons changed with the change in the size and shape of balls and who vociferously despised non-athletes; and while he was bookish, he was also dreamy and was often at the very bottom of his class, so that he was nearly as tongue-tied and queasy with the boys who sanctimoniously honored Algebra as those whose god was the Discobolus. But Victor Smithwick, a child of nature, flung down no challenge, and because their worlds were so divergent there was between them no exhausting and carking competition, the spirit of which was upheld by the masters at Sewell as a cardinal virtue, indispensable to American, Episcopalian men. Not racing with him, Andrew had never lost to Victor and the cocoon of shyness that bound him all winter released him as soon as he arrived in Hawthorne.

Ever since they had been very little boys, their companionship had been daily and all day long, uninterrupted by homework and unhampered by parental disapproval, for Andrew's parents, far away in Europe every summer, knew nothing at all of Victor. Andrew's mother would have been appalled that the boy had smoked cigarettes since he was nine and that he had been so long acquainted with the processes and the rites of sex that only the most extraordinary variation on the theme could interest him; and Andrew's father, who was a snob, would have said, "the chap's a bumpkin," and implied that there could be no possible reward in such a friendship except a sentimental sense that one was being democratic. From time to time, Cousin Katharine had urged him to widen his circle of acquaintances; but the other native boys his age were uneasy and even hostile in his presence since usually the shoes and shirts they wore had been provided by his rich and philanthropic relative, and those who were visiting great-aunts or grandmothers in the other summer houses were no different from the boys at Sewell: they beat him at tennis and crowed and some of them bragged shamelessly about their marks and seemed to have no aim in life except to study hard at Harvard. Cousin Katharine, who believed in the pleasure principle, and who was fond of Victor, had given up the effort to socialize Andrew and he was never seen on a tennis court again.

It had been an incessant pleasure and a summer-long protection against the fits and starts of melancholy that always plagued the winter and had especially beset the one just past when, throughout his parents' house, there had hovered a vague and massive mood that had slowed down everyone, even the servants, even the bromidic, optimistic governess, Miss Bowman, who had theretofore been indefatigable. There had been some wilting, asphyxiating emanation that had made itself known negatively, through silences, omissions, forgetfulness, sometimes on his mother's part, sometimes on his father's. They had seemed forever to be standing abstractedly at windows, staring out into the snow or rain, never hearing what was said to them. Often his mother had had a tray sent up to her room after his father, in dinner clothes, went out to join a client, and when her children begged her to join them at their early meal, she complained of a splitting headache and pointed to the bottle of Empirin compound beside her bed as if this were the explanation and the cure of everything.

Cousin Katharine, in whom the children had individually sought consolation, had explained that John Shipley was badly overworked—an architect of his abilities was much in demand—and that Maeve, sensitive and loyal wife that she was, reflected the strain; that these black humours would be dispelled by their annual trip to Europe and that the twins and Andrew would forget all about it once Congreve House was opened. It was a reasonable diagnosis, for their father did look drawn and their mother's eyes were listless, but they had none-theless been careworn and one time late in April, Honor had come into Andrew's room without knocking, had lain down on his bed and cried heartbrokenly. "What *is* it? What's the matter with everybody?" she had demanded through the muffling pillow. Never in his life had Andrew been so sad.

But he did not pity anyone except himself; he almost hated his mother for perpetually looking woebegone and he did hate his father for his irascibility when he snapped at the servants for no reason and greeted the slightest mishap with a towering rage, blaming Andrew if he could not find his briefcase; he was forever blaming someone and forever exonerating himself of charges that had not been laid against him: "It's not *my* fault you have a cold. You wouldn't have if you watched your health as I do mine," he said to Andrew who had not complained, had only sneezed and said, "Excuse me." He dressed them down before the servants, and Andrew intended never to forgive him for a public utterance (in front of a clerk in Brooks Brothers): "If you could learn to kick a ball around the field, you'd get some meat on your bones and then your clothes would fit. But I suppose that's too much to ask."

This spring, Andrew's need for Congreve House and Victor had been more urgent than ever, and he had counted not only the days but the very hours until he would alight from the slow local train at the Hawthorne station. As in every year, as the end of hibernation neared, he had begun to keep a notebook full of things to tell his friend and questions to ask him: What was the coldest it had been when Victor had fished for smelt through the ice? Had anyone escaped from the pen? How many days had school been closed on account of the snow? How often had Jasper, the retired, towheaded barber who chose to have his epileptic fits in public, been carried home in the Black Maria from the corner of Baldwin and Main? In exchange, he had to offer an account of a fierce and bloody fight between two drunks he had seen in the Park Street subway station; a description of a Norwegian sailing vessel that had tied up at T Wharf, having come across the open sea all the way from Oslo; there had been a trip to a bull-mastiff kennel that he knew would interest Victor and another one (made in secrecy, needless to say) to the morgue.

And as always, as the train toiled finally into the station and he heard the summer bee-buzz of an outboard motor on the lake and saw the gray carcass of a schooner that had lain atilt at the headtide of the river since anyone in Hawthorne could remember, he had gone to the door of the coach and over the engine's clangour and hiss had jubilantly cried, "Smithwick, I'm back!" though Victor lived miles from the depot. Still, this announcement of himself, unnoticed as it was—except by the affable stationmaster who nodded and said, "At your service, Shipley"—formally opened the holiday for him. In his exuberance he felt as if he had run all the way from Boston and still had enough energy in his legs to go straight on to Montreal. His tongue was abruptly loosed from the cat's hold and in his cousin's old-fashioned carriage on the way to her house, he chattered wildly, with himself as the center of all he said, until his sisters begged him to be still.

This year, he had run all the way only to find that there was no prize at the goal and, his place usurped, he was embarrassed as if he had spoken to someone he later realized he did not know; his shyness sealed him up again into an envelope he could not tear open. He and Victor had never written letters to each other (they exchanged comic valentines but that was the extent of their communication in the winter) and he had therefore not been prepared at all for Charles Smithwick's return. He was newly shocked each time he thought of the casual way Cousin Katharine had said, "Charles Smithwick has come on, to the unbounded delight of his mother."

It had been at lunch on the day of their arrival and as she delivered the information, she serenely fingered the pale green grapes on her plate and, as if nothing had happened, went on to extol to his sisters the charm and intelligence of the St. Denis boy, Raoul—the more remarkable, she thought, because his mother lacked both, though she was sweet, and his father had deteriorated through the years into nothing more than a business-man. She could not have distressed Andrew more if she had said, "Victor Smithwick has gone away," for he knew, because he knew Victor well, that so long as Charles was there to talk of submarines and Eastern ports, of storms at sea and of himself—a paragon of wit and strength and sex appeal—there would be no comradely clamming on the mudflats of the river, no studious explorations of the town dump, no endless rush and cataract of conversation, no badgering of Jasper ("Will you take a fit, Jasper, please? Pretty please with sugar on it?" mocked the dauntless Victor and often was obliged), no hunts for snakes or Indian artifacts.

And, indeed, Cousin Katharine, returning to the invalid in her chronicle of happenings and situations which she had been accumulating since her own arrival three weeks earlier, confirmed his fears by saying, "I was afraid that the return of the native might take Beulah Smithwick away from us but when I asked her if she could leave her Charles to come and sew for us—I have some lovely gold linen that came last week from Dublin—she said, 'That Victor is as good as Florence Nightingale with his big brother. He's not got eyes or ears for anything but Charley, Charley, Charley.' Whether that means he'll fetch the gruel on time, I don't know, but in any case, Beulah will be here tomorrow."

Honor and Harriet, entranced with freedom and the thought of dresses and of the charming Raoul St. Denis, had already cast the winter from them and Harriet sang,

"Gold linen from Dublin's fair city! How perfectly celestial!"

And Honor said blandly, "How glad for us, how sad for Andrew that Victor is the lady with the lamp."

His fingers lay nerveless among the grapes and as he watched his sisters bud and blossom in the sprightly season, the winter's gray rue washed dully over him; the light itself, streaming through the long, gossamer curtains, had seemed as spiritless as city light. Cousin Katharine had appeared not to notice his despair and this astonished him because she had always before sensed his troubles and had done what she could to ease them. She should have said, "That won't make any difference. Charles will soon be well and until he is, I daresay Victor will be glad to have Andrew keep him company while he plays nurse." But she said nothing of the kind. She was as unaware of him and as scatterbrained as the twins as she talked on of short-sleeved boleros made of pink piqué, of the droll, sky-blue modern house the St. Denis family had taken for the summer on an island off Bingham Bay, and of the birds she had seen on the walks she had taken; it was more important to her that she had found a phoebe's nest than that Andrew had lost his last friend. And after lunch, when he asked her frankly if she thought that Victor would have any time for him, she was absent-minded and offhand; she said, "I expect the three of you will play checkers a good deal." The three of them play *checkers!* That was the sort of irresponsible thing his mother might say, but in Cousin Katharine it was alarming. He watched her deftly arranging a vase of sweet peas to make them look Japanese; he had the feeling that she wished he would leave the room, and nervously he realized that she had not looked at him once since she had kissed him at the train. "Why don't you go down to the alewife run?" she said. "They tell me we're having a bumper crop this year." Still she did not look at him but frowned at the flowers and Honor said brutally, "He's afraid to go to the run without Victor." Cousin Katharine reproved her, but Andrew was not convinced; he felt disliked by everyone.

But he had not given up immediately. That afternoon he had rowed across the lake and had gone to the gate of the widowed Mrs. Smithwick's house, a crooked little cottage with an undulating roof and dented walls, painted the color of raspberry ice except for the shutters which were green. He had whistled his and Victor's fraternal whistle, a bobolink call with an added note, but in answer he heard only the fussy flight of a heron he had startled and which arose, a clumsy wedge of feathers, to fly to the opposite bank. Victor's pet vixen in a chicken-wire cage at the side of the house yapped peevishly at him; he heard a distant dog and a distant clump of voices, but no sound came from the house that crouched like a pink gnome at the end of a tousled vegetable garden. He could almost feel the sickness in the quiet air, and his imagination persuaded him that he smelled medicine. He whistled twice again and finally Victor appeared, closing the screen door softly behind him; he blinked against the sun and yawned and said "Hi," simultaneously. He must have been asleep in a room with the blinds drawn; the thought of his possibly having been lying companionably beside his brother on the same bed filled Andrew with unbearable envy. For a minute he could not say a word and simply stood there at the shabby picket fence, staring at his friend.

Victor was the most peculiar-looking boy Andrew had ever seen, so freakish that it took him several days at the beginning of every summer to get used to him; after that the ugliness fascinated him. He was a parody of a boy in whom all the components had originally belonged to another species; he was as various, said Cousin Katharine, as a duck-billed platypus; Honor and Harriet called him the boy from Mars. His head consisted of a woodchuck's upper lip from which obtruded two large oblong teeth, a porcine nose that pointed skyward, a pair of amber cat-eyes, round and feral. He wore his tall ears high upon his head and they were red; his pigeon-toed feet were huge and his hands were pebbled all over with big pied warts and they were scarred with the marks of a jackknife with which he tried to dig out the unsightly nubbins. His long black hair lay on his conical head like rags and usually there was something in it, a crumb or a burr or a small twig. Once Andrew had seen a green worm in it and when he reached up to brush it off, Victor said, "Leave um be. I put um there. He's measuring me a hat." Victor, whose mother was a fortune-teller as well as a dressmaker, believed in signs —another thing in Victor that Andrew's father would have taken exception to.

That afternoon, he stood in the slanting doorway under a lucky horseshoe, looking doubtfully at Andrew as if he could not remember at first who he was and then, grinning, he whispered loudly, "Did you hear? My brother's home." When Andrew diffidently asked if they might go for clams one day soon when the tide was right, Victor, still whispering, said, "Who, me? I told you: my big brother's home."

The rebuff was genial and his manner was even generous as if Victor expected everyone to be as happy as he was. "I'd like to meet him," said Andrew.

"He's sleeping."

"I mean some other time. Maybe tomorrow? I could row over here right after breakfast."

"Well, I don't know . . ." Victor looked down at his feet and meditatively twisted a string of his hair around his index finger. "He has to sleep a lot. Charles sometimes sleeps all day. And when he wakes up, well, he sort of just likes to have me around." He smiled proudly to himself, still looking at his splayed basketball shoes. "He doesn't even care a whole hell of a lot about Billy Bartholomew comin' ridin' up here."

"My father bought me a slick new rod," offered Andrew. "And a landing net. Could you go up on the lake tomorrow? We'd take a picnic?"

But Victor shook his head. "I've got my work cut out for me," he said. "I guess you wouldn't fool around with fishing and stuff when your own brother was sick."

Andrew was mortified, and he did not give Victor the Hitler Jugend knife his father had brought him last year from Berlin, a knife exactly answering the description of the one Victor last summer had said he longed to own. It had been selfless love that had made him keep the knife, unused, for Victor and that had made him use up three weeks' allowance in having the initials, "V.S.," in Gothic type, burned into the handle where the *Hakenkreuz* had been; in the box from the shop in Germany, there was a card that said: "To his best friend from Andrew Shipley." The long box stuck out of the pocket of his sailing coat, but Victor had undergone so great a change that he did not even ask what it was, though he was by nature a prying boy. After a minute or two of awkward silence, he went into the house, nibbling between his rabbity teeth a tiny lettuce leaf that he stooped down to pick and over his shoulder he said pleasantly, "See you downstreet some time."

Andrew rowed back across the sun-struck lake, helplessly angry and certain that the whole of the summer would be as empty as this shell of an afternoon. It was so much worse, this negligent, smiling dismissal than an out-and-out quarrel; Victor, for all practical purposes, was not on speaking terms with him, but because the snub had derived from brotherly love and family ties were said to be sacrosanct, Andrew had no grounds for revenge. He could not himself imagine ever being in the least interested in any member of his own family, except Cousin Katharine, but he knew that his apathy was shameful and knew that Victor was behaving as everyone should. But though he was unjustified, he hated the intruder, Charles, and ambiguously he hated Victor too. He rowed slowly over the cold blue lake with islands in it where, in all summers past, they had fished for pickerel and frequently had caught eels instead and pink, whiskered horn pouts, hideous past description. On that small island yonder they had found a fossil of a beetle and farther up, where the lake widened, they had rescued a tourist who had had a heart attack and had fallen out of his rented boat. Was nothing like that ever to happen again?

Late on that same day, he drove with Cousin Katharine to Bingham Bay to buy lobsters at the pound and he gave Victor's knife to a total stranger, a man he had never seen before in his life. It was just at sundown when they reached the harbor and as his cousin made her transaction, Andrew went to stand on the dock to watch the fishermen baiting the trawl for the next day's hake catch. One of them, scraping the berries of blood off his hand with his pocket knife, hummed up and down the scales; untrue but firm and loud, the sound proceeded from his Roman nose which was pitted all over like a strawberry. Presently he looked up and shading his eyes against the evening sun, he smiled at Andrew and then he smiled at Cousin Katharine's gleaming and anachronistic black brougham, drawn by Pegasus, the bay, and Derek, the roan; Adam wore a tall hat and his summer-weight livery was bottle green and his gloves were hand-sewn yellow kid. Cousin Katharine maintained this striking equipage less for eccentric than esthetic reasons and even her friend, old Mr. Barker, who had a passion for motorcars, was forced to concede that it was far more pleasing to the eye than anything he owned, including a beloved Pierce Arrow which he had painted off-white.

The fisherman immediately recognized the brougham, for it was famous throughout the region, and he said to Andrew, "How do. My name is Congreve Smithwick." Both names were common in Hawthorne and its environs but the coupling of them seemed, on this day, deeply significant and when the man had finished tracing the complicated lineage that related him by blood to Katharine Congreve, Andrew, on an impulse, brought the knife out of his pocket and handed it to him; it was still in the cutler's box and the gift card was still beside it. Cousin Katharine called to him just then from the door of the pound to help Adam with the pails and before Congreve Smithwick had had time to see what he was to thank the boy for, Andrew was gone. It was as if he had paid Victor back by depriving him of what he awfully wanted but all the same, in some way that he could not quite define, had left behind a life-line by giving it to someone who bore his surname.

On their return to Hawthorne, through the fragrant, tree-darkened lanes, under the brilliant early stars, he was exhilarated by the rush of summer in the country, imagined that he had misinterpreted Victor's behaviour and that on the next day he would be waiting beside the gate at Congreve House, alternately yodeling and whistling the private whistle, summoning Andrew. They would go then to swim in the warm salt river where seals played and sometimes teased the unwary by rising suddenly to the surface of the water and looking them straight in the eye; a pup once had nosed Andrew's stomach and had barked in his face, so close to him that he could have counted the bristles on the foolish little snout, and he and Victor had laughed so hard that they had nearly drowned. Here, at low tide, they would dig for clams in the velvety mudflats and Andrew would give his harvest to Victor who would sell them all at the general store. As often as not it was Andrew's own clams, bought by Cousin Katharine from Mr. Breyfogle, that went into the Friday chowder at Congreve House.

In this solacing delusion, generated by the look and the smell and the sound of evening, he put his head on Cousin Katharine's shoulder, withdrew it, interlaced his fingers with her gloved ones, saluted a black and white dog that barked at the horses, behaved, in general, with such abandon that Cousin Katharine, her affectionate self again, smiled down at him and said, "How you flatter me to like the summer in Hawthorne so much!"

He leaned into the orbit of her flowery perfume and thought delightedly of the first ceremonious dinner at Congreve House when they would have lobster and minute green peas, clover-leaf rolls and brandied peaches. Afterward they would darken the drawing room and make the magic lantern cast on the wall its watery, wavery pictures of John Drew as Hamlet and Maude Adams as Peter Pan and its scenes of Windsor

Castle and the Bridge of Sighs. After all that and a game of Hearts and a late meal of sandwiches (there were no sandwiches in the world like those that came out of Mrs. Shea's kitchen; they were made of anchovy and olives and watercress and were cut in the shape of hearts and diamonds, clubs and spades), there would be the first night in his remarkable sleigh-bed in the room with the window seat and the Franklin stove and two stuffed pheasant cocks on the bookcase. He would barely be able to sleep for excitement and for the bleak admonitions of the owls by the lake and the flicker of fireflies in his room and the anticipation of the morning, a drench of sun, of dew, of grass and lights and shadows.

He laughed to himself and to his cousin said, "Do you know where my clam digger is? I'll need it in the morning."

2

But Victor had not been at the gate on the next day or on the one that followed, and the habit of waiting for him grew on Andrew like gluttony. He promised himself that if ten cars passed westward on the road before the church bells rang for three, Victor would telephone. If his guess was correct and they had ham for dinner, Victor would be at the gate next day.

Often the waiting was an end in itself so that for brief periods he forgot what he was waiting for. He seemed, at these times, to wait for nothing but the passing of the listless time, told by the bell that Paul Revere had made to hang in the belfry of St. James's church. Each hour there came to his inner eye the image of the verger, a fat, lame idiot who, being enamoured of the bell—for the ringing of it was the only art he had ever mastered and his aged mother had to lace his shoes—wore a small replica of it on a string around his neck so that his shuffling, sidling approach was heralded by a dulcet jingle. If one greeted him, he bashfully shook the little bell in answer and from his freckled, lunar face, there came a babyish gurgle, ineffably kind. In other summers, Andrew and Victor had teased Poor Hollis, as he was known, by climbing up into the steeple and throwing down acorns on his head. But this summer, he was too inert even to gather the nuts and the memory of the smell of bat dung sickened him a little.

For hours his lazing body floated away from him, as light and shapeless as the luminous clouds swimming through the aqueous sky. He read fantastic apotheoses into the clouds and the intricate patterns of the elm leaves: pink, hairless tapirs; vast polliwogs; Rip Van Winkle still asleep. Or he mused on the vireo's nest that hung, purse-like and pendulous, from a branch in one of the trees and pondered the clever and courageous instinct that in autumn would take its tenant south, to Louisiana perhaps—he liked the name—where Cousin Katharine had one time trod upon a water moccasin and another time had fainted when a night-blooming cereus had finally opened out in an explosion of perfume. The vireo might build its nest in a chinaberry tree. *Chinaberry tree:* he envisaged twigs dripping breakable lozenges like the filmy pink beads Aunt Dora had given the twins for Christmas or like the yellow pearls his cousin plaited in her hair when she wore it in a coronet. If the bird came whirring to its nest, he lay quite still and listened to his heart. Deep in the pine-woods to the west of Congreve House the blue jays bickered. "'Tis!" "'Tain't!" they nagged.

But all of a sudden, his lethargy would end in a pang and he was alive with bitterness; his stomach ached as if he were starving. And then he could not help his thoughts from straying backward to the irretrievable days when Charles Smithwick had been no more than a mythical hero, as insubstantial and therefore as tolerable as someone in a book. He thought of how, in the old days, when he and Victor were clamming, Victor would pause, holding his digger up-ended and pointing down the river that vanished in the summer haze, he would say, "The high sea is there," and his tone was so rapt and his desire to follow in his brother's footsteps was so keen that it was as if he had stripped the intervening seven miles of their forests and farms and hills and dingles and were looking directly at the North Atlantic; as if, in his revery, he could stride titanically to the very pier of his imagination and board the very battleship his mind's eye saw moored there. With a sigh, he returned to his tame digging and did not speak again. But later, when they started back to the village to sell the clams, he would indicate that he had thought of nothing but the sea and ships by saying, "Do you know where he is now?" And because "he" always meant Charles, Andrew clothed a faceless stick figure, six feet three, in a middy blouse and bell-bottomed trousers and situated him, in the posture of a trapeze artist, atop a mast. "He's in Panama, the lucky stiff," Victor told him. Or Charles was in Yokohama or in Manila and from these exotic harbors, he sent back snapshots of himself, embracing native girls ("One of the local products, not for export"), striking a comical attitude with a knife between his teeth ("Yours truly as Captain Kidd"), standing stiffly at a quayside with a waste of sea behind him and looking, in such solemn portraits as these, as if he had just got his comeuppance from a superior. Charles was so strong, said Victor, that he could have been a wrestler if he had wanted to or a circus strong man, "one of them that lifts the weights," and, indeed, he had considered both professions but in the end he had elected the navy because he liked to be "on the move in a big way." He liked to ride on things, said Victor, on trains and trolley cars and motorcycles, on horses, in rickshaws, on every kind of water-going craft. One time when the high-school track team had gone to Portland for a meet, he had got so interested in riding on the streetcars that he had altogether forgotten to go to the stadium and Hawthorne High had lost because he had not been there; his specialties had been the broad jump and the shot-put and people who were in a position to know said that he could have been top man at the Olympics. Last summer, Andrew's father had gone to the games in Berlin and after hearing him describe the Finns, Andrew doubted that anyone—and particularly Charles Smithwick—could have beaten them.

And while this Galahad and Douglas Fairbanks and Admiral Byrd rolled into one was not handsome—this was evident from the pictures and Victor himself who lived in a glass house and should not have thrown stones admitted that he was "no looker"—he had not one but several girls in every port. When he had left Hawthorne, he had left a string of broken hearts behind him and Victor was by no means sure, he said and smirked, that he had not left some children.

For proof of his popularity, Victor once showed Andrew Charles's high-school autograph book, inscribed in purple ink and brown and green, with rococo capitals and luxurious serifs; the "i's" were dotted with hoops and the "t's" were crossed with unfurling banners. The signatures belonged to Dorothy, Edie, Trudy, Flossie, Janet, Josie who all enjoined him never to forget some rendezvous or secret. "Remember the night you and I didn't go to the Junior dance accidentally on purpose?" "By any chance did you ever watch the sun rise from Coot Isle?" "Is it fun to get stuck on the top of a ferris wheel—or isn't it?" Andrew and Victor had gone through the book carefully and matter-of-factly, as if it were a table of statistics, sitting side by side in two rocking chairs in Mrs. Smithwick's parlor-sitting room and all the while the old, moulting parrot that could not talk but could only laugh, chuckled pruriently as he paraded up and down in front of them on the floral-patterned Congoleum. It gave Victor an obscure but assertive pleasure to point out one of Charles's former girls in the village, settled already into the fat or the gaunt lean of bucolic motherhood, hauling along a child by the hand or carrying a baby in her arms. And though the girl had been the one robbed of her youth, it was the husband Victor defended by saying, looking coldly at her, "Charles was smart. She would have done that to him if he'd of given her half a chance. You take these girls, you give 'em an inch and they'll take an ell."

In Mr. Breyfogle's store, spare, reddened men collected amongst the bins of dusty navy beans and the racks of gutta-percha overshoes and while they waited for their groceries, they cleaned their square fingernails with Bowie knives. "How's the admiral?" they asked Victor. "What's weather like on the bounding main?" and Victor, haggling with the grocer over the price he was to get for his clams although it was fixed and had been from the beginning of their contract, smiled, sunning in his brother's glory and repeated the text of Charles's last letter or postal card. Charles was generally regarded as the most interesting of Hawthorne's younger citizens and though he had not been home once, until this summer, since he had gone away, everyone kept so well informed of his activities through his mother and brother that if he had stepped off the train unexpectedly one day, no one would have been at a loss for words but could at once have asked him specific questions about his ship, his officers and his friends.

What chance had an untraveled twelve-year-old to compete with a celebrity like that? He could do nothing but wait for Charles Smithwick's departure, either through death and burial or recovery and the return to his ship. And whether the news from the tip-tilted house was good or bad, his spirits rose in the same degree. If Beulah reported, "Charley's perky as a squirrel today," or mourned, "He's bad again, Miss Congreve, my fellow's low," Andrew's satisfaction was the same. The *status quo,* however, depressed him and he could feel his mouth drooping when at lunch Cousin Katharine, imitating Beulah, said, "Charley's holding his own, thank you. Not well enough to leave us lonesome but not poor enough to make us blue."

Though he did not have in them the blind faith that Victor had, Andrew furthered his interests through incantations; on wishbones, first stars and on loads of hay, he wished that Charles would die; at night, genuflecting quickly (he did not think it necessary in the summer to kneel since Bowman, a phrenetic High Church convert, was miles away out West) he prayed Christianly for the immediate restoration of the sailor's health, calling on heaven to make him "better than new" so that he would be able in the future to resist all disease and never come back to Hawthorne again. He did not care at all which fate awaited Charles; he wanted only his removal and the end to this heavy stupefaction that had gone on like a bad sleep for months. His resilient sisters, busy with the business of girls, their enormous correspondence with their school friends (they were extremely popular), their needlework, their lessons in ladyhood at Cousin Katharine's feet, their dates with boys who drove from miles away to see them, had entirely forgotten the miasma of the winter. But Andrew, though he could not distinctly remember the details of it, felt it still drugging him and dragging him, pushing him mysteriously down and down and to his alien, absent friend he called "Help! Help!" But Victor would not listen and the quagmire sucked.

Day after day from his hammock, he watched the traffic on the road: Victor rushing up or down the hill, fleet-footed for his brother's sake; Billy Bartholomew, the loafing old blacksmith, sprawled bareback on his white horse on his way to visit Charles; Mrs. Smithwick scuttering past, her sewing finished for the day, with a pot-shaped basket full of food for him; Dr. Taylor, a child-sized man from Bangor, honking nervously at every tree as he drove past in a rattletrap coupé to minister to the famous invalid. Far from the center of the world, Andrew lay torpid and individual on the periphery of it. Lethargically he shuffled through his favorite daydreams, of being on a buffeted boat in the Baltic Sea with Victor, of catching one of the river seals and training it to balance a ball on its nose, of having an eye on the end of his finger. But nothing seemed worth while and he continued to mark time, waiting for Charles to die.

3

He would lie in the hammock until the spurs of light began to recede from the ground and a general shadow to invade the lawns and meadows. The sound of early evening came on the timid wind in the high tree-tops, of cows ringing their bells in the small pastures that lay all around, of children calling good night to their friends as they went home for supper, of the final stutter of an outboard motor as it came to shore. His sister, Harriet, came out the front door and called to him, "Tea, Andrew, tea!" and, almost absent-mindedly, she assumed the five positions of ballet, framed between two of the classic pillars that stood before the house. After a moment, Honor appeared, to look for tail-feathers that the peacocks might have dropped and as she sought, she sang, "On the first day of Christmas, my true love brought to me a partridge in a pear tree . . ."

He was absorbed then into a mauve and female hour and with his sisters and his cousin, all three of them as soft and beautiful as flowers, beside the swan pond, he ate *pâté* and cake, listened to Cousin Katharine read aloud his parents' letters and those that came each week from the hortatory governess, played "I Went to Boston" and was, in spite of himself, consoled.

"Don't you get bored doing nothing all day long?" Honor would cry; she was a restless girl who never finished anything. "I would *die.* Mrs. Shea says you look 'laid out.' "

And Harriet said, "It's exactly what Mr. Baxter told Daddy. He is 'markedly anti-social.' " She elongated her face to mimic the elegiac headmaster at Sewell and they laughed because she did it well.

But Cousin Katharine, full of tact and affection, said, "I *like* to see you cogitating in my hammock. I like to know that the man of the house is within hailing distance."

And though he knew that this was nothing more than flattery and that she was facetious when she said "the man of the house" he was warmed with a fugitive glow and when she offered it, he took her long smooth hand and touched her round ring paved with rubies. He almost wished to be a small child then, a baby even, and be held in her arms and rocked and crooned to.

There was a short space of every day in which he was taken out of himself and caught glimpses of a larger world as he had used to do when he voraciously read history and the lives of Napoleon's generals. Just after they had finished their light, delicious meal, Cousin Katharine, who was pensive at this hour, told them a story that some trifle in the course of the day had brought to mind. They sat some time after Maureen had cleared away the tea things, hearing her account of an odd meeting in Rome, a curious twist of fate in Vienna, a dream that had come true. This artful, graceful, fanciful woman, their mother's age (yet seeming, because of her white hair, to be a generation older and seeming, at the same time, because of her light heart, to be the Shipley children's contemporary) did not accommodate her manner or her facts to the youth of her audience, just as she did not alter her mode of living because the times had changed.

"There is only one time," she said, "and that is the past time. There is no fashion in *now* or in *tomorrow* because the goods has not been cut." And so her anecdotes were as archaic and yet as timeless as her carriage and as the ostrich-feather fan which she carried with her when she went out to dine with Hawthorne's summer gentry. It was not that she "relived" her stories but that she seemed to exist in two tenses simultaneously. The children moved with her from memory to memory as if from case to case in a historical museum and they were excited, as sight-seers would be, to find in one display a shard identical to one they had seen in another gallery: if a Bavarian named Max Pirsch whom they had originally heard of in a tale of a ball at a baronial house in Munich reappeared on the passenger list of a steamer that had taken Cousin Katharine to Budapest, they were as satisfied as people who recognize in a novel a place where they have actually been.

In her rarefied world, she countenanced no change, and she had faith that the Dublin and the Rome where the elder Shipleys went each year were in every particular the cities she had known as a girl and had not revisited for eighteen years. Once she had commissioned Maeve Shipley to buy her some gloves at a shop in Venice—no substitute would do and she was firm on this point—and when Maeve wrote to say that the shop was no longer there nor anywhere, Cousin Katharine was shocked and disbelieving and she said, "Maeve went to the wrong street or she's playing a trick on me." She did not choose to recognize political alterations in the countries she was fond of; Mussolini and Hitler she looked on as demented eccentrics whose day would soon be over, and she would not be persuaded that their power, moral and philosophical, was more than superficial. In her reflections, she was like someone looking at a Chinese painting, allowing his eye to begin at the bottom and to travel slowly upward to the top of the mountain and the houses beside the waterfalls, as large as the ones in the valley; there was no progression in time because there was no perspective and therefore no shrouding of the past; the present was exactly the same size as the past and of exactly the same importance and except in the most minor and mechanical of ways, the future did not seem to exist. Andrew had always clung to her in her unchangingness, as he had clung to Victor. After his first fears on the first day, when he had believed that every single part of the world was spoiled, and even Cousin Katharine was different, he had been reassured: she was the same as ever. She never spoke to him of Victor, but he reasoned that this was not out of a lack of sympathy or understanding, but simply that she did not want him to see that she knew he was humiliated.

Often these stories of hers had no point that Andrew and his sisters could see and were no more than the descriptions of a scene, but so warmly did her gray, lovely eyes and her articulate long hands support the role of her fluid, gently monotonous voice, that they were carried with her and they looked as closely, heard as vividly, smelled as keenly as she did. The parks and the palaces of foreign cities were brightly projected for them, and the rivers of Germany and the bare, gray islands of the Outer Hebrides.

One day, she put on the tea table a fragile, spiraling seashell and she said, "I found this in the pocket of a jacket I haven't worn since the day I acquired it. The day seems like yesterday but actually it was eighteen years ago."

"The year you went abroad with Ma and Pa!" cried Honor, for Cousin Katharine, their mother's first cousin and best and lifelong friend, had gone to Europe with the Shipleys on their honeymoon, a fact that Honor and Harriet found so debonair, so airy and jocose that they brought the subject up whenever they could. They had gone on John Shipley's fabulous yacht, the *Empress Katharine,* which had long since been sold to a Cuban parvenu who had changed her color from midnight blue to apple green (in moments of ill humour, John Shipley fumed, "How dared that Dago take such liberties?") and Honor and Harriet, now that they had grown sophisticated and outspoken, took extraordinary pleasure in the knowledge that they had been conceived in the middle of the ocean.

"The *annus mirabilis!*" exclaimed Harriet.

"Yes, that was the time," said Cousin Katharine,

picking up the shell again as if the touch of it would transport her to the far time and place. "We had gone for a picnic to a beach near Naples, taking the funicular and then carriages and though, when we started out, we congratulated ourselves on selecting a perfect day, we had no sooner got to the seashore than thunderheads began to gather and the air was so heavy that we could feel it pressing down on us like mattresses. I remember it all, down to the clothes we wore and the word 'Bulgaria' printed on the shells of our eggs. We had forgotten to bring salt and the wine was undrinkable. Maeve hated the blue lizards that went slithering through the ruins and what disappointing ruins they were! They were nothing but hunks and heaps of rubbish from which we couldn't get a sense of history at all. A band of children materialized out of nowhere to beg from us. One little girl was blind and she sang us an uncommonly sad song. Another child juggled two of our own oranges and a big boy, about fourteen, did a very wild dance—I think he was supposed to represent a whirling dervish. Your papa paid them handsomely to go away."

"Our papa disapproves of fun," said Honor.

"Not fun," said Harriet. "He disapproves of children."

Ignoring them, Cousin Katharine continued, "It was Ronnie Pryce who gave me the shell. He picked it up and said, 'Put this in a pocket to remember this day.' And so, you see, I have done as he asked. Just after that, a storm came up and as we scrambled for the shelter of the carriages, we could see the lightning far out at sea and suddenly, quite magically, the ruins that we had been so contemptuous of became weird and splendid in this new light and we all grew thoughtful in spite of the wet."

Ronnie Pryce, as they all knew, had been one of Cousin Katharine's many admirers. Long ago they had seen a picture of him standing in a formal garden beside his father's Georgian house in Gloucestershire; fair, silkenly mustached, he had looked so aristocratic and so English, so reticent and dignified that it was hard to believe that he had been a practical joker, fond of exploding cigars and spurting boutonnieres and, as Cousin Katharine described him, "a man in whom garrulity was a malignant disease." In another photograph he wore his Lancers uniform and when Honor had seen it first, at the age of eight, she had asked, "Is that the king?" It was only years later that the children understood their cousin's answer, "If that were the king, don't you suppose that I would be the queen?"

Harriet picked up the shell. "It's pretty," she said, "but it's awfully small. You couldn't use it for anything. You couldn't even hear the ocean waves in it."

"Why did Mr. Pryce ask you to remember that day?" asked Honor. "Did he propose to you?"

"Did he?" Harriet was enchanted. The twins literally could spend hours speculating on why Cousin Katharine had never married. This was the darkest of all tribal mysteries and Andrew was sure that not even his mother knew the answer. "What did you say to him?" insisted Harriet.

"If he did, and I don't recall that he did—he was certainly much too line and rule, in spite of all his buffoonery, to propose marriage in a cable car or in front of a troop of mendicant urchins—I must have told him 'no.'" She laughed, finding the memory of the man ludicrous but sweet. "Perhaps the day was memorable to him because he was to leave Italy that evening to go back to England and from there to Australia where almost at once he made a fortune raising sheep. He *looked* rather like a sheep. And baa'ed continually."

"He went to Australia because you broke his heart," exulted Harriet. "How many people's hearts have you broken, Cousin Katharine? Tell us! We promise not to tell."

"Ah, where shall I begin in that long list?" teased Cousin Katharine. "I can't. It's far too long and I must concentrate on the conquest of Mr. Barker who's to be my dinner partner tonight."

"Mr. Barker's eighty!" screamed Honor delightedly.

"But he has at least eighty million dollars," said Harriet. "And his cars are perfectly stunning."

"I know for a certain fact that you broke Raoul's father's heart," said Honor. "Because Raoul told me. Do you know what I said when Raoul asked me why you never got married? I said, 'The answer should be very obvious. No one in the whole wide world was good enough for her.'"

"When did you see Raoul alone?" said Harriet sharply.

"Oh, once upon a time." Honor went to the edge of the pool and dabbled her fingers in the water. "What difference does it make? He thinks that you are me and I am you. He got so rattled once he called me 'Honoret.' He'll call you 'Harrior.' "

Poor Hollis rang the bell for six and Cousin Katharine got up to go and dress for dinner, taking her shell with her and patting Andrew on the head as she left, saying, "You are my favorite child because you mind your own business."

"Andrew is the strong, silent type," said Honor. "You may *think* he minds his own business. But he doesn't. He listens at keyholes."

With Cousin Katharine's leavetaking, he was suddenly lethargic again, too sad and bored even to defend himself against his sister. Besides, her charge was true. He loved to eavesdrop and read other people's mail; locked diaries tantalized him.

Cousin Katharine said, "You must not forget, you three, that tonight is the night for letters to the voyagers," and she moved across the lawn, forgetting them all, humming an Irish air to herself.

"It was awfully snide of you to say that to Raoul," said Harriet, still angry. "It implies that his father wasn't good enough for her."

"Well, he wasn't. That fat, terrible thing? The only person I can possibly imagine being worthy of Cousin Katharine is the Prince of Wales. Or was."

"He isn't tall enough for her," said Harriet.

Disputing, the twins went off to the picking garden to cut flowers in the cool of the dusk and Andrew, left alone again, returned to his grief which was all he had to keep him company. Victor would not come this night or any other night to invite him to go and watch the fish in the alewife run by moonlight or to play grave-robbers in the creepy churchyard. Last summer, Andrew would not have depended so heavily on the tea hour and his sisters' silly prattling; he would, half the time, not appear at all but would still be prowling with his friend who, wise, ragged, raffish, prodigiously *au courant* with scandals and crimes knew, through his clairvoyant mother, what murders were to be committed, what houses robbed, what bastards born and what escutcheons blotted. He knew by a sixth sense where to go on the lake on one particular day at one particular hour to catch bass, knew by the stars or the moon or the color of the sunset where a salmon would await him the next day; he knew the habits of birds and the deer that came to drink at the lake's edge and the stoats and the skunks and the porcupines. Days in advance, he knew when a caravan of gypsies would come to camp on the ridge above the lake; he knew by their first names the itinerant tinkers and revivalist preachers and traveling salesmen.

At this hour, in other days, they would be scuffing slowly up the hill from the village to Congreve House and Victor would be yodeling. The grotesque, good-natured warbling had always grown louder as they approached the summit and at the gate, it reached its peak, Victor's signal of good-by. He would go on and not look back, taking the winding lane to his mother's incarnadine and rhomboid house to feed his vixen and laugh at the parrot who laughed at him. His voice came rippling thickly back; in one little hollow, it caught an echo and after that, Andrew could hear it no longer. With that, the day was done. He plaited his way between the shadows of the maple trees that bordered the drive, walking carefully as if a sudden jolt might knock out of his head all the sensations and impressions and witticisms he had garnered through the day. But when he had opened the front door, he raced across the entrance hall and took the stairs two at a time, sped to his room and wrote down everything before he could forget. Afterward, a family child, he washed and went downstairs to apologize for missing tea. He sunned in the memory of the day that had passed and in the thought of the one to come.

Now he lay on his back on the grass and waited for the first star to appear. Patient, contemplative tears that never overflowed ebbed and surged in his eyes as he considered how everyone he knew was supported and comforted by some intimate conjunction: Victor had Charles and the twins had each other, his father had his mother, Maddox had the roses that might as well be people the way he carried on, and Mrs. Shea had God. Cousin Katharine, universally adored, had everyone. She was the world round which all lesser worlds revolved; her houses were the Shipley children's second homes;

she was their sponsor, playmate, teacher, second mother, their father's second wife, their mother's second self. In the winter in Boston, she came two or three afternoons a week to the Shipleys' house a little before tea to talk to Andrew's mother in her bedroom as they sewed or addressed invitations to the cocktail and waltzing parties they gave jointly. They were as forthright and sometimes as quarrelsome as sisters.

Andrew, listening at the door (his sneaky habit was so obdurate that his father had spoken of "taking steps"), heard his cousin call his father a wastrel and his mother reply, "How *can* you be so presumptuous, Kate, when you're not married to him?" Sometimes, though, the shoe was on the other foot and he heard Cousin Katharine defending John against Maeve's charge that he was irresolute. "What do you expect," retorted Cousin Katharine, "in an age when the will has ceased to exist?" He had never heard anything more revealing than this sort of thing; the one thing he was sure of was that neither his mother nor his cousin particularly liked his father, and it was no wonder: a man as cross as that could not expect to have friends. And yet, when the three of them were together, they seemed to have a wonderful time.

Cousin Katharine and his mother had effected an armistice by the time they went down to the library to wait for his father who walked home from his office in Franklin Street (he was a great one for exercise and health foods, a faddishness for which the two ladies often teased him), arriving punctually every day at half past five. He always paused in the doorway a moment, surveying his domain, and then he advanced across the rosy Aubusson to kiss his wife as she sat behind the urns and pots and to present to her the wine-red carnation that he brought her every day; and she received it with a quotidian smile of love (although, with his own ears, Andrew had just heard her say that he was, in some ways, weak and, being weak, was cruel), put it in the silver vase that yesterday had held its predecessor and asked him whether he would have rum in his tea or cream. Then he bowed to kiss the other lady's hand, murmuring his pleasure in seeing her as if he had not seen her two days earlier in this same place and had not had with her this very morning his daily conversation on the telephone, lasting for three minutes, shortly after ten.

Though this short section of the day was jocularly known as "the children's hour," since at no other time except at Sunday lunch were the family together, it was nothing of the kind but belonged to the three adults who, in their solidarity, excluded everyone from their twilight eucharist. Their jokes were so old and complex and personal that even they could not have dug down through all the laminations to the source of them. Their gossip was esoteric and to an outsider it sounded, often, as if the people they excoriated and anatomized were creatures of their own invention and not, as they really were, men and women they had lunched with or had seen at the theater or were going to dine with that evening. They seldom used proper names but spoke allegorically of "our charity" and by the laughter in their voices indicated that they did not feel charitable toward him at all, of "our court jester," and "our Karamazov." There was "the *arriviste*," "John's club Macaulay," there were "Maeve's poor ladies" (at the instigation of Cousin Katharine's mother, Aunt Alma, who was public-spirited, Mrs. Shipley headed armies of women who knitted furiously for the destitute of half the world) and there were Cousin Katharine's "young men," a retinue of dazzled youths who came in droves from Cambridge on her "day" to be inspired to sonnet-writing by her beauty and her charm. In speaking of these people, in terms as incomprehensible as a foreign tongue, such was their community that they gave the impression of being three aspects of the same person and not three separate persons. This indivisible trinity, established long before Maeve and John were married, was looked on as the most winning friendship in Boston. Cousin Katharine, who believed in the stars, counted it beneficent that they had been born under signs congenial to one another, Cancer, Pisces and Virgo. In anger or frustration, the children called their parents by their zodiacal symbols, their father "Fish," their mother "Crab"—though, actually, it was the other way around—and, until they were reprimanded by Miss Bowman, they had, in moments of familiarity, called Cousin Katharine, "Cousin Virgin."

On these snug afternoons of winter when the thick velvet curtains were drawn in the bay against the sneak-thief wind in the bony trees of Mount Vernon Street and the orange fire flicked and lapped the shining andirons, Honor and Harriet, protected by each other and by their inborn pride, sat apart and read while they drank their tea. But the lost boy, diffident in the farthest corner of the room, was as random and unfixed as a floating island and sometimes he blushed darkly though no one saw. He pretended to be reading the inscriptions on his father's yachting trophies, but really, out of the corner of his eye, he was enviously studying first one group and then the other, the three friends and then the twins. The miracle of his sisters' identity baffled and enraged him as if, in His production of the Shipley family, God had played favorites. The unity of their outward pattern and color gave to them an inner oneness, like a culture or a nationality, so that their responses to everything, unrehearsed, were exactly the same, neither of them taking a cue from the other but both simultaneously exclaiming in delight, dismay or scorn. He thought it unlikely that twins could ever know the slightest twinge of loneliness; nor would he ever if a magic spell could invest with dimensions the image of himself in a looking glass. He was at times as frantic as his cousin's cat who, believing herself to be two cats, boxed her reflection in a mirror and hunted for herself behind it.

These people were as cool as that smug cat or as the horses, Pegasus and Derek. Peggy received offerings of sugar lumps and apples as his just due and gave in return no more than a perfunctory nudge of thanks and retreated at once into his lofty ruminations. Like Beth and the horses, the peacocks and the swans, his friends and relatives were all engaged in something of their own so that they were perpetually self-sufficient. Often, even so, they beckoned to him, they called, they sometimes went so far as to wheedle and then, when he came abreast of them, they had retired into their private and inscrutable worlds, as concealed and convolved as the flesh within their hiding clothes. He had never forgotten and never failed to smart when he thought of it, an incident in the first summer in Hawthorne. They had gone to the seashore, to Pemaquid, and had found a plot of sand although the coast was rocky there. Harriet and Honor wore faded blue jackets and pleated white skirts and their black hair was braided into pigtails that reached to their waists. Harriet cried out that she had found a ladybug on a whelk shell but when he ran to see, the fine sand squelching between his toes, she would not show him; she held the shell in her eclipsing hands and though he stood at her elbow, complaining, impatient, perplexed, she would not look up but kept her cool, large eyes fixed tenderly on her phenomenon. What had made her court him if she only meant to send him away? She had let Honor see and as if he were going to steal or defile her shell or her bug, she had said to her twin, "Don't let Andrew see!" Yet she had called *him*, by name, had cried over the windy roar of the waves, "Andrew, come and look at what I've found! A ladybug on a seashell!" He had to pretend that he did not care; he had appeared to be interested in nothing in the world except a parade of snails inching toward the withdrawing waves, between the tracks of sandpipers, but he had listened, yearning, to his sisters' merry speculation on how on earth the ladybug, idling in a place so out-of-the-way, would ever get home in time to save her children.

Just so did Cousin Katharine sometimes evade the consequences of her invitations. She would say, "Be a pet, Merryandrew, and bring me my knitting," but by the time he had found the tapestry valise she kept it in, she was out of the mood, was telephoning the pastor's wife to beg from her a start of lovage or was telling her own fortune with a deck of Tarot cards; or, worst of all, had decided to write a letter to his mother and father beginning (oh, he had seen it written there in her old-fashioned, grand calligraphy) "My darlings."

Victor Smithwick was the only one who had ever *really* paid attention. Victor had *really* belonged to him for five solid summers. The evening wind up off the river said, "Heavy, heavy hangs over thy head, what will you do to redeem it?"

"I will wish on the star," he moved his mouth to form his answer to the wind and scanned the sky and wished on Venus and then stared northward until another star appeared, a minuscule point of blue, perhaps not big enough to make the charm work. His superstitions had become so labyrinthine that he did not trust his way among them. But the small star would have to do for he could see no other and he wished that Charles would die. Then he turned to considering what would happen after the wish had been granted and Charles was in his coffin. Would they bury him in his sailor's middy? How many days must pass after the funeral before Victor would come and call for him with his digger and his pail? A week at the most, he thought. Seven days of marking time? A hundred and sixty-eight more hours like this? He could not wait! He pleaded with Victor to shorten the time of grieving. The daydream made his heart race and he hugged himself until, like ice-cold water in his face, crudely down his back, reality awakened him and he whispered, "Oh, hell fire. Charles Smithwick is immortal. He is an immortal snot."

His mind, fumbling and prehensile like a baby's hand, groped, then wearied, but even when he fell heavily into his familiar lassitude and seemed actually to sink into the springy sod, his loneliness stayed like a bone in his heart.

He heard Maureen exclaim, "It's the prettiest summer in all my life," as she stood in the back door, breathing in the pastoral smells and heard Honor, her hands full of pansies, agree as she and Harriet came up from the garden, "It is! It's the divinest summer that ever was!" He hurled a pebble at the swans to ruffle and deflate them but they did not turn their haughty heads nor were even the cocky cygnets disturbed.

"It's the worst summer in all *my* life," he paraphrased Maureen, who was in love with someone though no one knew with whom. And because the summer was the only part of the year that counted, he went on, "It's the worst *year*, in case you'd like to know."

His sorrow winged assertively down on him like snow until the sun was altogether gone and the peepers began to chirp and the daft loons cried in the cat-tails and another meal was nearly ready in the cool, vast dining room. His sisters, learned and frivolous by turns, would either discuss capital punishment or describe the dresses they prayed their mother would bring them from Paris. Andrew, without an appetite, would try to gather into his spoon all the bits of chive on the surface of his vichyssoise.

The girls gave their flowers to Maureen who buried her smiling face in them and then all three of them went into the house. His solitude was a cage or a suffocating glass bell and he felt that everyone in the house was looking at him, making fun of him because he was unpopular. For a moment he felt close to Ronnie Pryce who had been rejected even after he had given Cousin Katharine the seashell and he had a wild wish to write to him in Australia and ask if he might come to visit. Now that Hawthorne had lost its meaning, it was a waste of time to stay on. Abruptly he got up from the grass and went into the house and to the telephone in the library and asked the operator for Victor's number. He was going to say, "Listen, Victor, you come over here tonight or my cousin will fire your mother." But the line was busy. In a panic of claustrophobia and in an agony of disappointment, he swung the cage of cutthroat finches and made them squawk and twitter with alarm and then he stood still, his hands limp at his sides, and let his slow tears fall.

CHAPTER II

My True Love Took from Me

HAVING ARRANGED the lilacs, the last and the most beautiful of the season, in twin tall alabaster vases on the mantel in the dining room and having reminded her cook that today was Tuesday and, since she was therefore at home, an undetermined number might be present at tea, Katharine Congreve went up to her sitting room for her customary mid-afternoon hour of privacy, pausing in the door of the drawing room to enjoin her cousins to wear something pretty for Raoul St. Denis who was driving over with his parents from Bingham Bay.

The supple, slender, black-haired girls, sedulous copies of their mother as she had been at their age, looked up from the handkerchiefs they were hemstitching for Christmas presents and Honor, smiling, beginning with a happy laugh that candidly anticipated the meeting with the boy who had set them both off into dreams of love and of engagement rings, said, "We've talked of nothing else for hours. We've decided on the lavender shirred batistes. Do Southerners like lavender?" And then with a dramatic moan, suppliantly holding out her hand that still wore its silver thimble and addressing her sister, she cried, "But what good will it do us? He's already in love with our old, old second cousin. Every man in the world is in love with Katharine C." And returning for a moment to childhood, plunging with her whole heart into a new mood, she lay at length on the sofa, hung her head over the side of it and seriously asked, "Cousin Kate, when you were my age, did you *long* to walk on the ceiling?" Her twin said, "Honor is mad," and neatly bit a thread.

Miss Congreve assured them that the lavender batiste dresses would be appropriate, admonished Honor not to let the blood rush to her head and Harriet to use her scissors and not her teeth to cut the thread and then proceeded up the curving stair, pleasurably observing a hummingbird as it gyred in the bittersweet that grew beside the window of the landing. Fair, not rare, this day in June was like all the days of all the summers and as she rose, step by step, up the spiraling stem of her beautiful house, serenity ripened in her face and she parted her lips in a fond smile, cherishing everything she surveyed and smelled and heard, the dimming medallions of the wallpaper and the Audubon prints that ascended the wall; the commingled fragrances of sunning foliage and old, oiled furniture and flowers everywhere, within the house and out, all bound together by the fresh salt breeze, a constant wraith in the curtains, a perpetual touch, feather-light and tentative, on the pages of open books and the tassels of velvet table covers; the multitudinous bird-song, the far-off bells of buoys.

She was not really contented anywhere except in Congreve House and she reflected on a wasted summer when she had gone to Puget Sound, unwillingly accompanying her mother who, as Progressive as Katharine was Conservative, had gone to attend a convention of formidable women and then had lingered on when she had found a whole colony of vigorous sympathizers in the innumerable causes to which she had dedicated herself: she was a Baconian, an anti-vivisectionist, an advocate of buttermilk and rat control. Except for that year and two others when she had cruised with John and Maeve on the *Empress Katharine*, she had come to Hawthorne from May until October since her infancy. But Congreve House, after thirty-eight years, still took her breath away and she never came up the avenue of maples without rejoicing in her immaculately proportioned and pedimented front door and the seven classic pillars of the façade. Large and white and regal, ensphered by orchards and gardens and acres of lawn, Congreve House had been built at the top of a monarchical hill and because its construction had been supervised by Katharine's great-grandmother, a Huguenot from Charlottesville who had made few concessions to the North (there still existed in this otherwise homogeneous region a small settlement of Negroes, descended from her servants and bearing still her maiden name of Delessert), it had a Southern amplitude, a height and a depth and a spaciousness of rooms and prospects that recalled the airy generosity of the houses of Virginia. This long dead ancestress, whose hauteur was centralized in a stony hooked nose, looked forth from a journeyman portrait that hung in the library, appearing to be staring out of countenance the shelves of books confronting her that dealt with the War between the States.

The long, embrasured windows of the house commanded, at the back, a view of the wide blue lake ringed with thin pines that cast their Oriental images blackly over the waving water. From the drawing room and the dining room, one looked out on the green swirl of the tidal river, spangled with the silver wings of gulls and the white pouches of spinnakers. From the east windows and those on the west, Katharine looked toward meadows, magisterial and vast, two oval yellow seas bounded by black country lanes. Beyond the western meadow there was a dense blue forest where the sun could never penetrate and where there always hung a gun-blue haze between the trees, where, in certain places, there were dells as green as Ireland and the mossy earth was bejeweled with monkshood and bluebells.

Her friends and relatives granted that her house was splendid, was perfect of its kind, but the life in Hawthorne! They flung up their hands and cried, "You're beyond me! It may be an ideal place for a waif of ten or an invalid of fourscore years and ten, but for an active woman in the prime of life! You owe it to yourself, Kate, to try Newport or the North Shore." Her critics' dismay was understandable enough in terms of themselves, for they were gregarious and uncontemplative and when, once in a blue moon, one of them made the long, uncomfortable journey to visit her, there usually arrived, soon afterward, an urgent telegram summoning him back; the pretext of business or of ailing uncles would not have deceived a child and, in a flutter of relief, the visitor scampered back as fast as he could to midday cocktails upon the humid sands of Bailey's Beach.

Hawthorne had nothing at all to offer any generation except the oldest and the newest, no club, no proper swimming beach, no summer theater, no sailboat races. Katharine's fellow summer colonists, as old as the hills, occupied (and had since they were children) vast, sprawling cottages that hovered on the outskirts of the demesne of Congreve House and which, with their gingerbread and their trailing porches and their purposeless stained-glass windows (a murky, morgue-like light entered Mrs. Wainright-Lowe's dining room through the leaded bodies of Paul and Virginia) appeared unkempt like tasteless but kindly frumps in the entourage of a famous belle. The cottagers entertained in varnished drawing rooms, darkly paneled in chestnut, wherein were situated copses of wicker furniture upholstered in cretonne and round tables on which stood stereopticons and albums, quadrupedal jardinieres planted with oxalis, chipped alabaster figurines and all the other outmoded bits and pieces that were unpresentable in town but "good enough for the country." In every house, since Katharine could remember, there had been a commingled smell of vanilla and of lemon oil which, like willow-ware tureens and cracked Waterford bud-vases, she would always associate with midsummer and septuagenarians.

Katharine had endeared herself to the halt and stooping citizenry because not only did she continue to return loyally each year but also intrepidly to withstand the inroads of what Mr. Barker, in spite of his worship of fast automobiles, petulantly called "these ultra-modern times." The customs in Congreve House remained the same that they had been in her father's day. She had conceded to electricity, to modern plumbing and the telephone but to no ungainly fads like radios or vacuum cleaners, canned soups or boisterous evenings of The Game. Her dinner parties were long and she dispensed with no formality (Hawthorne heard, more sorrowfully than angrily, that in Bingham Bay, the ladies did not withdraw and Miss Margaret Duff predicted, "Next thing you hear there'll be mixed swimming parties *au naturel*"); at her occasional balls, usually outdoors on a platform festooned with crepe-paper lanterns, there was only waltzing and the music was slow to oblige stiff knees. The servant staff was smaller, the tennis courts had given way to an herb garden, new objects had been introduced into the rooms, but nothing else had changed upon this lordly hill since her father, whom she had idolized, had died.

In great peace, she mounted the stairs, slowly as she did every day, slowly and then even more slowly until, three steps from the top, she was nearly immobilized as if her feet themselves were reluctant to leave the deep grassy carpet and her hand to quit the wide white banister.

Confronted by the portrait of her father that hung at the head of the stairs, she did at last stop still, her daily habit, and renewed her memory of his black eyes whose vital brightness the paint had not obscured and his full, versatile mouth, one corner upturned and the other set implacably, and his strong bones, having in them a Hebraic aggressiveness or a Hellenic one, a validity and an inherent pride so that they flattered rather than were flattered by the moon-white skin that rose to perish in tight, coarse curls of blue-black hair. Her own face, deriving from his, had been softened to a female role, the colors modified (her eyes were gray and a cloudy pink suffused her cheeks), and the aspect transformed from that of a humanist, steadfastly ironic, to that of a leisured, tranquil woman. These fine long faces were civilized. They were the faces of people so endowed with control and tact and insight and second sight that the feelings that might in secret ravage the spirit could never take the battlements of the flesh; no undue passion would ever show in those prudent eyes or on those discreet and handsome lips. For there was no doubt here, no self-contempt, but only the imposing courage of sterling good looks and the protecting lucidity of charm. So compelling was the integrity and the impregnable, intelligent self-respect that as Katharine looked at the masterful painted face, her source and counterpart, euphoria at her good luck extended her height and the length of her narrow hands and narrow feet and she felt as heroically proportioned as the statue of Minerva that stood in a summerhouse at the end of the pergola which her father had had made as a present to her on her fifteenth birthday, astonishing everyone who had imagined that, like other girls, she would have preferred necklaces or frocks.

"The poor Humanist is dead," she said and she said it in the same unaccented way she had done the first time she had said it when, finding that her father's heart had stopped in his sleep, she had gone into Maeve Maxwell's room and tugged her awake in the green light of early morning.

"Why did you go first to Maeve and not to me? *I* should have been the first to know, *I* was his wife." Even now, years later when wifeliness had lost all its meaning for her, Katharine's mother, a woman who insisted upon rights, upbraided her for this extraordinary defection and she could only repeat her apology and her explanation that she had been too bewildered to think clearly.

Who could ever understand or fail to condemn her that it had been essential to her own tears of grief that Maeve's fall first? If there had been no Maeve, no uncertain poor relation, no orphaned cousin, there might have been no tears at all. "And that would have puzzled you far more, Mother," she sometimes said in her imagination. For Katharine, who had never learned to demonstrate, could only imitate. She would never know, because of the timidity and the apologetic vagueness that obscured all of Maeve's human relationships, whether she had taken in that calm, comic use of the epithet, "the Humanist," spoken through a mouth that wore the same double expression this painted one did and she would never know, therefore, whether Maeve's immediate and authentic tears had come from shock at the news of the tragedy or shame at the way it was announced. "Don't cry," Katharine had said and the articulation of the word had permitted her then to burst into bitter, hopeless tears and to arouse the household with the sobbed outcry as she flung open her mother's bedroom door, "Father's dead! Oh, my God, my father's dead!"

When, later that morning, John Shipley had come to Congreve House for second breakfast, he had found his fiancée consoling Katharine, murmuring to her like a nurse or a mother, and he was touched at first only perfunctorily by the calamity but, on the other hand, was moved so deeply by Maeve's goodness that he had said, "You are an angel," before he had so much as offered a commiserating handclasp to Katharine; before he had composed himself to the atmosphere of sorrow, he had smiled, head over heels in love. Katharine's bereavement had been double that day but she knew that neither John nor Maeve had seen in her careful face anything but the loss of her father. "My skeleton would not have pained me so if John Shipley, mine by rights of discovery, had called *me* an angel and given *me* those ingenuous, amorous looks." She could not recall ever having cried again except occasionally in her sleep; then she would awaken from some irretrievable dream to find her pillow wet and her eyes streaming from a buried wretchedness.

She moved at last, turned all the way around to look down the stairwell and into the heart of a pale pink water lily in a milk-glass cuspidor on a table in the entrance hall. It must be replaced today, she thought, her affectionate husbandry overtaking her, and then a fresher memory flicked across her mind, of the quite unwarranted *succès fou* she had scored the week before when, telling Edmund St. Denis that this was, indeed, as he had suspected, a cuspidor, she had added, "But you see, I dignify the profane vessel with a pristine *nymphaea*." This kind of lapidary speech, while once it had been a conscious affectation, was natural to her now, as natural as her daily carriage drive or as her Japanese fans for hot evenings and her Spanish shawls for cool ones. These eccentricities, having so long been her second nature, were no longer eccentricities and she was surprised when Edmund, whom she had not seen for fourteen years, had laughed, exclaimed, repeated the word "vessel" as if it were obsolete or superlatively witty, had, in the course of his applause, used the phrases "a sense of humour" and "from the sublime to the ridiculous." He had seemed, in his torrential mirth, to be about to slap her on the back. He did slap his own soft thigh resoundingly. The tribute disappointed her; she had looked forward to the company of Edmund and his wife (a cipher, badly dressed, but oddly appealing) but she could not be at ease in the face of such voluble appreciation. Indeed, she was more than disappointed, she was affronted that a man she had nearly married could understand her so little: she had not meant to make a joke.

The boy, Raoul, had been embarrassed at his father's exhibition just as Edmund himself, when he was young, had been embarrassed by his own father when Katharine, just after her father died and a year before Edmund married Madeleine, had visited him in Louisiana. General St. Denis, a professional gallant, shamelessly lecherous, had grossly flirted with her and so monopolized her, fascinated by what he called her "black abolitionist tricks and dodgements" (he referred to nothing more regional than a few New England expressions and an indifference to hominy grits) that his enraged and jealous son had been reduced to plotting ways to steal her away for himself. The older man had not seemed to belong to his perfect and patrician house just as Edmund must seem out of place there now.

It had been a strange, exotic land. Through the vast, rank grounds at Thibodaux, thirty peacocks had strutted, and there was a cage where a summerhouse should have been in which there spat and grimaced and bawled an old, indecent chimpanzee. She remembered, feeling faint, the heavy-headed flowers and the great ubiquitous insects and the hypnotic air that sucked like a parasite until the mind was benumbed. The large family dined sumptuously and excessively beneath a fan that whirled and whirred like a colossal crazed bug. They spoke in the French of the region, these violet-eyed and small-boned women going plump, and the loving, hedonistic men, red in the face from all their luxuries of food and drink and infidelities. They had seemed, all of them except Edmund, continually to flirt—with each other, with the household dogs and cats, with the servants—until all experience became with them no more than an elaborate structure of artifice. When it was not an interchange of *double entendres,* conversation had been occupied with the perverse nature that smothered the land, with the purple water hyacinths that choked the bayous, the plagues of river rats and termites, the fevers and the nameless affections of the Cajuns and the Negroes, the snakeskins cast on the verandas, the tree-toads in the magnolias, the crocodiles seen from pirogues in the hidden waterways. Ceaselessly, the warm rains fell, rotting and mildewing; she remembered how the backs of books had been swollen and soggy.

Katharine, bred to a thriftier landscape, had liked no part of it except the peacocks and, of course, young Edmund with whom she had almost persuaded herself, in this tropical air where the senses overpowered the logic and the will, to fall in love. Then she had believed that his mind had been like the scenery, rich and dark and teeming. Just back from a studious year of *Sturm und Drang* in a solemn Paris atelier, his mind, though it was not unusual, was passionate. But now, the exercises in copying Rembrandt's drawings forgotten, the etching tools discarded, one would not know his mind from any other. Concerned so long with cotton gins and oil and the millions that fluffed and gushed from them to make for himself, his wife and his son what he was bound to call "the good life," he seemed to have forgotten everything he had ever known. He could never, except in the flesh, revisit Paris. When she had spoken of it to him the other day, he had not the faintest recollection of the ape, did not remember that his name was Julius and that when he was in a friendly mood, he let his keeper put a baby-bonnet on his head. At the time, the two of them together had spent their mornings morbidly watching him. He had congratulated her on the excellence of her memory—as if that satiric beast could ever be forgotten!—and said, "I bet we did some fine philosophizing!" Invisibly she bridled at his ridicule of himself.

It was alarming and disarming and sad to see how like that Edmund the young St. Denis was, limber and tall and fair, his oval, olive face full of poetic and boyish solemnity that would go—oh, how rapidly it would go!—when he had reached the man's estate of real-estate and fortune-building and surrender to the second best; when the skin-deep college education or the *Wanderjahr* had paled like the tan of a winter holiday and the mind was left to rust and blunt like a knife left out in the rain and instinct and reflex replaced imagination.

"Stop this. Stop this infantile tirade," she counseled herself and set her hand against her heart, pounding with anger, and entered her sitting room, turning in its lock the ponderous brass key, vehemently as if she were shutting out a heated argument that had come to an impasse. Inexorably, like clockwork, this rage assaulted her each day, having its origin in something different every time but scaling swiftly to the same pinnacle of passionate and unforgivable disappointment. Sometimes it sprang from the recollection of an endearing mannerism that the boy Andrew had unconsciously acquired from his father who had acquired it from *her* father, sometimes from the timbre of the twins' voices, indistinguishable from Maeve's: and then, as the patroness of these three innocents whom she deeply loved, she travailed as she considered what they would become, tarnished with compromise, becalmed by convention.

At first she did not recall what had set the detonation off today and then she did: five minutes ago or ten, she had happened to look across the lawn at Andrew, limp in the hammock, looking, in attitude and countenance, so like John Shipley that she had desired all the clocks in all the world to stop just then at that point when John Shipley returned to her in the person of a boy of twelve. Progress, change, stereotype, dilution: "Their minds! What will become of their minds? Andrew's, Raoul's, Honor's, Harriet's?" On second thoughts, though, the girls would last as Maeve had lasted; like hers, their naïveté was imperishable.

The fever passed and to her reflection in the pier glass opposite, she said wryly, "It might be well to consider what is happening to your own mind, dear." And gathering her selves together she went to her desk where with a blue quill pen she began, facing the problem, to write in her journal, a massive album of tooled Italian leather which contained the history of twenty-three years of her life, on India paper, in an ample hand. She wrote:

June 16

Last night the whippoorwills were tireless and I read late. It was a struggle to keep their flagellant cries from influencing the rhythm of Thomas Browne. The melancholy birds and the melancholy prose kept me awake when I longed to be oblivious of both. I think I shuddered and wailed aloud when I read that dour forecast of Judgement Day "when many that feared to die shall groan that they can die but once" and "when man shall wish the coverings of mountains, not of monuments." Finally, well past two o'clock, the heathen whippoorwills got the upper hand and I could not take in another word. So until I could sleep, I played a new kind of patience that Celia Heminway has taught me, long and intricate and perfectly suited to her invalidism and to my insomnia. I did not give up until I had once defeated Sol. Maddox's lamp went on for a moment as I turned off mine and I watched him, wakeful with love, come out of the stable and go down to the garden with a lantern. The winter must be a sleepless grief to him when the snow and the ice implacably mask the rosary, exiling him. Mrs. Shea complains that he is sour and dumb. Poor, lonely, obsessed Maddox.

Poor, lonely, obsessed Katharine. For I am snatched by moments of hallucination when reality disgorges me like a cannon firing off a cannon ball and I am sent off into an upper air where there is no sound and my senses are destroyed by the awful, white, paining light. I know that it is only a matter of seconds but because there (wherever *there* may be) time does not exist, it is also eternity, unchanging, looking forward to no equinox, no winter, no spring, no night, no day. Upon a matter so indefinite, having no attendant symptoms, no preamble, no pattern of any kind, I can consult no one. What or whom do I serve? Solomon himself could not tell me. If there were vertigo along with it or a headache or a twitching of my nerves, I might go to a neurologist or even, though I should loathe so craven a capitulation to the vogue of half my friends, to a psychiatrist. Or if there were premonitions beforehand or visions during or afterward, if it resembled at all the *déjà vu* or a bad dream, I could speak to Beulah Smithwick and let her sixth sense explicate and extricate me. If fear or regret attended it or any other vaporing from a tangible cause, I could find the proper physic for myself. But there is no fear except the fear within the experience itself which is, to be sure, a fear of the utmost intensity: it is ideal and has no object that I can name. At the same time that I rise, ejected from the planet into the empyrean, I plummet through the core of the world.

I took this dangerous journey for the fifth time last night, embarking under the prosiest of circumstances, at Peg Duff's when, after dinner, she was showing us her newest cactus, a huge globe with a gray hide and yellow spikes that curled like talons;

at the top of it there was a sort of fontanel covered with a downy growth and I was seized with a frightful desire to stab into it with the paper knife that lay beside its tray. Above the table where she exhibits all these abominable armed bladders and bulbs, together with her Western gear, her tomahawk and arrowheads and a lariat that she declares once belonged to an illustrious cattle-rustler, she has with her infallibly bad taste hung two della Robbia reproductions, more simpering than most and, because the workmanship is so bad, more lifelike. The association between those plaster baby skulls and the organic, living cactus made my impulse monstrously immoral; but as I stepped back, unable to find a suitable comment to make, Mr. Barker, from all outward appearances a good and gentle man, explored the soft fungous top with the fingers of one hand while in his other, he balanced the sharp Scots dress dagger with which Peg slits open her morning mail. And he said, "Wonder what's inside?" and Peg replied, "Know what you mean. Looks like baby hair." In varying degrees, in different ways, I knew that all the others had been possessed as I had been, but this coincidence of our crime did not absolve me, and I was swept upward, outward and pressed down by . . . by what? Shall I call these moments "trances"? When it was finished and I had, so to say, come back into the room, something peculiar and irrelevant took place: I seemed to smell something hot and acrid and the smell seemed to proceed from the array of plants. I spoke of it, not sure a fire had not broken out somewhere. But no one else, though they all sniffed vigorously, caught the odour and Peg said, "Smelling the wide open spaces. Sun on the desert sands. Dunes, you know, like the Cape." My suggestibility was remarked and then the subject was changed. I lasted the evening, played bridge and even concentrated well enough to win five dollars. But when I walked home alone through the fog, my legs were weak as if I had been through an exhausting physical ordeal; I felt that the straps of a tight harness had bruised my back. The first light had come before I fell asleep.

She closed the journal, returned her pen to its bowl of shot and went to her front windows from which, through the interstices of the Dutchman's Pipe, she looked down at the languid figure of the boy in the hammock, his bare, shadow-dappled legs ivory against the crimson, his intelligent large head turned upward to the house. The look of John in him was embryonic for he was still a child, but nonetheless, it was there, beginning, a breathtaking, reminding vulnerability, a pure and open wound of youth. In the healing, he would change. Katharine who had never healed, had never changed, and but for her white hair, she was the same as she had been at nineteen when her lover married someone else, at seventeen when she had sworn to marry him.

At seventeen when, recognizing her first real love, she had gone to the summerhouse one night and prostrated herself before the figure of Minerva, the protectress assigned to her by her learning-loving father, and had vowed by a majestic galaxy of Roman gods and Christian saints (Teresa of Avila, John of the Cross, Aquinas and Augustine, heaven's intellectuals) to marry John Shipley to whom, translating as she went, she read *The Georgics* at his request in payment for the bouquets he brought her; she had taken those naive offerings as symptoms of the absent-mindedness of his infatuation, for no garden in Hawthorne yielded anything like the flowers of Congreve House.

Unlike Edmund St. Denis, she did not make fun of that prefiguration of herself nor even of the melodrama of a passage in her journal that she remembered having written in the beginning of her rapture, "I thanked him for the flowers and could not help from putting him on tenterhooks by telling him he should take care what he puts in his nosegays for girls who have studied the language of flowers. And then I told him that when Maeve comes on Monday week, he will bring her nothing but red roses. He said, 'I shall bring nothing but stinging nettles and deadly nightshade to anyone but you.' This speech, though it was pretty, seemed to me headlong and I was relieved to have Papa come in just then to ask us to play croquet. But for all my precautions, I am devastated by the fellow. Papa believes that he will be another Bulfinch. I pray for that. I do not need to pray for his proposal because of that I'm certain, but I do beseech all the powers that be to make him an eminent architect." (Another Bulfinch! Oh, Papa, for God's sake, let us sit upon the ground and tell sad stories of the deaths of kings.)

It had not been more than a week later that Maeve Maxwell arrived, having spent the earlier part of the summer with Aunt Dora Congreve. Maeve, Katharine's father's ward since her infancy, had been brought up almost as Katharine's sister; together they had gone to Miss Winsor's and then had spent three years at a convent school in France. They bore a strong family resemblance (Hibernian but of the Protestant complexion) and it had been a natural error, in those days, to speak of them as "the Misses Congreve." The Misses Congreve, rather than the "Misses Maxwell" since the latter name was not borne by such luminaries as the former and therefore did not spring so quickly to the tongue; Maeve, erroneously congratulated once on having so brilliant a father as George Congreve had flushed and answered, "I'm only his niece. Katharine's the cream, I'm the skimmed milk."

There was a sisterly, rather than a friendly bond between the girls, and the very fact that they were not sisters but were cousins made their intimacy circumspect and incomplete; Maeve could not forget that she was a burden thrust upon an uncle who had never liked his sister, and she was continually remorseful that the money that had been left her was insufficient to cover her needs of schooling and clothes. Her humility exasperated George Congreve and filled Katharine with such unbearable guilt that, fleeing from it into resentment, she was often coldly cruel. And like everything else, Maeve accepted the cruelty without a murmur.

But when she had come on that summer, Katharine

was so much in love that she overflowed with love and welcomed Maeve with abounding grace and affection. She had not confided in her (it was a miracle that she had been able to hold her tongue since she could put her mind to nothing but John Shipley) but had described to her in full detail the Norman Gardiners' young house-guest whom Maeve was bound, she said, to adore. He had gone sailing with his host, Dick Gardiner, and Maeve did not meet him until the evening of her birthday when a supper and dancing party was held in her honor.

There had been fireworks and dancing on a platform on the lawn; the whole natural world had seemed a background constructed for this one particular night in Katharine's history to accent and deepen her triumphant blossoming. She had been so enthralled by the splendor of her father's gardens, the perfection of the moon in the sky and the clownish paper moon in the tulip tree, the green flares of the fireflies and the sparkle of the violins, the jasmine petals floating in the Moselle *Bowle* in the cool, columned temple to Minerva, the bonhomie of all the young guests lustrous in the promise of their lives to come and, above all, by the joy of a moment when she met her father's eyes and knew by the look in them, wholly altruistic, that he knew and approved and hoped for her that her young man would propose marriage to her on this spellbound night—she had been so secure in the clouds, so busy at her Spanish castles, so self-assured that, in the beginning, she had heard no dissonance in the hour's unfolding melody.

There had been no doubt of it, Maeve, that night, had never been lovelier nor had her simplicity ever been more winning. Ignorant of the cause of it, she had turned toward Katharine's ripe warmth like a leaf turning to the sun. In their bountiful mood, they had gaily worn identical frocks of rose-red *mousseline de soie* and had adorned their Psyche knots of black hair with garnet rosebuds; their beautiful slippers had been ivory satin overlaid with an Arabian design in silver threads, presents from Uncle Daniel Thornton who had enjoined the young ladies to save them until their coming out. But they had agreed they could not wait. Both pairs of slippers now stood in the bibelot cabinet in Katharine's sitting room; they had been worn only that one time and the reason Katharine and Maeve gave each other was that, exquisite as they were, they did not fit. Nor did they ever wear those diaphanous dresses again; they hung still at the back of Katharine's closet, smelling of ancient sachet.

Late on the evening of the ball, just before supper, the fireworks were announced and even then, Katharine had been too much interested in watching Adam and Maddox moving down into the meadow, suppley cleaving through the silvery grass, their arms laden with rockets and pinwheels, to see that Maeve and John, who had danced the last dance together, were standing beside her, hand in hand. A crimson girandole mounted with a hiss into the sky and fell, a fountain of blinding orange fire; the fine, showering colors were unreal and chemical, plangent pinks and purples, sharp blues and violent greens, and the rapidity with which the rockets vanished, leaving for only an instant afterward the image of their course and the echo of their explosion, so excited her that she had been lightheaded and tears had started to her eyes. As the last Catherine wheel revolved insanely on its separate planes of scarlet and green, sizzling and thundering as the wild spokes fired each other, Katharine, in an ecstasy, turned to face John Shipley. No longer than it took the Catherine wheel to spin itself to nothing and leave the summer sky to the stars did it take her to see that he could not, could never see her. So cold that her joints themselves were locked and frozen, so icy that her smile could not relax, she stared at them who, in their oblivion, stared at each other.

It had been a long, long, silent struggle in which, from the start, Katharine had had no chance, for her adversaries, blind and deaf to everything except each other's eyes and voices, had not known that a struggle existed. Throughout that tortured summer and the next one after that, two mortal summers, delaying the formal announcement of their engagement because of some parental restriction imposed on John, they had bruised her; undetected, unsuspected, the cancer spread until its progress and its malevolent pain became the armature of her whole thought and conduct.

As if it had been yesterday, she remembered her demeaning anguish when, on idle afternoons, they begged her to read aloud to them *The Georgics*. (It was always *The Georgics* they asked for, though what did they care for the pruning of vines and the keeping of bees?) They sat the while demurely far apart, stealing glances and mouthing pet names. In the intoxication of their romance, furthered—even created—by this house, these grounds, this lake, this river that Katharine's father and grandfather and great-grandfather provided them with, in this lavish, extravagant Roman holiday, they had had energy and lunacy to spare and had showered her with it. They had imagined that she had deliberately brought them together and to her, their ambassadress, had proposed that the three of them be a triumvirate for life. They had even gone one evening, after a moonlight horseback ride, into Mr. Congreve's writing room off the library where he was reading Tibullus, and had asked him to draw up a document in Latin to testify to this intention. Katharine's father had half turned from his desk and, angry at the interruption, said, "Are you drunk, Shipley? What sort of rambunctious romp is this?"

That night, when John had gone back to the Gardiners' and Maeve had gone upstairs to bed, Katharine had returned to her father at his lucubrations and that time and only that time, they had spoken of Maeve's intrusion. "Was it the real thing, Kathy?" he asked, and when she nodded, he stroked her hand and said, "Poor dear. I had hoped for you there'd be no compromise." The oil in one of the canisters of his student lamp was low and the light expired behind the fluted green glass shade as they watched. At the coming of that half-darkness, Katharine gave up, sighed deeply, brought in another lamp from the library and, Spartan to commend herself to him, she said, "First things first, Papa," and returned to his hand the pen he had set aside. It struck her, as she watched him poise the nib again over the margin of the page of poetry, that like her father, note-maker, student for study's sake, she would never participate, that she would read astutely and never write, observe wholeheartedly and never paint, not teach, not marry God. Untalented and uncompromising, she would not commit herself: her life had seemed to her to stretch upward in a dark curve and as she ascended the stairs, she seemed to tread heavily through all the days of her future years.

Maeve's wedding, in Hawthorne's St. James's church, had followed on the heels of George Congreve's funeral at the same altar, and where his coffin had stood in the drawing room, there stood the bride and bridegroom, embowered in the finest of Maddox's roses. The brevity of the interval, called indecent in the town, had been insisted upon by Katharine herself who had wanted all the business of Congreve House finished, for without her father as her champion she could not have endured much longer to look upon the lighthearted lovers. Maeve, having no relatives closer than the Congreves, could not be married anywhere else, and Uncle Daniel Thornton had come up from Newport, rather grumpily because he hated to be disturbed, to give her away. There had not, at least, been the indignity for Katharine of seeing her own father in this role. Her extremely busy mother who had had little in common with her husband (she had ordered her weeds with the same efficiency and good sense that she employed in replacing worn linens and in the same way put on her face the look of widowhood) and nothing at all in common with her daughter, had gone back to town as soon as she had buried her husband behind Minerva's temple ("I want my bones to be alone," he had said. "I'll not be buried with a multitude. You must plant me under my own fig tree in my own backyard") and dispatched her niece in a flurry of rice. She, Alma Congreve, had been too much concerned at the time with raising a private fund for an ex-sexton of Christ Church in Cambridge who had suffered a nervous breakdown, to think it odd or even interesting that the newlyweds, moved by Katharine's great generosity in the midst of her bereavement, had determined that they would postpone their honeymoon until she could go with them almost a year later. Their insistence on preserving the fiction of the triumvirate had made her think, at first, that they suspected her disappointment; later on, when they were in Europe, she realized that to them it was not a fiction, for they continued to believe that she had made the match between them and with the greatest good humour continually and publicly thanked her.

Ten years later, Mrs. Congreve was once to remark in passing as she sat in her daughter's Boston drawing room, knitting cardigans on the double quick to send to a Dublin temperance house, "It strikes me as unorthodox, to say the least, that you went abroad with Maeve and her husband so soon after their marriage. Wasn't it actually their honeymoon?" But Katharine's affirmative answer was lost on her mother whose questions were usually rhetorical and who went on with a rushing and detailed account of a charity bridge tournament she had attended the day before when, to her certain knowledge, a doctor of good repute had reneged twice and had not been caught out. She was too busy and too obtuse to realize that Katharine had been "keeping up appearances" for, like the honeymooners, she had never dreamed that her daughter was in love with John, whom she referred to, even now, as "Maeve's husband" or as "Dick Gardiner's friend."

After they all had gone, leaving Katharine alone in Congreve House, through some miraculous, compensating providence, she had been stricken desperately with typhoid fever and it was then that her hair had turned to white. The faithful Maddox and the faithful Beulah Smithwick had attended her and when she was well enough to have a mirror brought to her, she had amazed them both with her delight in this transformation. Her calendar had not changed since that time; she remained, in looks and in interior complexion, the girl John Shipley had listened to as she read Vergil's recommendations to agrarians on how to pass the winter.

2

A sigh like a sob shook her as she thought how, in the end, the patience of her charm and her rigid rejection of the second best had finally won her a Pyrrhic victory. For John Shipley, grappling in his forties for his twenties, had been fooled by his needless need and, as greedy as Ponce de Leon, imagining a source of rejuvenation, a new start, rebirth, a second chance with no strings attached, had returned to her. Except that he did not look upon it as a return; he believed he was seeing her for the first time and the bitterest pill of all the galling pills she had had to swallow was the knowledge that he had scarcely been aware of her those years ago but had only been impressed, snobbishly, by her situation as the only daughter of a remarkable man in a showplace of a house.

Now, though, he *must* divorce his wife, *must* marry Katharine, *must*—this is how he stated it—"save himself." *Must, ought,* words dear to the Puritan tongue telling lies between its veiling teeth and coating the vile mendacities with an ethical vocabulary. "I must save myself *no matter what!*" It was not, as she had once imagined it would be, honey-sweet; it was sand in the mouth and under the nails to see his notion of his salvation thus debased; to see him yanked like a trussed and hobbled victim toward the destiny she herself had set for him when she was seventeen on a pallid summer night, when she had loved and desperately required him, and had pressed her hands against Minerva's giant, marble sandaled feet; to see him cowed to incest and Maeve abandoned sordidly for "the other woman."

Maeve had not guessed who the other woman was; conventional and more old-fashioned, in spite of everything, than Katharine, she pictured to herself a dancing girl who kept her husband away often at the sacred hour of tea, caused him to pick humbling quarrels, mantled the house with deceit and gloom. Pacing her bedroom floor she said to Katharine, her confidante, "I want to know and I cannot bear to know. I want her to be the very soul of vulgarity with bad perfume and ankle bracelets and at the same time it revolts me to think of my successor as a tart." Katharine, warming her cold hands at Maeve's hearth, consoled her cousin with a truism, "If she's a tart, it won't last," but could find nothing to console herself for her hypocrisy, could not escape the memory of his insistent declaration that he must save himself, *no matter what,* and that only if she helped him could he succeed.

Their complicated history had begun most honestly and naturally with a conversation one afternoon when John had come to Katharine's house for tea since Maeve was gone for the day on some errand of good will. He had brought with him a portfolio of sketches he had made the summer before of the houses in Gardner's Crescent in Edinburgh; he had drawn the pleasing Augustan conceit well and she expressed her genuine delight in his deft eye. He was as pleased as a schoolboy, and eagerly and with impressive scholarship he talked to her of architecture as if he had only just begun his career and as if nothing could impede the fulfillment of his talent. On that innocent autumn afternoon, he had seemed to her as serious and as frank and charming as he had been in the very beginning and though she had felt a dim stirring of her old emotion, she had essentially been a generous friend, glad to see the renascence of his enthusiasm which, conversationally, at least, had seemed long ago to have died. For, early in his marriage, he had lived too much for his marriage and for his second love, his yacht, the *Empress Katharine*. Self-indulgent while he had the boat, incurably restless after the sale of her, he had never really worked at anything.

The sale of the *Empress*, seven years before, had been urged by his father, a commanding parent in a severe goatee who, being his son's employer in a venerable family firm, had objected to the cruises that had begun in July and ended in September and had been conducted, so he said, "as if Ash Wednesday never followed Mardi Gras." Ever since that time, John had gone each summer to Europe and these tours, even longer than the cruises, were called, a little fictitiously, "business trips," but if the business involved in them led to no contracts, led, indeed, to nothing but the depletion of an expense account, their purpose was ostensibly so elevated that the elder Shipley, who had his soft spots, was satisfied; though he described himself as "a practical man, a mason, merely," and was content to remodel department stores, he revered the artistic persuasion and he liked to think that his son was greatly gifted. "I think John's got something," he said. "I think he's by way of being a pioneer."

For many years John had been endeavouring to evolve what he called "an absolute design" for municipal buildings, but "pioneer" was a misnomer, for he was a revivalist and it was his ambition, before he died, to see a Palladian circus in every principal city of the United States. For an enterprise so daring and so elegant, it was natural that he require an annual refreshment of his memory in the classic cities of the continent. Therefore, for these seven years, he had gone abroad to look at Bath and Paris, Dublin and Edinburgh and Cheltenham, and while he was no closer than he had been before to the renovation, along the ingratiating lines of the eighteenth century, of the police courts, land offices, city halls and vehicle bureaus of Detroit, St. Louis and Bangor, he had an imposing collection of notes and sketches and his father, defending him against wags who claimed he spent his time golfing in Ballybunion and gambling in Monte Carlo, said, "These things take time."

Maeve, in every particular a constant wife, faithfully accompanied him, though Katharine remembered that once on the eve of departure, as she sat surrounded by luggage tessellated with the stickers of hotels too numerous to count, she said, "I wish I could once go to the North Shore with my children. It's sinful of me, I'm well aware, but there are times when perfection tires me." For Katharine, the arrangement could not have been more felicitous; Congreve House was too big for her by herself, she loved the children and they loved her.

It had not occurred to her until their tea *à deux* on Brimmer Street when, in his stimulation, the color rose to his cheeks and his eyes grew lustrous, that he ever had done anything in Europe but play. And even then, she mistrusted the evidence; the sketches might be nothing more than the result of training and facility. Certainly she had never taken seriously his plan to revolutionize the business centers of America and behind his back, with friends and relatives, had laughed at him. No one scolded him for deluding himself; he could afford to; he was rich; and insulated by fatherly and wifely trust, he could go to his grave believing that he had worked hard toward a worth-while aim.

And he might have done so if, on the coppery October afternoon when Maeve had gone to Concord to serve tea at a charity bazaar, he had bought a drink for a tart in an ankle bracelet in the bar of the Touraine Hotel instead of coming to Katharine's house and letting her see the drawings which he was taking home to file with all the others and then to forget. And so also might he have done if he had not, in the course of their subsequent impersonal talks, gradually begun to include himself in his talk, to speak of what he meant to do, then what he could do, then what he *might have done,* and then what he had not done. Suddenly the wasted years of his procrastination gaped open at his feet and in terror of the fading, academic blueprint of his life, he turned desperately to Katharine, persuading himself that she was the catalyst that would turn his whole world gold. But his terror had not burst just yet, it had unfolded slowly and had masqueraded as something else entirely; it had shown itself, through unresolved gestures, the warmer than cousinly greeting kisses, the pretexts for telephone calls and those for presents of flowers and books, it had shown itself to be the mild aberration of a man who knew he could rely upon his lady not to take him seriously. And she was reliable; she did not lose her head.

And finally, then, the terror worked itself out of the maze of his confusions and he had come running to her, begging her to tell him that it was not too late. (Too late for what? At the time she had not questioned but now she did. Too late to persuade the town fathers of Bridgeport to build a railroad station after the manner of Robert Adam?)

So they must save him, together, *no matter what.* But there was a matter: there was the matter of his children. She loved them warmly, especially the lonely boy who, last winter, had sometimes overcome his reticence and come to her for protection against the incubus that shambled through his parents' house. Doctoring him with lies ("Your father's badly overworked this year" and "Your mother's heart is delicate, but they'll both be as right as rain when they've come back from Europe"), she had felt, nevertheless, that in some intuitive, though still amorphous way, he knew and sensed in her drawing room that his father was a frequent visitor to it. It had been one afternoon when Andrew had come to call on her that she had suffered the first of the series of these seizures.

The day before, John had stood with his back to her, leaning his forehead on the mantel and running his fingers through his hair and had said, "I'm at the end of my rope, Kate. I can't pretend any longer or I'll be ready for an asylum. I'll admit I didn't bargain for this, I didn't want it, I don't want it now. But unless you help me, this is the end of me." She had told him to be still, had told him to pour himself a drink and then go home and when he would do nothing but stand there, woebegone, she finally crossed the room to him and in the spendthrift luxury of their embrace, promised everything he asked of her. She promised that if, at the end of the summer, after a fair trial (there is so much self-justifying in adulterers, so much good sportsmanship among ladies and gentlemen in doing dirty) he could not reconcile himself to the continuation of his life with Maeve, she would cast her lot with his, sell Congreve House, leave Boston and go with him to "begin again" in some outpost of the earth.

Childishly and criminally, they had picked out on the globe the island of Mangareva at the bottom of the world. Now somberly contracted to revenge for her ancient wound (she was an honest woman with herself and did not beat around the bush: she was and had always been "in love" with John Shipley and she did not love him and she knew that at the moment of conjugal commitment, the state of being in love would be annulled and she would never be accessible to him again through any ruse) she could not sleep that night and at last she took a soporific, left over from an illness of some months before. As the medicine began to solace her and she began to descend circuitously and slowly like a leaf falling to earth in a demure breeze, she wished, not thinking of John or Maeve or of the children but only of herself, never to awaken. For the first time in her life, she thought of life's alternative as delectable; with her whole heart she wished to die.

On the following afternoon, having observed that Andrew left his large schoolboy's tea untouched (Maureen imagined that all growing lads were gluttonous and on the days he came, set forth a trencherman's meal) she invited him to help her put together a jigsaw puzzle of the Taj Mahal. He was absorbed, head bent, his tongue between his teeth, his being concentrated on the restitution of a minaret. But when all the pieces were interlocked and the garish picture was smooth, Andrew did not smile in his characteristic shy, self-congratulatory way, did not seem to take any pleasure in his accomplishment. He turned away from the table and idly spun the globe and when it had stopped, he closed his eyes, pointing his finger at a spot in the azure matrix of the earth and opening his eyes again he read, "Mangareva. Who lives there?"

She recalled having heard from a psychiatrist at a dinner party that coincidence sometimes dogged the errant course of lunatics, and he had told her of a patient who, having escaped from his sanitarium, had gone to a distant city where he had never been before. Such was his sense of unreality that, requiring tangible proof that he existed, he had looked up his name, an ordinary one, in the telephone book in a public booth. And there it was, lightly underlined in pencil! Just as the man, terrified by a chimerical pursuer, tore out the page in the directory and went howling through the railway station, murderous with fear, until policemen came, so Katharine that afternoon, galvanized with guilt, had savagely spun the globe and screamed at the baffled child, "No one lives there! There's no such place!" and had shaken his shoulders. When the hurricane ended, she had acted quickly, had won him back by saying, "That wretched, wicked Fanny Lyndon did Mangareva as a charade and everyone got it except me. You're trying to humiliate me." He had seemed to accept the explanation and had laughed and amiably teased her a little further. But she could not be sure, and she had not been sure of him since he had come to Congreve House; she had felt his large, speculative eyes on her and often, as if he had mesmerized her, she let fall allusions to his father that, if he did know, he must surely be storing up. Just now when she had looked out the window, she had thought he was watching her even though she was hidden by the broad-leaved vine.

Trying to hush her heart and her hammering pulses, she stared at a portrait of herself as a bibliophile, painted in the library, her hand upon a massive, gold-clasped book, her sidelong glance upon a cage of finches. It had been painted in that memorable and awful summer of Maeve's birthday party, and until he died two years later, it had hung on the wall beside her father's desk. She recalled that when it had been unveiled, the servants had gathered at the outskirts of the group of guests and Maddox had exclaimed, "That isn't her!" Nor was it, for there was no strength in the face, only a retreating prettiness as shallow as a shell. She found herself irrelevantly curious to know how many days before the party the portrait had been finished and she opened her journal once again, leafing quickly through the early pages on which the ink had faded into brown. Two days, she learned, two days before the Catherine wheels lighted up the night and whirled, two days before she had been fixed upon her own Catherine wheel.

The figure was unwise: shutting her eyes against the insipid presentation of herself, she spun upon a wrenching rack and there came again that blinding, dumbing annihilation of reality. She did not know, as she had not known on the other occasions, how long the agony lasted nor did she know whether Honor's voice, singing, restored her to her senses (she noted the accuracy of the phrase) or whether, like the pyrotechnic Catherine wheel, it had ceased of its own accord. As virginal and hyaline as the June day, the voice winged upward:

"Who is Kath'rine, what is she,
That all our swains commend her?"

The wristwatch at her waist said four o'clock and crossing again to the window just as the church bell began to ring, she pulled aside the vine and called to Andrew, asking him to row her out to get a water lily. She must find out, she thought, and in so doing, she must watch her tongue.

Now that her hour of solitude was finished, her mind grew practical. It dwelt upon the number of nasturtium sandwiches she would advise Mrs. Shea to make, on the warning that she must repeat to Beulah Smithwick against scrimping on the sleeves of a blue linen blouse.

> "Who is Andrew, what is he,
> That all my acts imperil him?"

she softly sang. He is a child, she replied, who, like his father, will become a weak man. She sat down at her dressing table where stood a grove of silver-capped and gold-stoppered vessels filled with homemade creams and lotions for her china skin. My life is seeping out of me, she thought, the nightmare vitiates my charm. For a long moment she could not lift her hands that lay, palm down, upon the cool and silvery marble. But finally the life came back to them and she clasped them over her breakable heart and she said, "Lackamercy on us, this is none of I."

CHAPTER III

The Sea's Souvenirs

HALF IN the hammock and half out of it, Andrew tortured a beetle in the grass and fretfully murmured obscenities. A squirrel sassed him from the crotch of the tulip tree and Beth, three feet away, insolently sat with her back to him. Nothing could make him feel worse, when he was feeling bad to start with, than the insult of a cat. He hated them all, and most of all he hated this black bug whose legs he slowly amputated. Between the dirty words, he talked as he worked to an imaginary twin who sat on the grass at the base of the tree. This interested and adventitious homunculus, although it was his twin, was, nevertheless, much younger than he and surpassingly ignorant.

"When I have finished killing Charles, I'll take you downtown," he said to it. "How would you like to eat an alewife at the smoke-house? What is an alewife? Why, it's a sort of herring. Okay, just hold your horses till I get this done. This will be about the only chance I'll have because day after tomorrow, I'll be too busy to bother with you."

"You mean because day after tomorrow you're going eeling with Victor?" asked the twin.

"Eeling!" he exclaimed. "My God, you don't know anything, do you? Do you think I'd catch an eel on purpose?"

The poor kid quickly changed the subject. "When will the funeral be?" he asked.

"Ten in the morning probably," replied Andrew. "Depending on the tide."

"Why depending on the tide?"

"Because we have to go clamming right afterward."

It was mid-morning but the dew was not yet dry in the shade of the elms; drops of it depended like beads from a spider web that was strung from tree to tree. Andrew had been awake since daybreak, stirred out of sleep by two wrens that had held a shrill colloquy in the vine over Cousin Katharine's window. Looking out at them, with the strong, fresh breeze on his face, he had seen his cousin's lamp go off. For a moment he was so thrilled to think of the two of them awake in the sleeping house at five in the morning that he had thought of knocking on her door and asking her to go for a swim. But he knew that the lake would be cold and anyhow, there was something too intimate and isolated about this hour of the day; alone with her in the aboriginal morning with nothing else to distract her, she might read his criminal mind. She had not come down to the dining room while he and the twins were eating their breakfast and her tray, which usually went up at half past seven, had not gone up by the time he left the house at nearly nine. There was a funny feeling in the house; the maids and the twins were quiet, and no one seemed able to settle down to anything. It was always that way whenever Cousin Katharine's routine was disrupted in the slightest.

"Cousin Katharine stayed up all night," he told his twin. "All night long she was reading my mind."

"Maybe she just turned on the light for a minute," suggested the twin.

"Listen," he said to this impudent Doubting Thomas, "listen to me. I'm boss around here. I said Cousin Katharine stayed up all night and that's what she did, no ifs, buts or maybes." The twin blubbered at the scolding and more kindly Andrew said, "Come on, half-pint. Charles Smith*wicked* is deader than a doornail."

He had decided to go down to the village because of something Harriet had said the night before when they were playing three-handed bridge. She had said he should be ashamed of himself for behaving like a baby; he couldn't fool her, she said, he wasn't reading in the hammock, he wasn't doing anything but pretending it was a cradle; she thought that anyone should have more pride than to advertise to the whole wide world that he had no friends and no resources. He had flung down his cards and told her to go to hell. But she was right and he *was* ashamed and all night long he had pitched and tossed and pummeled his pillow and deranged the bedding.

It took great courage to leave the hammock and to expose himself to the town; his mouth was as dry and his heart was as erratic as it always was when he had to be in any kind of play or exhibition. It was like a dream of going to school in his underwear. But he steeled himself; he got up, full of determination. To Honor who called out from the drawing room to ask him where he was going, he replied, "I've got some errands to run downstreet." She saved his life then, for in fact he had no errands at all but she asked him to take the morning letters to the post office. There were five altogether, the three they had written to their parents (Andrew, having nothing to say, had only made a few brief comments on the health of the animals, all of whom were well) and two in Cousin Katharine's hand, one to the Shipleys and the other to Aunt Alma. When he was out of sight of the house, he held these last two up to the light but the letter paper was thick and he could not make out a word; he would have given much to know what she had written about him.

He idled down the road and through the town, keeping up appearances by smiling to himself and, from time to time, if he passed anyone, faking a chuckle. He paused to look at an unfamiliar skiff tied up at the small pier and to speculate on its owner and its purpose and to deduce that it had sailed in from Bingham Bay on the early wind. It occurred to him to board it and get a lift to the docks to hunt for Congreve Smithwick and reclaim his knife with which to cut out Charles's heart; but for all he knew the man was out on a tuna boat, so he abandoned the idea. Lined with white houses, each with a picket fence, a square of lawn or a spring garden, a pair of lilac bushes, this road was as familiar to him as his own face and so pleasing were his sensations as he walked along it that for the time being he took heart and was happy and independent. To the ignorant little wraith beside him, he made much of the stock rural-joke Christian names on the letter boxes, Silas, Reuben, Hiram (he found them marvelous, not in the least comic, exactly as he would have found it marvelous and reassuring to know a colored man named Rastus, a dog named Fido, a cat named Tom), stopped dead still to gather and remember smells, smells of skunks, of tar, of some late riser's percolating coffee, of peonies, weigela, salt air, wood smoke. He and Victor had always felt it their right to look through open doors and windows and he did so now, frankly stood and stared at women combing their hair or punishing their children or disemboweling chickens or shelling peas; at an old man, infirm and useless, rocking himself to sleep in a Boston rocker as gently as if he were a mother and a baby in the same person and then jerking suddenly awake at a sound or the intrusion of the sun. He examined the packages on top of the letter boxes, read the addresses of the senders, applauded or deplored the knots in the string. Now and again he opened a letter box itself and diligently and with no interest at all read the postal cards and quickly leafed through the sale catalogues from Montgomery Ward, bridling with indignation at the pictures of corsets.

Eventually he came to the fish run, a complicated conduit a few hundred yards below the crescent head-tide where every spring the alewives left the river to spawn in the fresh water of the lake above. He stood on a plank over the canal for a while and watched the obdurate fish that progressed by fractions upstream through the fast-moving water, or simply held their place for seeming hours, with their fins immobile and their unseeing eyes glued upon eternity. From the smoke-house came a strong and putrid reek which, on windy days, penetrated to the outskirts of the town; Cousin Katharine, at such times, closed all the doors and windows and went from room to room carrying a long burning joss stick high over her head. The smoked alewives which were bony and tasteless—until age imparted to them an unintentional pungency—and had a skin like yellow isinglass, were shipped to Haiti where, it was said, they were considered a delicacy, a fact that had led the cynical manager of the run to observe that he would not "care to sample their home-grown carrion." Once Charles Smithwick's ship had called at Port-au-Prince and on the back of a view of the Citadel, he had written that he had bought a Hawthorne alewife and that eating it had made him "(home)sick." Oh, that Charles was a wit all right, all right.

"He's a wit in a pig's valise," snarled Andrew's loyal twin.

Not because he liked them, but because it had always been a part of his and Victor's ritualistic day, Andrew begged a fish from one of the men and in the fuming shed he ate the woody, salty flesh in flakes; they were as dry as pine shavings. The genial, stinking man, pausing to wipe his sweaty face, smiled down at Andrew and said, "I suppose you and your side-kick have been too busy listening to Charley Smithwick's tall tales to come and see your old friends."

Andrew was amazed; he had thought the whole town knew that he and Victor were not speaking. He said "Yes," but he dared not elaborate lest the lie be discovered and he become really the laughingstock, and as soon as he decently could, he sped from the smoke-house and went to the general store where, with urgent thirst, he drank a bottle of tepid raspberry tonic. There in the cool of the vast room, partitioned into aisles with cases of notions and shoes and graniteware kitchen pots, he heard the news that had accumulated since this time yesterday. There had been a fire in a henhouse and you should have smelled the feathers! And a breaking-and-entering, a motorcycle accident on Route One; a boat had capsized in the harbor at Bingham Bay; a ventriloquist named Theophilus Sabatini had come to town and would be heard nightly after the first showing of the movie. Charles Smithwick had gained five pounds in the last week; Mr. Breyfogle was out of green split peas but he had plenty of the yellow.

The martial Miss Duff, barking out orders to Mr. Breyfogle for dried apricots as if she were requisitioning ammunition, turned and pointed her finger at Andrew like the man in the Moxie ad, "Is your cousin sick?" she demanded. He choked on a swallow of tonic and shook his head. "Her light was on all night," she accused. "I know because a damned rat kept me awake myself."

"You ought to try this here new 'Rightaway Rataway,'" said Mr. Breyfogle. He had a long pointed nose and beady black eyes and he looked exactly like a rat himself.

"Ought to try a shotgun," said Miss Duff, "and would if the damned outlaws weren't so wily."

"Did you say Kate was sick?" asked Mrs. Wainright-Lowe bustling up from the back of the store where she had been pawing a bin of new potatoes like a ragpicker. Mrs. Wainright-Lowe was a grass widow and she was fond of trouble. Mr. Wainright-Lowe had, for all practical purposes, vanished off the face of the globe though there was a rumor that he was living in Tibet and another that he had settled down in peaceful bigamy in Omaha. She lived with her elderly bachelor son who called her Mumma. Putting upon her round, small-eyed face a look of sympathy transparently malicious, she said, "You don't suppose she ate something at your house last night that poisoned her, do you, Peg?"

"If she did, she brought it herself."

"Oh, I wouldn't be so sure of that," returned Mrs. Wainright-Lowe. "One man's meat is another man's poison, as they say. As a matter of fact, Brantley and I both remarked that we felt a little under the weather this morning. I wasn't going to mention it to you but since Katharine is sick . . ."

"Rats," said Miss Duff and turned back to Mr. Breyfogle who, evidently under the impression that she was speaking of her own rats, held out for her inspection a can of Rightaway Rataway.

The whole town seemed to know that Katharine Congreve's light had been on till morning and everyone was wholeheartedly interested. The occupants of the summer houses of Hawthorne, whose chimneys smoked from just after thaw until the first frost, greeted Andrew one by one with solicitous inquiries as they sauntered or bustled, according to their humour, into the store and later when he sat on the porch, petting Miss Duff's beagles. It gave him a vicarous importance and he was careful not to deny or affirm any of the hypotheses that the ladies and gentlemen proposed; he tried to give the impression that he knew all about it but was not at liberty to tell. Between interviews, he dropped his role and studied the matter analytically, but he came to no conclusions; he could not imagine what on earth she had been doing and he did not believe she had been sick; Cousin Katharine was above sickness except for flu occasionally when there was an epidemic.

"Perhaps she had a guest," suggested Mrs. Tyler.

Miss Duff exploded with outrage, "The light was *upstairs.*"

They were standing just inside the door and evidently

Mrs. Tyler caught sight of Andrew for she hastily amended, "I meant a guest of the animal kingdom. My rats and squirrels often give me insomnia."

"Don't talk to me about rats!" roared Miss Duff. "They're driving me stark staring mad."

They moved out of earshot of Katharine Congreve's relative but he could see that they, together with Mrs. Wainright-Lowe, were continuing the conversation avidly.

Now he watched the deliberate approach of old Mr. Barker who laughed continuously (some said because he was happy and others, because he had nothing else to do) as he took his two-hour constitutional, covering the whole of the little town, his choleric Negro valet following a few steps behind, armed with an umbrella if it should rain and a palm-leaf fan if Mr. Barker should have one of his attacks of vertigo. He waved his stick at Andrew and called out, "I hear your daddy's yacht came into Bingham Bay last night, and I also hear that our own Empress Katharine is indisposed. Convey to her my distressful solicitude and beg her to call on me, her humble servant, if there is anything her heart desires." He laughed, taking none of his speech seriously. "It's my personal opinion," he shouted, cupping his hand to his mouth in a stage gesture, "that she was up all night reading *Gone with the Wind* though she would never own up to it."

Miss Celia Heminway, speeding to the post office in her wheel-chair, on hearing this aspersion, stopped dead still and, glowering, said, "Speak for yourself, Rodney. The trash *you* read!"

He continued to sit on the porch, his back against a tall milk can, knowing that he was the cynosure that morning of every eye. Aloof and smiling enigmatically, he watched as much as he was watched; he watched the parade of summer people whom Victor, even though he had known them all his life, looked on as *sui generis*, "the people from away," and watched the town's indigenous freaks and skeletons whom Victor did not find odd at all but who comprised a gallery so unusual, small as it was, that on the two or three occasions Andrew had described its members to boys at Sewell, no one had believed him. Every single person indicated in one way or another that his rich and beautiful maiden cousin had not gone to bed till morning. The French Canadian game warden of great age and rumored lunacy (he sometimes thought he was General Pershing and tried to drill the trusties when they were working on the highway) and whose hobby was reputed to be raising snakes, came riding his skinny brown mare down from the headtide for his weekly purchase of provisions; he had a reckless greed for macaroni, thereby earning for himself the nickname Yankee Doodle. As long-legged and as lean as his horse, he loped up the steps and Andrew could have sworn as he passed by, that he caught the fishy smell of snakes. He looked at Andrew with his crazy, batting eyes and he said, "Tell her to try a spoonful of honey in a glass of gin." Behind him, Miss Duff made a sound as if she were throwing up.

There was a vile old beggar woman known as Em Bugtown who sometimes wandered away from the county farm at the edge of town and went from door to door asking for food or snuff or silver spoons; it was said that she had been beautiful, been rich, been—despite all this—jilted by her fiancé and then, defying everyone who loved her, had turned to dipping snuff and so had gone from bad to worse. She had come drifting like a hobo up from New York and finally had settled here, an eyesore when she was abroad, a burden to the taxpayers when she stayed put. She smelled of onions and she wore a yellow rag, limp with Musterole, on the back of her neck to alleviate the headache she had had ever since her lover disappeared. Early this summer she had come to Congreve House and had hammered loudly at the spotless door and when Mrs. Shea came to shoo her off, she planted herself solidly on the front lawn, bony arms akimbo, and shouted, "Hark, Lady Congreve! You'll pay for your black sins." Cousin Katharine laughed but she turned a little pale and said that it did not seem fair to be so threatened simply because she would not part with her coin silver teaspoons that had been in the family time out of mind. But Cousin Katharine, who had never borne anyone a grudge, did not fail, when she made her weekly visit to the poorhouse with baskets of fruit and bunches of flowers, to take the old wretch some tins of snuff and packages of cigarettes nor to talk to her for a quarter of an hour. "Miss Bugtown and I," said Cousin Katherine, "according to Miss Bugtown, are in the same boat. She asked me whether I got 'the go-by' by letter or by mouth and when I told her 'both' I thought for a minute she was going to hug me." This morning Em Bugtown came ranging down the hill in a huge pair of sneakers, busily munching her toothless gums.

"Pick up your feet, Em Bugtown!" cried Andrew, for it was this injunction that Victor used to make her swear. She halted, peering this way and that to find the source of the voice, her mouth still browsing greedily over itself. Seeing Andrew finally, she took a stance in the middle of the road, her feet far apart and she shook both fists at him; from her ribby lips there came a stream of words so venomous and nasty that his arms and legs and the back of his neck erupted into goose-flesh. When she had finished with her imprecations, she became malevolently unctuous and actually rubbing her twiggy hands together she said with a smirk, "You don't go scot-free for robbing the poor and defrauding the helpless, do you, dear? Didn't go to bed at all last night? But I, for one, am truly sorry for her." Humming villainously, she moved on in the direction of Mr. Barker's house undoubtedly to ask for spoons.

He saw the man with one diminutive ear (it was no bigger than a clove of tangerine and Andrew would have given both his normal ones for it) and the man without a nose but only a great bandage where it should have been; and Jasper, the epileptic; and the fabulously corpulent Bluebell James who had had a bastard baby every year since she was twelve. Every one of them spoke to him and tried to seem casual when they asked after Miss Congreve.

Not the least interesting of these autochthons was Beulah Smithwick, that sly and frowsy necromancer who could foresee the future and disclose the past in a pack of filthy playing cards or a pattern of wet tea-leaves. She came to town at a trot every morning, carrying a covered basket in which she put her small supplies of two eggs, four potatoes, half a pound of pork liver, a loaf of bread, which she left then in the cold-room of the house where she was sewing that day until it was time for her to trot home. She loitered a little in the streets—yet seemed to skip when she stood still—to gossip in a voice as high and unrelenting as a whistle with a single note. It was Andrew's sisters' fancy that Beulah and Yankee Doodle Lafontaine were married but very secretly and that they practiced black magic with the snakes and the tea-leaves. One year, when a band of gypsies came in the heart of summer and through the bird-watching binoculars, Honor and Harriet and Andrew had spied on the fat little women sidling in and out of Beulah's cottage on what errands they did not dare imagine, Honor had sworn that one of them had given her the evil eye through the glasses because the very next day she broke out in hives and she would not be persuaded that they had come from eating wild strawberries in the woods; she spoke of "the time Beulah's house-guest hexed me." Beulah wore a ruffled mobcap and winter and summer, rain and shine, around her neck, there slackly hung a many-tailed fur tippet the color of a mouse. "How come your mother wears fur in the summer?" Andrew once had asked Victor and Victor, shrugging his shoulders, countered, "How come your lady cousin rides around in that old-time whatsis?"

Remembering that, Andrew turned his face away from the street and gazed into a stand of pine trees on the far bank of the river, carried again into the past in spite of the potentialities of this morning's mystery. For one of the most puzzling aspects of Victor's snub was that next to his brother, he had admired Cousin Katharine more than anyone else in the world and Andrew had never deceived himself that it was partly because of his kinship to her that Victor had so favored him. But unless they were meeting secretly (anything was possible in this unpropitious year) he had ignored her as completely as he had ignored Andrew. It was true that he had seldom come nearer to Congreve House than the kitchen garden except during a party, but all the same, he knew the interior of it as intimately as Andrew did for, making no bones about it, he toured it in the winter when it was shut up except for the kitchen and the two bedrooms where Maddox and Mrs. Shea slept. Similarly he entered all the boarded-up, dust-sheeted summer houses, inspecting them methodically and uncritically. He said that if one kept "a sharp look out" it was possible to learn everything there was to know about a person just through his belongings. In speaking of Mr. Barker's house, he once had said, "I think it's funny for a man to keep a box of cowbells under his bed." His eye had wandered as he contemplated this vagary and then, "I bet he's afraid of the dark and has them handy to roust out his man," a hypothesis that was very likely true since Mr. Barker, who was many times a millionaire, had long ago been threatened by black-hand letters, presumably from a band of kidnappers. He had immediately retired for protection to a private sanitarium for nervous complaints, where through a gross misjudgement or a snarl of red tape, he had been put into the violent ward. He admitted freely that ever since, he had had horrifying nightmares in which the kidnappers and the psychiatrists pursued him in gyroscopes.

And speaking once of Cousin Katharine's house, Victor said, "I figure she keeps those spriggy shoes in the china closet to remember something by. I figure she wore them on some red-letter day or other, but I haven't figured out yet why there are two sets." The "china closet" was a bibelot cabinet in the upstairs sitting room and the "spriggy shoes" had been worn by Cousin Katharine and Andrew's mother at a ball he had often heard about. When he told Victor this, Victor winked and said, "It's funny to keep a keepsake for getting two-timed." But when Andrew demanded an explanation of this cryptic statement, Victor said only that he had been joking. Another time, he said, "You know last winter when I was in your house? I found out something. I found out why she never got married." And then, when Andrew asked why, Victor stood on his head and upside down, in a strangled voice, brushed him off. "April Fool," he gurgled. "I found a mice nest in a hat of hers, that's what I found."

Beulah Smithwick was a woman to whom gossip came unsolicited and copiously like particles of iron to a magnet and who, though she was trustworthy with confidences, enjoyed holding character up to a strong light. Like all inveterate gossips, she claimed she did not gossip at all but that she had only a friendly curiosity to know "what made people tick." And it could be assumed that in the winter, when she was snowbound and half the time the erratic telephone was out of order, she used her son as her sounding board and interlocutor so that it was natural that his mind had been sophisticated early and natural that he should know as much and even more about Cousin Katharine than Andrew did. For she had known Miss Congreve from childhood since she had been a maid in the house, twelve years old, when the infant Katharine had been brought up for her first summer in Hawthorne. Through the crude country boy, Andrew had learned that his cousin's gilded cradle had been made in the shape of a shell and had been lined with pale pink China silk; her frocks and bonnets and peignoirs had come from Paris and so had her saucy nanny who taught her to say "*ma bonne*" before she said Mama or Papa. Beulah had watched her gorgeously unfold, emerge magnificently from her adorable chrysalis. And Beulah had, moreover, watched Maeve Maxwell grow from a thin and tearful little orphan into a woman nearly as confident and nearly as beautiful as Katharine.

When Victor, borrowing his mother's recollections, spoke of Andrew's mother, Andrew was at once excited and discomforted: it was like a double vision or like a dream within a dream. As if he spoke of someone he had read about or someone he knew and Andrew did not, he would say, "She and the other one . . ." (and by "the other one," he meant Andrew's own mother). "She and the other one took off one night in the middle of the night and rode horseback to Bingham and stowed away on a tuna boat. They found them before they got past the lighthouse but—" and now he quoted his mother verbatim and his voice even partook of her screeching timbre—"it was a scandal that rocked our town." Then, speaking for himself again he added, bored, "Nothing happened, though." At such times, Andrew felt like an immigrant to a country where he spoke the language brokenly but had excellent connections.

He thought of how flattered he had been by Victor's envy of Andrew's relation to her, how he had questioned him on the interior of her house in Boston and had been delighted to know that she had a chemical laboratory in the basement where she had once successfully made gunpowder. His cat-eyes widened and his mouth hung open in fascination when her name was mentioned or when he saw her, tall, white-haired, dressed in her lovely clothes, her flowing cloaks and her Spanish shawls, her broad hats and her veils. He liked to see her going past in her carriage for her afternoon drive, bowing and smiling like a public personage on her way to pay visits of half an hour or to leave her card together with one of the small mementoes she always carried with her in a rattan basket, sprigs of lavender, spills of colored paper, dried morels. She greeted everyone she met by name and by her friendly questions, to do with a sick child or the progress of a new wing on a house or the loss of a dinghy or the preparations for a wedding, she indicated that the concerns of all her neighbors were her concerns.

When Victor called her "ma'am" he sounded as if he were addressing a queen and sometimes, forgetting his manners, he stared at her, dumb and spellbound. He was rigid at the lawn parties, the midday picnics, the strawberry teas and the evening fetes with dancing round a maypole garlanded with roses. And while she organized the other children into games of blindman's buff and snipsnapsnorum, he stood apart, unwilling to be distracted from his contemplation of her. And while she fed the others to repletion with profiteroles and lemonade, he could not eat. Once, though, he had agreed to join in a game of post office which Cousin Katharine herself had organized and he had got a special delivery letter from his hostess and had been required to go with her to the writing room off the library, the "privy chamber," as she called it, a term that made the country children blush and squirm with giggles. And here, behind the damask portieres, he had received a kiss from her. His look of surprise when he came out had imparted to his hodgepodge face an unbelievable dignity which had stilled the tongues of the others who had been on the point of teasing him. He had stalked directly to the finches' cage over the terrarium and Andrew had seen him put his lips to the grating as if he hoped the birds would permanently tattoo the kiss on his lips with their sharp beaks. Ever since that time, however, he had shunned even post office and he stood speechless on the sidelines, unable to participate in anything although, because the etiquette his mother had schooled him in demanded it, he would stand on his head, he would even yodel briefly if Miss Congreve asked him to.

Cousin Katharine had not had a single party this summer, not for children and not for ancients. Andrew had not thought of that before but now that he did, he could only come to the conclusion that there was something wrong with her. "Something is rotten in the state of Denmark," he said to one of the beagles and at that moment Beulah Smithwick fluttered up the steps and shrilled at him, "What's this about my darling lady being sick? Say it isn't so."

"It isn't," he said and on an inspiration he added, "She was up all night cutting out paper dolls."

"Cutting out paper dolls?" Mrs. Wainright-Lowe inquired with great interest through the screen door. "I think you're mistaken, Andrew. I think Miss Duff's hot crabmeat hors d'oeuvre gave her an upset."

Beulah flicked through the tails of her tippet and underlining every word she said defensively, "Shellfish does not disagree with Katharine Congreve and I am in a position to know, having known her from the bassinet."

"I wasn't impugning Miss Congreve," said Mrs. Wainright-Lowe. "If I was impugning anyone . . ." But just then Miss Duff, who was about to be impugned, marched out the door, ordered her dogs to "Heel, damnit," and charged off. Beulah went into the store, haughtily refusing to look at Mrs. Wainright-Lowe again.

Now that the dogs were gone and now that practically everyone in town had spoken to him, there was again nothing to do and no attitude to strike. Turning a little to the left, he said to his twin, "This is the most boresome summer A.D." It was indeed a summer not in any way superior to those of his school friends whom he had formerly pitied since they were either shunted off to camp to learn the doubtful art of making fire with sticks or to grandparents, set in their ways and in the belief that a child's sole commission in life was to be seen and not heard.

He and the twins had had one awful, unforgettable summer, to be sure, when Cousin Katharine had gone out West and they had been sent to the Stygian Newport villa of their Uncle Daniel Thornton, a queer fish who kept his own appendix pickled in a jar under a glass bell in the library. All that summer he had sought to improve his wards' minds by a nightly reading from *The Decline and Fall of the Roman Empire* and every morning after breakfast, no matter what the weather was, they had had to sit in the library, in full view of that pale inner worm of his and write an essay—or rather a *pensée,* as he more stylishly put it—for Uncle Daniel was in love with the written word and called himself "a member of the scribblers' fraternity," though he had been published only once, with an epithalamium in dimeter, in *The Harvard Advocate.* The rest of the time in Newport had been divided between orderly excursions to Bailey's Beach with an acidulous Fräulein hired for the season (their governess, Miss Bowman, who was from Santa Fe, had been refused house-room by Uncle Daniel who did not favor the West which he called "the ultramontane colonies where nothing flourishes except the solecism") and equally well-ordered afternoon picnics with suitable children as bored as they. The whole summer had had the languid, empty air of convalescence.

But so had this present one. They had not gone once to Bingham Bay to hire a boat to sail among the islands of the wild Atlantic; nor roasted corn on the rocks at Pemaquid; always before, Cousin Katharine sitting sidesaddle and wearing a perky derby and a regal habit of dark blue poplin, had taken them for moonlight horseback rides. They had not even played croquet or *boccie.*

Conceivably the world was coming to an end.

2

Billy Bartholomew, the blasphemous and long-winded blacksmith, was sitting in the doorway of his shop directly opposite the store, alternately reading a newspaper and observing the doings of his fellows with a misanthropic eye. Billy disliked almost everyone and he especially disliked Katharine Congreve who took her horses to Bingham Bay to be shod. Through innuendoes, through a maze of hints about "someone, naming no names, not a thousand miles away," through a crabbed castigation of the rich and of summer people and "certain parties that get themselves up like Lady Astor's plush horse," the shaggy, baggy, cantankerous old man had, in the past, lambasted her to Andrew when the notion took him to, when Andrew and Victor were calling on him and when he was reminded of her existence by the sight of her maids going into the drugstore or by the spectacle of Miss Congreve herself in her splendid carriage, her coachman dressed to the nines, Pegasus and Derek trotting along in their infuriating shoes. He had the caution never to make a direct attack but circuitously, speaking of "*some* people who are ruining the country by refusing to buy in the domestic market," of "people who come down here in the summer and think they can lord it over us," of "hoity-toity spinster women who think they know it all," he arrived, eventually, at his old wound which he loved and cherished and kept open, bleeding for all the town to see.

Although Billy was garrulous and tiresome and usually angry, Andrew needing company made his way across to the cool, cavernous barn, piled to its rafters with wheels and broken springs, the skeletons of sleighs, old lanterns, splayed creels, rat-chewed landing nets. On top of the cold anvil there was a battery radio which Billy kept tuned to a Canadian station; over it there came a watery wail from Toronto and, at certain times, the exultant voice of a young woman who advertised "live honey" which could be ordered through arrangement with one's local grocer; in the background, the static sometimes gave the impression of bees producing on the spot.

"Glad to have this unexpected honor," he said as Andrew sat down on the floor beside him. For some time then he read aloud the obituaries of people he did not know and the fillers in the Bangor *Courier*. In a rich, ministerial voice, he intoned, " 'There are more rats than people in New Orleans, Louisiana.' What do you think of that? *More rats than people.*" Then, in two different voices, as if he were reading a dialogue, he presented a question and answer:

"Question: Why is neatsfoot oil so called?
Answer: Neat is an old Anglo-Saxon word meaning ox or oxen. Neatsfoot oil, used principally for dressing leather, is a fatty oil obtained from the feet of cattle."

He fell silent and leafed through a magazine called *The Northern Farmer*. From time to time he looked up and sneered at someone in the street. "How Albert can call that thing a car is beyond me," he said. And some time later he observed, "There's Jasper walking like a fiddler crab, sign he means to take a fit today."

Billy's pleasure, apart from mustering odd data, was to inveigh against the government and against women for both of whom he had an unremitting hatred. He led his lean (he himself was stout and red and hairy) embittered wife a wretched life, and their exchange of vituperation in public places was as much a part of the local scene as the springtime arrival of the alewives or the daily passage of Miss Congreve through the streets. Anything that was low or uncomfortable or dishonest or ugly was, in Billy's mind, either womanly or governmental and he liked to confound the two abominable species by speaking of "all those women in the White House and in Congress" and calling Mayor Curley "a damned flapper." Of his horse, an irascible white gelding with one blue eye, he said, "When he gets my dander up, I call him Carrie Nation, but generally I call him something sweeter." His sweeter name was Dave. And all the murders he recounted—he did this well; he had a histrionic flair and a sincere appreciation of bloodshed—had been committed by women whose victims, always men, had died through fiendish, housewifely tricks; they had drunk arsenic with their morning coffee, had eaten ground glass in their rice pudding and died a dog's death, had been decapitated with hatchets as they read the Sunday papers. A relative of his who had gone West and rashly had married a native had been eaten to death by a pack of dogs belonging, significantly enough, to his mother-in-law. Billy's nickname for Mrs. Bartholomew was Lizzie Borden.

"The blue, or sulphur-bottomed whale is the largest living animal, attaining a length of more than 100 feet and a weight of 150 tons," he read, picking up the newspaper again. He exhaled a breath of beer though it was not yet noon; he made the beer himself and drank it green and bottles of it, in the dark recesses of the smithy, sometimes exploded like a clap of thunder. "Here's something else," he said. " 'Dried skinks are still used medicinally in certain parts of the United States.' Doesn't say what parts or what for. That's typical of these women on the papers; they leave out half of what a man wants to know. Also I am fully of the opinion that a good part of the time these facts are not true. For example, do you believe as it says right here that 'the jaw is the strongest part of the body'?"

Andrew, to please him, said he doubted it and Billy yawned and put *The Courier* aside. "It's as plain as a pikestaff that the horse-drawn carriage as a means of transportation is done for," he said gloomily. "Now you take Charley Smithwick, when he was a little shaver he wanted to be a blacksmith and he spent more time with me than he did away from me learning my trade. He would have been a good man, but I never blamed him for throwing me over for Uncle Sam when it became the self-evident fact of the matter that the horse-drawn carriage was a gone goose. Charley, I am happy to report, has begun to rally. It is my conviction that he is one of the two or three people I have ever known who was worth his salt."

"When is he going away do you think?" asked Andrew.

"He oughtn't to go back too soon. He ought to lay around his mother's house for a good long time. Else how can he get the strength to become—as it is my full opinion that he will—the kingpin of the whole U. S. navy shebang? I am persuaded that within my lifetime I will see that young fellow bring his ship right up to headtide." The fact that Charles had neither received nor been ambitious for promotion was ignored by everyone, and he was called "the captain," "the skipper," and "the admiral" and it was believed by many in the town that his finger was on the pulse of the world. "You can't tell me," said Billy now, "that being right there on the spot in Tokyo and Shanghai and all that he doesn't know all there is to be known about this so-called Far East. But he's tight-lipped even with me, his tried and true old friend. He knows a lot he can't put out."

The eulogy went on and when he began, "I'll take my share of credit in the molding of that young man . . ." Andrew surreptitiously leaned toward the radio and concentrated on the phrenetic pops and ululations from Canada. When he ended, "You mark my words," Andrew sat up straight again.

"So the former *Empress Katharine* has come to the

Bay," he said, "and her Ladyship has got the pip. My, my, there's a lot going on in the world. A lot more than meets the eye, and a lot of it that don't bear too close examination, if you get my meaning."

"I don't get your meaning," said Andrew nervously. "I don't get your meaning at all."

"Well, you know, like I said, there was a lot that Charley knows about those Chinamen and Japs that he's not telling every Tom, Dick and Harry. Well, everybody's got something like that, haven't they? Not so important but something to keep in the dark all the same. I bet if you were of a mind to do it, you could tell me a good deal I'm mildly—*mildly*, I repeat—curious to know. Why lights are burning in the middle of the night or whatever."

"I could tell you a thing or two about Charles Smithwick if I wanted to," said Andrew.

"What about Charles Smithwick?" demanded the blacksmith, clenching one enormous fist as if he were looking for a fight. "Be careful how you talk about Charles Smithwick."

"Oh, just about what's going to happen to him one of these days," said Andrew and ducked out the door and ran up the hill toward Congreve House. He had turned in at the gate before he realized that he had not mailed the letters.

He debated whether to go back now or to wait until after lunch. Seeing Cousin Katharine feeding the swans and not looking in the least unwell, he decided to wait and to spend the time now trying to find out why she had behaved so eccentrically. He hailed her, and she greeted him warmly. If he had had any idea of broaching a serious subject to her, he had to put it aside. She would talk of nothing but the downy woodpecker fledglings that this morning had at last flown out of the nest down near the summerhouse.

There was one thing though that, detective-like, he noticed: there was a long slim glass of pernod on the iron tea table and when she had finished with Helen and Pollux, she began to drink it, not in sips but in big swallows. He had never seen her drink in the middle of the day before. He wondered if, all of a sudden, she was going to become fast and cut her hair and even dye it. He half wished she would. But there was not even a suggestion of a crack in her façade and when she saw him looking at her apéritif, she said, "I was longing for Paris today. Nothing brings it back to me more clearly than this delicious drink."

"No," Andrew said to his importunate twin who had been asking too many stupid questions, "I will not take you there again because there is absolutely no point in eating alewives. You can go by yourself if you want to."

The twin business had begun to bore him, and there was no end to this day in sight. At lunch, each time he had opened his mouth to say that everyone in town knew that Cousin Katharine had stayed up all night and that the *Empress Katharine*—called now, horror of horrors, *La Paloma*—was in the harbor seven miles away, someone had interrupted him. Finally he had moodily asked to be excused before dessert and ever since had been lying in the hammock drafting in his mind a series of black-hand letters to be sent to Charles Smithwick, Billy, and Honor who, at lunch, had called him a gas-bag though the fact was that he had not got a word in edgewise. He had not gone to the post office but had put the letters in his bureau drawer and had told himself that he would mail them when he got good and ready.

He watched Brantley Wainright-Lowe pegging along the road in shorts and a tennis visor and he saw Miss Duff, dressed in a mechanic's coverall and a baseball cap, riding past on her motor-bike to hunt for bargains in summer squash and hand-hooked rugs. "Rockabye, is it, day after day?" she hollered and was gone with a threatening pull at her police siren. She disliked boys and declared that they did nothing but crack their knuckles and ask each other riddles. "Pop! Pop!" she would say to him on meeting him in the road and give him a hard look. "When is a door not a door? Really!" He was too busy with other things today to resent her implication that he was a lazy and overgrown baby, though he filed it away to consider later, for he had found that slights and insults often served to distract him from his deeper grievance; for one whole day he had been sustained by Honor's charge that he handled his knife and fork like Mutt.

He turned over in his tree-hung cradle, his back to the road, and gazed upward at the lightning rods and the broad arched doors of the barn; the iron whale was veering east. As he watched, he saw Cousin Katharine come round the side of the house, her arms full of lilacs. She appeared and disappeared behind the sweep of columns as she approached the door and then for a moment she stood framed by the two central ones, looking into the rosary opposite where she had perhaps heard a bird, so motionless and tall, placed so symmetrically that she looked to be a part of the house itself, like the cool, impassive statue of Minerva. Today she wore a full skirt of yellow linen, a tucked white blouse with wide sleeves that were inflated with the breeze, and a ribbon crossed at her neck and pinned with a cameo; her white hair rose from her forehead in a high pompadour. She listened for a moment and then she turned and though she looked directly at him, she did not call or wave or smile, seemed not even to recognize or see him. He was nonplused by this preoccupation—or was it displeasure? He was accustomed to preoccupation in his parents and lately this had been their usual role, but not in her, *never* in her for her greatest virtue was that she immediately welcomed and attended anyone who came within her orbit. For an awful moment, there flashed preposterously across his mind the thought that she really *had* read his wicked thoughts and knew he wanted Charles to die (at night before he went to sleep, he could not help it, he kept seeing Charles's bloody, decimated body strewn all over the highway and he was sometimes paralyzed with fear that he would talk in his sleep) and she had stayed up all night long writing to his parents to tell them that they should lock him up somewhere before it was too late. He knew a boy, Teddy Throckmorton, who was only one year older than he who had gone berserk, out of a clear sky, and had threatened a cook or a maid or someone with a straight razor and had been taken away to an insane asylum. At Sewell it was rumored that he was in a padded cell and that he ate out of a bowl on the floor like a dog.

Possibly he was going crazy; it was possible that he would kill Charles without even intending to. He'd better read a book, he thought, or his mind might do something dreadful, and he picked up *Life on the Mississippi.* Over the top of it, though, he watched his cousin. She went in in a minute, closing the front door softly so that the knocker would not sound, but the image of her there persisted, poised perfectly in the exact center of the stage. Or like a judge at the middle of his long, legal pen, sentencing the prisoner to death.

> "I sent thee late a lilac wreath,
> Not so much honoring thee,
> As giving it a hope, that there
> It could not withered be,"

sang Honor; her voice was reedy and clean, as pellucid as a shallow, amber pool. She sang and stopped, unable, perhaps, to continue with her paraphrase or asked, perhaps, to put the lilacs into water. The house was silent. At the back of his mind, Andrew heard Poor Hollis ring the bell for three and heard the insatiable gulls caw hoarsely over the refuse from the smoke-house. He continued to stare at the expressionless face of Congreve House and at the after-image of Cousin Katharine. *Did* she know? Did she know that as he lay here hour after hour under his great-grandfather's elm trees he wished and prayed for the death of someone who had never done him any harm? Together with the fear and the guilt and the dismay at his atrocious inner nature, there was a kind of obscene pleasure in it and he thought how he might most dramatically blackmail himself by writing an anonymous letter to her, telling on himself. "Madam, you harbor a serpent of the male sex," he would write and sign it with a skull and crossbones.

The more he thought about it, the more convinced he became that all last night she *had* been writing to his father about him. The letter had been very thick. He was not sure that he would ever mail it.

He turned from Charles to Cousin Katharine and back again, living through the afternoon. Alternately he stared at the house and stared at the road. An hour passed. He saw Beth, pregnant, wearing her kittens like saddlebags, adroitly mount the Dutchman's-pipe to her mistress's windows and just after the bell at St. James's rang for four, its last note loitering and dissipating then in a spray of fading echoes, the owner of this belvedere appeared, assisted the cat and called down to Andrew, "Will you take me out to get a water lily for my spittoon?" and vanished, letting the vine fall back into place like a curtain.

She must want to get him alone to give him the third degree. His heart was as loud and jazzy as a dance band, but he got up and called back as naturally as he could, "Sure! Now?" and she reappeared in a blue silk wrapper. "I'm changing for a swim. I'll meet you there. Just you and I, no little girls allowed."

The twins, hearing this interchange, came to the downstairs windows and Harriet cried, "As if we cared!" and Honor happily caroled, "As if we'd get our hair all wet when Raoul is coming!"

"Beth will go with us," said Cousin Katharine, coming again to the window. She had always taught her cats to swim. When he came to think of it, Cousin Katharine was awfully peculiar; he had always before taken her for granted but suddenly he no longer did. Why, for example, was she so attached to such old-fashioned pastimes? The game of patience while she drank her tea if she had no visitors; the simple needlepoint; the making of potpourri with sun-dried rose petals; the outmoded customs of reading poetry aloud, and mounting butterflies on pins. She even smelled old-fashioned, of some fastidious, countrified scent (Maddox made it for her from an arcane receipt) no more conspicuous and no more nameable than the general sweetness of a rural garden just come into bloom. She moved in a nebula of this and of dove-gray chiffon or lilac lawn, regarding the works of Robert Browning and the Roman poets through a shell lorgnette or watching the birds which she described in a black ledger with a thin gold pencil, rejoicing in them all except for the puffin which she found absurd and the cowbird which she deplored on moral grounds. The cat was always doomed from kittenhood to wear a bell of piercing tone.

If insanity ran in the family, who was she to have him put away?

For a moment, he was inexplicably exhilarated and he set off at a run, taking the longest way through the meadow, a field of timothy full of daisies and nests of voles and stands of wild iris. A bright snake flicked past him and he ran after it and though he could not catch it, he shrieked in the direction of the kitchen, "There's a snake here, Mrs. Shea!" Instantly, like a jack-in-the-box, the woman rose from the steps and vanished into the house, slamming the screen door behind her to finish her Hail Marys trembling as she stood upon a chair. Maddox, who was clipping the box beside the stable, paused and laughed unkindly and at once resumed his look of sullen disapproval. "If you throw any more rocks at my Seckel pears, I'll snake *you,*" he said sourly.

Honor came to the dining room window to scold, "You're mean! You're a beastly boy and you'll never go to heaven. You tell Mrs. Shea there wasn't a snake."

But he cried back, "I was only telling the truth. There *was* a snake. There are millions and trillions of snakes in the grass." He stood still, his eyelids burning in the sun, and chanted, "Grass snake, water snake, bull snake, viper, red snake, green snake, cobra, adder." But the joke, like all jokes these days, palled and he sighed and his smile faded. No prank seemed worth the effort when there was neither confederate nor claque. Morose again, he plodded on.

When he had changed into his swimming suit in the damp bath-house (he hated it here; it was tiled like a public lavatory and daddy longlegs ran on stilts up and down the slippery walls) he sat in the tippy rowboat waiting for Cousin Katharine, carelessly startling two young turtles that were sunning on the rock at the lake's edge; their place was taken by an enormous butterfly that shuttered its pansy-yellow wings three times before it flew away. He plucked the beggar's lice off his socks and swaying the boat lightly as if he were still in the hammock, he crooned, "Charles Smithwick, die, oh, Charles, get well, oh, big fat nitwit, Charley Smithy, go to hell for leather."

A stream of images like a motion picture passed before his eyes: Charles was swimming off the dangerous rocks at Pemaquid and a squall was coming up; under the darkening sky, the phosphorescent spindrift shone; it was a sinister sight. Charles was too far out! He could not get back! For the third time he went down! Months later, flaccid and fishbelly white, the body was washed to shore sixty miles south at Kennebunkport. Then: someone was ringing the bell in the firehouse to summon the volunteer brigade and the cry went up through the streets of Hawthorne, "It's the Smithwick house! It's going up in flames!" Beulah was in the sewing room at Congreve House, sewing a fine seam, and Victor was at the store, but Charles was in his bed in the burning house and he died before the marshal came. Charles Smithwick ate a poisonous mushroom. His lifelong enemy stabbed him through the heart. His mother, mistaking the bottles, gave him iodine instead of Castoria and he writhed to death before the doctor had even finished cranking up his car. As they were leaving the graveyard, Victor said to Andrew, "Let's go smoke."

He was frightened again and when Cousin Katharine came down the path, he bent his head, pretending to be tying his sneakers. She was wearing a long red linen cape over her bathing suit and a straw picture hat that tied under her chin, making her look not much older than Honor and Harriet. Her cat came trotting after her, mewing conversationally, her high tail waving like a plume. She leaped neatly into the boat to sit squarely in the middle, winking her shrewd eyes.

For a long while Cousin Katharine said nothing significant. Under the white sun of summer as he slowly rowed her from this archipelago of lily pads to that, he listened to her casual stream of talk, but at the same time he followed the paths of the blue devils' darning needles that skated through the reeds and watched the holiday fishermen try for bass; once someone in a red motorboat got a strike and Andrew rested his oars to watch the catch. The struggling fish arched angrily as it twisted through the air and when it was landed, Cousin Katharine clapped her hands and cried, "What a sight! Oh, what a day!"

But on a day like this, he and Victor should be fighting with the valiant bass (his new flies, ordered for his birthday from Abercrombie and Fitch, had never been taken out of their cellophane wrappings) and automatically he looked across the water in the direction of the Smithwick house, but all he could see of it above the trees was its single solid chimney from which arose a line of smoke as narrow as a pin. And then, a minute later, from far off, he heard Victor's lighthearted approach and Cousin Katharine said, "It's a pity your friend hasn't a quieter talent. Couldn't we teach him to juggle? It would be just as droll as yodeling and it would disturb the peace far less."

Hating Victor, Andrew cut the water deeply, wounding it, and said, "He'd juggle if Charles told him to," and under his breath he went on, "He'd suck eggs if Charles said suck eggs."

"Yes, he is devoted to his big brother, isn't he?" said Cousin Katharine. "I don't think he's been to our house once this summer."

"He'll never come to our house again. Not as long as I'm there anyway."

"What a ridiculous, unworthy notion. Someone has to look after Charles."

"They could hire a nurse."

"And what would they pay her with? You shouldn't say such selfish things, dear, they make a bad impression. And you should remember that Charles can't stay forever."

"Charles *can* stay forever," said Andrew grimly, gouging the water. "And he will."

They were near the end of the lake where the water petered out in a marsh beside the road and when he glanced up, Andrew saw Victor just rising over the top of the hill on his way home; from his wide-open mouth the yodeling poured copiously like something from a pitcher. Cousin Katharine waved and called, "Hello! I hope your brother's well today," and softly to Andrew she said, "Do you suppose it's related to gargling? I must try it some time."

"Hello!" cried Victor exuberantly. "Charles is okay. He went out in the yard."

"Splendid! Give him our fond regards."

Enraged, Andrew set his jaw.

"You got the cat with you?" bellowed Victor and when Cousin Katharine assured him that Beth was there and if he looked closely he could see her flattened out now in the middle seat, taking the sun, he slapped his behind with the magazine he was carrying and shouted, "Oh, boy! I hope she don't get seasick."

"If she does, we'll give her Mothersills in her cream."

Tee hee! Ha ha! Shut up, said Andrew to himself, shut up and that goes for your damned old brother too. Not very long ago, he had heard about a man who had got a cactus spine in his finger that worked itself into his blood stream and finally got to his heart and killed him like a poisoned arrow. It wouldn't be hard at all to send some cactus spines in a black-hand letter.

"Won't you come for a row with us?" asked Cousin Katharine. Victor shook his head and flippantly replied, "No, thank you kindly, ma'am. I got to get this Albert Payson Terhune installment to my brother p.d.q." And beginning to yodel again, he marched on quickly, swinging his arms as if he were doing calisthenics.

Andrew turned the boat and doggedly rowed on. "The Smithwicks are a touching family," said Cousin Katharine. "I hope the chap recovers. If anything should happen, if Charles should die, I think poor Beulah would die herself. She very nearly did when her husband was lost at sea." She was speaking of the terrible shipwreck, before Victor was born, that had cost the towns of Hawthorne and Bingham Bay eighteen lives. He did not look at her for fear she was looking at him.

"Perhaps we should take him strengthening things, calves' foot jelly and beef tea and all those other things in books. Do you think a bottle of my father's best burgundy would restore him? We must go and call on Charles one afternoon, you and I. It isn't Christian not to cheer the sick."

Andrew, feeling very sick himself, smiled politely. "I hope Charles gets well soon," he said.

For a short space of silence, he kept his eyes averted from his cousin's regard which, nevertheless, he could feel upon him like the silent, examining scrutiny of Dr. Townsend to whom, last winter, he had lied about the pain he had; and exactly as the doctor had finally touched the flaming spot in his right side and said, "Here, boy, you do your part and I'll do mine and between us we'll rout this bellyache," so Cousin Katharine said to him at last, with utmost gravity and sympathy, "Wouldn't it help to tell me what it is that's troubling you so terribly this summer? You can trust me."

Involuntarily, he relaxed as he had done when the doctor had seemed to enter with him into his pain and keep him company and even to feel himself the short, blazing dagger-thrusts of the diseased appendix. He remembered how then he had willingly answered all the questions. But a real thorn in the side was one thing and a figurative one another and his moment of ease was followed by deep distrust of her intrusion on his privacy. Grasping out of the air a plausible reason for his brooding, he told her that last year he had especially hated school.

"But surely I remember that your mother told me you liked it much better than before," she said earnestly. "Didn't contract bridge take the lower school by storm? And didn't Maeve tell me—I know she did—that you played every afternoon at Johnny and Allen Webster's house?"

He shook his head. It was true that half the boys at Sewell could think of nothing else but bridge last year and he had gone, twice, to the Websters' house but he could never fix his mind on the game, never was sure what was meant by "trumps" and after some *gaffe* that caused the other players to scream at him in rage, though he had not the slightest idea what he had done, he was expelled from the foursome. If his mother had said that to Cousin Katharine and had believed it, it showed how little she knew of the way he spent his time. When he did not go to the Public Library to read the New English Dictionary, he prowled through Scollay Square, counting the sailors as his cousin counted birds, and in the doorways of abandoned buildings, smoking cubebs stolen from his mother's cook, waiting for the summer.

At first he said that it was Latin that had made him miserable (this was an outright lie for Latin was the only thing he had ever liked in school) and then he said, in quick succession, that it had been Chapel, History and Algebra. It had been Miss Bowman's interminable quotations from Poor Richard and *The Autocrat of the Breakfast Table* (the Lord knew Bowman was enough to set one's teeth on edge. He and the twins had long outgrown the need of a governess but she was kept on, combining the roles of housekeeper and secretary to Maeve although she did not relax her vigilance over the children; energetic and stoutly self-improving, she read hard books on economics and psychology and as she did so gnashed her teeth as if she lay on Procrustes' bed) and her insistence that he recite the Gettysburg Address immediately after brushing his teeth, night and morning, as an exercise in memory.

In a way everything he said—except his attack on Latin—was true and it all made far more sense than if he had said he was ready to commit suicide or murder just because some dumb country hick had never stopped to see his brand-new fishing tackle nor even whistled as he passed by. Victor had left no notes beside the lantern on the gate, he had not one single solitary time called Andrew on the telephone: he might *at least* have done that and still kept his eye on the invalid; they had sometimes talked for half an hour until other people on the party line impatiently snapped at them; Miss Duff once had roared, "Deputy sheriff going to hear about this. What if you're trying to get a doctor for an emergency and can't get through because boys are saying riddle me this, riddle me that until the cows come home?" They had retaliated by putting a ticktack on her living-room window when she was there alone on maid's night out and scaring her half to death.

"But there's no Algebra to stump you now," said Cousin Katharine, "and poor old Bowman is far away. Isn't it more that other thing you sometimes came to me about? That feeling at home you couldn't put your finger on?"

Of course! How could he have forgotten? But strangely enough, as he began to speak of it, she interrupted him to praise the way he was so capably managing the boat with its dangerous keel and to direct him toward a far patch of floating flowers. And as if they had been engaged in nothing but small talk, she began to plan a picnic on Stork Island to which they would invite the Smithwick boys.

Rhetorically she inquired whether they should have whole lobsters or put the meat into sandwiches; should they color the hard-boiled eggs with beet juice in the old-fashioned way? And should they roast corn or should the meal be cold? Perhaps it would be a greater treat for the Smithwicks to go to Pemaquid; but she did not like the waters there, for there was no hope at all for a swimmer if anything went wrong. (His mouth was dry.) She wandered and lightly talked about the picnics of the past, beginning in a fairy-story way with, "Once upon a time, the world was a picnic and Maeve and I were allowed to drink champagne when we went to the Bois at holidays, taking innumerable hampers and silver spoons and tablecloths and chinaware. So cumbersome and so very elegant! The inconveniences, as they are called these days, didn't disturb us in the least. We were as gay as larks in spite of the fact that we had no paper plates and ate off the breakfast Quimper."

Her bewildered boatman rowed on, the recipient of her bright-eyed reminiscences and speculations, her prophecies and her stray, unprefaced facts that she interpolated without rhyme or reason; as they skirted round the smallest and the nearest of the islands, she asked him if he was aware that on a certain island in the British Virgins, the natives formally disputed whether God could laugh. Fastidiously and with close attention to its good points and its flaws, she rejected lily after lily like a woman shopping for a hat, and as they zigzagged back and forth, she talked continually, her even, undemanding voice lulling, taking him willy-nilly away from the sharpness of his discontent and his suspiciousness and even leading him part of the way into her remembered adult world. She told him about a cruise she had taken once with his parents to the Caribbean and she described to him the extraordinary fish they had seen and the sea birds and the strange plants with stranger names, the shake-shake tree and the fiddlewood and the monkey-can't-climb.

"I meant to tell you," he interrupted, "the *Empress Katharine* came into Bingham Bay last night."

"Oh, that makes me very sad. Don't tell your father when you write him. She meant so much to him."

"I know she did," he said and to prove to Cousin Katharine that he did know, he told her about one afternoon last winter when, after the tea tray had gone, he had established himself in a corner of the library to read his father's second-class mail. Though he was really absorbed in it, thinking how extremely useful a home elevator would be for someone like Miss Heminway in her wheel-chair, he could not help hearing a passage between his parents who did not seem to know that he was there. His father was standing before the case of yachting trophies looking down at his mother who was sitting on the fire bench with her head between her hands. His father said, "For God's sake, Maeve, *this* testifies that I have done something with my life," and he gestured toward the loving cups. And his mother answered so softly that Andrew barely caught the words, "Oh, yes, you were an emperor in your fashion."

Cousin Katharine frowned. "Has no one ever told you that eavesdropping is a vicious habit?"

"They weren't telling secrets. That's all they said. After that they had a drink and talked about whether they should go to Europe on a big boat or a little one." Actually, his father had said something else but he did not repeat it to Cousin Katharine because it had been so rude and it had been about her. He had said, "You've grown so like Katharine that half the time I don't know whether I'm talking to you or her. You are mad to imitate a manner that you perfectly know sticks in my gizzard. The infuriating *reasonableness* of it!"

Cousin Katharine smiled. "No, I suppose you aren't repeating anything you shouldn't, so let's forget it. Poor John! That yacht *was* a beauty." Now she saw the flower she wanted at the far back of the lake and as

Andrew turned the boat toward it, stirring up a school of pickerel, she trailed her fingers in the water and began to talk again. "There is no water in the world as clear and clean as this. This is what Madeleine St. Denis envies us the most and I don't wonder because it seemed to me, when I visited there, I saw nothing but stagnant water. Louisiana was like something drawn by Doré, every inch of it covered with tendrils and naked roots and vines and that hairy moss hanging from the oak trees."

From their new position, Andrew could see clearly into the Smithwicks' yard and there, indeed, was a lengthy figure stretched out in a canvas deck-chair, the face obscured by a straw hat with a ruptured crown. Victor was standing on his head in the garden path. He looked as if he had been in that position for hours.

His cousin's self-supporting monologue went on. ". . . Like the stagnant water of a moat I remember in Chantilly. We drove out from Paris for Sunday lunch. I have never eaten such melon since. It tasted of the sun . . ."

Victor turned a back somersault and through the straw hat that capped the inert rope of flesh there came a booming voice, "Good enough, you landlubber you," and Victor patted his open mouth, favoring this time a war whoop instead of a yodel. With half himself Andrew watched the brotherly horseplay and the other half was drawn into the embrace of Cousin Katharine's voice.

"After the meal, in all ways perfect for a perfect summer day, our host and the other men practiced tight-rope walking in the park while the ladies of the party sat in a tree-house admiring one another's jewels. One of them had a golden cowrie shell in which she kept her heroin."

"*Honestly?*" he gasped and when she nodded he felt a quiver of delight run straight through him.

"While all this was going on, John took Maeve and me for a row around the moat. I can remember to this day the disgusting smells that came to us and how the oars dredged up the mud and brought to light the odious things that grow in stagnant water, a horrid, reptilian green. In some places we had to lie down flat in the boat when we went under trees that bent from bank to bank. Once John lost his balance and through some stupid accident, splattered your mother with his oar and totally ruined her velvet dress. It was no loss, really; we had agreed that it was a shade of violet that never suited her. But she was terribly nervy all that summer and when this happened, she burst into tears. She cried all the way back to Paris."

Now they had come to the lily of her choice and as she tugged at its snaky stem, the fascinated cat sat up to watch, thrust out a paw as if to help and then was quiet, her tail curled around her feet. There was to Andrew a new and exquisite quality in the air, a smell, perhaps, or the stillness of his cousin's sweet past life, or the foretaste of enjoyment, the source of which was undefined. In the end, the world might change and the cornucopia be filled again. The name "Paris" took his fancy, acquiring for him a dimension it had never had before and the words "park" and "moat" and the image of

Frenchmen walking tight-ropes and of women sitting in a tree captivated him. He leaned forward in the boat and said, "What happened afterward? Did you show your jewels too? Did Mother cry in front of all the others?"

"Maeve went into the house to set herself to rights," said Cousin Katharine, dreamily, intent upon the elusive stem of the water lily, "and the rest of us had a *cassis* under a false sycamore that was bound round and round by a thick vine that corkscrewed up the trunk like the serpent going up Eve's apple tree. The *cassis* was made on the premises. It is odd the way one will carry off an isolated and prosaic fact like that from the scene of disaster. Why should I remember that Peter's *cassis* was made by his servants out of his own currants? There, I've got it!" Her eyes shone and she cradled the lily in her hands, showing it to the cat. "A prize, isn't it, Beth?"

"What was the disaster? Did the tree-house fall down?"

"I shouldn't have said 'disaster,'" she said, "because the ruin of a dress hasn't quite got that stature, particularly for the bride of a very rich young man."

"Oh, was that all?" He was disappointed.

"Yes, but actually there was more to it than that, for she found out the next day that she was going to have a baby—or babies, as it turned out—and that was what had put her so on edge. I shall always remember the taste of *cassis* when I think of the day that the Shipley children were first announced. John and I toasted her in vermouth *cassis*, for our host had given us a bottle of it to bring back."

His interest flagged and he turned again to the boys in their desultory garden. They were so near the bank now that when Charles took off his hat, Andrew could see him clearly. He was quite as unusual-looking as Victor but in a different way; he had a flattened nose and his eyebrows were black although his hair was the color of sand. His forehead was a gleaming bulb from which that strange stiff hair rose straight up like a tall lawn. He did not much resemble his pictures because his illness had whittled him down to the bone. Beulah said his legs were rubber and his blood was water and he hadn't the strength of a newborn babe. If he stayed out too late in the dewy evening, he might catch a chill and die of double pneumonia.

Charles began to read his magazine; the parrot wandered out the door and stood, laughing privately, beside the canvas chair; Victor turned a clumsy handspring and seized his wrist and howled with pain.

"Who told you the *Empress Katharine* was in?" his cousin asked suddenly.

"I can't remember," Andrew said. "Everybody knows everything in this town. Maybe it was Mr. Barker and maybe it was Bluebell James. They all knew your light was on all night."

Cousin Katharine shivered. "Go back," she said. "I'm nervous about this boat."

He knew enough not to ask her a direct question and docilely he attended to his own business, turning the boat once more and cutting off the pantomime of the Smithwicks' contentment. He felt again the clutching void of summer with nothing to look forward to except more of these long, long days fading gradually into the gloomy winter. He wondered, without caring a pin, whether his parents, in Dublin now, were any gayer than they had been when he had seen them last, sitting far apart in the back of the car, as it took them to the station for New York, looking, as Honor had said, as if they were going to a funeral.

"They make me furious," she said. "*We* can't not answer when we're spoken to so why can they?" and Harriet said, "I'm glad they're gone."

As soon as the car was out of sight, the house had seemed to shake itself from a deep sleep; from the maids' sitting room had faintly come the sound of a victrola playing "On the Sunny Side of the Street" and Hal, the choreman, covering the furniture with muslin shrouds, began to sing "Santa Lucia." The children waited in the ghostly drawing room for Alfred to bring the car back from the South Station and take them to the North and all at once all three of them, for no other reason than that it was summertime, began to laugh. He thought of the silent house, shut up against the sun, holding the hush in its halls and niches and he wondered how he could ever be happy there again. Or anywhere until he was old, at least as old as Cousin Katharine. Much farther away than Ireland, more indistinct than dreams, his bemused parents seemed irrevocably gone. He said, "Supposing our house burned down or supposing they decided never to come back again, would Honor and Harriet and I live with you?"

"Andrew!" She was shocked. "The house *can't* burn down, they *will* come back. You must be careful what you think or it may happen! You must be careful what you wish for when you are young for you may not want it when you are old. What if we heard when we got home that your house *had* burned down? Wouldn't you feel as dreadful as if you'd set it on fire yourself?" He did not reply.

Now they had reached the little pier and Cousin Katharine, gently laying the flower in a mossy cave at the base of a tree, waded into the water for her swim. Knee deep, she turned again, "This must be a secret between you and me, but I'll tell you what I was doing all last night. I was planning the most wonderful party we have ever had. We shall have dancing and champagne, but the chief thing will be fireworks. Not the noise-for-noise-sake ones, for those I hate. But fountains and wheels and roman candles. Skyrockets and beautiful blood-red Catherine wheels."

As if she were descending to a bed, she entered the water; in her mild wake came Beth.

"What is a Catherine wheel?" asked Andrew.

"A spinning rack," she called. "A stupendous round of sparks. Some of them look like rose windows. They're gone before you know it."

"Was that really what you were doing, Cousin Katharine?"

But he did not believe her when she said it really had

been. For a while they swam in silence and then, still silent, they climbed up the path to Minerva's temple where Mrs. Shea had left glasses and a bottle of cold birch beer. They sat on the marble benches that encircled the gigantic, helmeted goddess, sipping the herbal brown drink with the summer day lying all about them; there came, to their heedless ears, through the topaz atmosphere, the sound of the rowboat dipping in the meek south wind. The careful cat dried herself and washed her violet-veined ears.

This afternoon had been a series of multitudinous beginnings that had come to nothing; now the sun had illuminated everything, now all was dimmed as a shadow intercepted the halo of June. Was this talk of Catherine wheels and lobster sandwiches nothing but a blind under the cover of which she was seeking his central, pertinacious sin? She had said *you must be careful what you think about or it may happen, you must be careful what you wish for.* Drawn to his obsession, he could think of nothing else and in this quiet and in this nearness to her, omniscient, judging, he could not help it; he said, "Do you think you can make somebody die by wishing for it? I mean, like a dog that had bitten you? I mean like using those dolls the way they did in *The Return of the Native?*"

"You must *not* say these things. You must *not* think these thoughts! Believe me, no one in the world is so detestable that you should wish him dead."

"I was thinking about a snake I saw in the meadow," he said.

"I know you were! I know it!" Her voice was flooded with relief and to his terrible embarrassment, he saw tears standing in her eyes. Perhaps it *was* true that she was sick and hurting somewhere. But while for her sake he wanted to be purged of his vileness, his interior voice went on and on relentlessly, "Charles Smithwick, die, die, die."

They went single file back to the house, Andrew in the lead. Cousin Katharine came fragrantly behind him, her cat on her shoulder, her water lily like an offering in her hand. She was so tall behind him! Her female shadow enveloped his; she was looking right through the back of his head and reading everything that was written there. When they reached the front door, the cat leaped, purling, from her shoulder and Cousin Katharine leaned against the lintel for a moment, bending her head forward as if to kiss his cheek. She did not, but the mass of her hair swept over his eyelids softer than snow.

"Oh, Cousin Kate, shame, shame!" came Honor's taunting voice. "You're showing preference!" She stood at the foot of the stairs holding a pair of ballet slippers by their ribbons. "If Bowman ever hears that you baby the boy, she'll send you straight to Coventry."

"Be quiet!" Cousin Katharine put her fingers to her lips and bade the children listen; in the pear tree at the entrance of the picking garden, a thrush was singing; when the intricate and formal song was finished, Cousin Katharine clapped her hands. "Bravo!" she cried. The children were infected by her cry and shouted in unison, "Encore! Encore!" until they were hoarse. Andrew snatched one of the ballet slippers from Honor's hand and running halfway down the lawn he whirled it like a boomerang and let it fly off to land in the dead center of the hammock. They raced for it through the sunlight, but even the whistling in his ears did not drown out the voice and even as he put the length of the long lawn between them, he knew that Cousin Katharine knew everything. Her eyes were inescapable. He was inundated by a wave of scalding anger and reaching the hammock first, he grabbed the ballet slipper and threw it into Honor's face. She was so surprised that she only looked at him.

"I think you're going crazy," she said. There was hardly any outrage in her voice. She seemed to be stating a fact. He did not trust himself with her and turning, without apologizing or refuting her declaration, he ran like the wind down to the orchard and when he was at the farthest part of it, he stopped and screamed.

CHAPTER IV

The Late Wedding Ring

A LETTER from John Shipley was waiting for Katharine when she and Andrew came back from the lake. In its thin, square European envelope, it lay on the table in the entrance hall, and though she changed the water in the cuspidor and took her time, painstakingly posing the lily so that it lay oblique to the burnished valentine of its pad, and though in this procedure, her hands were steady, she was invisibly assaulted. Her hands, moving with such deliberation that this might have been the creation of a masterpiece upon whose laurels she was to rest for the remainder of her life, in her imagination mauled the letter, and more vividly than she saw the chaste flower, she saw St. Stephen's Green and him upon a bench, writing to her, using a book as a desk, the opal mist of Ireland and the sweetness of being in love hanging between his faculties and the red-haired children playing among the beds of public flowers.

Importunate at her elbow, Harriet said, "Aren't you going to open Daddy's letter? Please open it and see if he promises to bring us the plaid raincoats."

Katharine shook her head, said she was busy as Harriet could plainly see and the girl, respectful but still impatient, fingered the foreign postage stamp and asked, "Then may I open it and read it to you?" With the unkind prerogative of the person in charge, Katharine severely changed the subject and more sharply than she meant to, she said, "Go up at once to dress. Honor is ready, why aren't you?" Wounded, Harriet ran upstairs without a word, but at the top she leaned over the banister and said, "I'm sorry I was nosy, Cousin Kate."

There were several further domestic interruptions before she could go to her room. Maureen had come in an excessive flood of tears to confess that she had broken a sugar bowl, not valuable, not pretty, and Katharine, aware that the girl for some time had been "carrying on" with a profligate and married lobsterman, feared that this undue display over nothing at all meant, perhaps, that she was pregnant and that in the midst of upheaval and revolution, a husband would have to be found for her. But for the time being, she refused to think about it and comforted the girl by saying that she would deduct a dollar from her week's wage. Mrs. Shea, wringing her hands and almost weeping, had reported that "the boy" had frightened her with a tale of a snake in the meadow and she could not, would not, therefore, cook fish for dinner, the bellies of mackerel being what they were, Miss Congreve knowing how she felt. She revised the menu, endeavouring to keep a rasp of exasperation from her voice. Then Maddox had appeared at the windows of the dining room to announce, sepulchrally, that his prize Dr. Van Fleet rose bush, a new and costly importation from Long Island, had been mortally felled by the blacksmith's dog whom he begged leave to shoot. Aggrieved by her refusal, he added reproachfully that a band of village children who had come to gape at the peacocks had littered the lawn with empty Walnetto boxes and gum wrappers. And Harriet's feelings were hurt and Andrew . . . Once more greeting her father's eyes, when at last her household let her go, she recalled his solacing precept, "When you are unsettled, consider yourself *sub specie aeternitatis.*"

But the strength she gained from his advice failed to serve her when she read the letter from Dublin in which John's consideration of the two of them under the aspect of eternity lacked, she could not help but feel, responsibility and compassion, was rash, was honest (bull-headedly) and unethical.

> The only anachronism in you [he wrote] that I find fault with is your caution. You once called it your "indeciduous Puritanism" (how like you to use a botanical term) but I beg you to name for me any people more incautious than the passionate men of Salem. While I deplore their violence, I

> honor their conscience and conviction, and while I deplore the cruel act you and I must commit, I love what makes it necessary. In obedience to you, I have taken this trip, prolonging my agony and Maeve's, and nothing has changed. My decision is incontrovertible and this dissembling is torment. There are times when I am close to anger with you. Yesterday we motored down to Tara and because the day was clear (the only one we've had so far; the rain has not improved my state of mind) we could see the whole of Ireland from the summit—or tell ourselves we could—like the assembled kings and poets and when Maeve innocently said, "If only Katharine were here! This is the sort of panorama that she loves," I leaped down her throat. I snapped, "Is it some special virtue in Katharine? Wouldn't anybody in his right mind love this view?" She cried when she defended you. I tell you this to show you how wretched I am, so cantankerous in this deceit that I am driven to attack what I love above all else in life. Will you not summon me back?

But in a sober postscript he wrote:

> Do not imagine that I do not have doubts. There are days when I am suicidal, thinking of the children for whom I've done nothing, to whom I shall now do much worse than nothing. And I say to myself, "This is their last happy summer." I hope they are the happiest they have ever been.

Stripped of the integument of middle age, John Shipley stood before her, twenty years old, and for one callow, callous moment, she leaned on him, abiding by his decision, a yielding woman trusting a man's strength. But then, miserably, she thought of Andrew and of the lures she had thrown to him. He had seemed to rise to every one of them, though she could not be sure. She could be sure of nothing, only that he bitterly hated someone but whether it was his father or herself, she did not know.

Within a child there lies an unforgiving heart, she thought. So then for a child, must one repudiate one's victory and love and life and go on existing in a state of need? John Shipley, in his anarchy, would say no, and the world would say yes, but in the end it was not John's place to answer the question, it was only hers. And she could not answer it now for she must change for tea and put upon herself an air of insouciance with which to confront her friends who had said that she was ill. She was ill but not as they imagined. In the boat with Andrew she had heard herself saying things she never meant to say (no one should ever know except herself the envy that had grated on her when she had learned that Maeve was pregnant); she could not bear to think that any fiber of her will could relax and she was afraid it had already begun to happen and that the ganglion of her being was beginning, slowly, to atrophy. It would take strength to live through tea.

Before the first caller came—Mr. Barker in his debonair Mercedes—she wrote a note to Boston to order the fireworks for her ball, a mixed assortment, she instructed, with a preponderance of Catherine wheels. As she looked through her address file for the name of the novelty shop she knew would send them to her, she came across the name of the stonecutter who had made Minerva and later had designed her father's tombstone. Under his fig tree in his own backyard and under the aspect of eternity: what peace awaits us all!

2

Old Mr. Barker, who wore a monocle, handed up his cup to be refilled and to the St. Denis family he said, "You fellows needn't tell me that in Dixie you've got any gardens that will put these in the shade. Even in a drought—and we had one last year to make you think of the Gobi—the gardens of Congreve House are a veritable paradise."

"Hear! Hear!" cried Edmund.

"Isn't it wicked?" cried Mrs. Wainright-Lowe and in elaborate mock indignation, she shook her dimpled fist at the roses climbing up the stable wall.

"Wicked is the word," echoed the old man, still addressing the Southerners who, as if they had been relegated there by reason of their being newcomers, sat a little apart from the regular Tuesday callers on the rim of the pond. "You take my word for it, this seemingly good Christian woman says incantations when the moon is full and does her plantin' when the Widow Smithwick's crystal ball gives her the go-ahead sign."

Edmund guffawed and nudged his son who rebuffed the gambit and became absorbed in lighting a Turkish cigarette. The decadent aroma drifted on two thin blue membranes of smoke, a European smell, a smell of snug cafés, bringing to Katharine a burst of fragmentary memories of morning conversations in Rome and Venice and Madrid in the middle of sight-seeing (how rapacious for churches and galleries and historic houses she and Maeve had been!) and bringing, as well, a bitter-sweet nostalgia for those cities and the hopes they had held, round every turning, from every yonder elevation, before the intimations of one's immortality had ceased. Those ascending days of loving girlhood, long, long before Maeve's ball which, a few minutes before, she had told her company, to their exclamatory delight, she meant to duplicate in August. She was committed, having allowed the twins to run back to the house to write down the event, permanently in ink, on the Phillips Brooks calendar that listed, otherwise, only the probable date of Beth's *accouchement* in July.

On either side of her, Maeve's copies in their lavender dresses watched Raoul, lips parted, innocently preying. She wondered which of them would engage him in an adolescent holiday flirtation—Honor, audacious and piquant, or Harriet, serene and soft. Their resemblance to their mother today was so remarkable that even old Miss Heminway who could barely see had spoken of it, saying, "You can't miss your alter ego when you've got her double strength, right here." Katharine tried to catch Raoul's eye to see whether either of them had succeeded, but Mr. Barker, following in Edmund's raffish lead, winked at him through his owlish eyeglass and Raoul deliberately looked away and up at the weathervane on the barn.

She was touched as she had been earlier when she thought of Raoul by the youthful intermixture of his nonchalance and his uncertainty, this arrogance with which he refused to join his elders in their buffoonery that was united to the humility with which he examined his surroundings, praising the house and the swans with his large, heavily lidded eyes and remaining silent except when he was asked a question. Rebellion, intellectual or filial, had caused him to obliterate his Southern accent but a soft, slow trace of it remained. His father's diphthongs, on the other hand, and his inflections were as pronounced as Mr. Barker's Mississippi valet's, to such an extent, indeed, that after they had met him for the first time the twins, imitating him between convulsions of glee, had said, "You *didn't* think you'd marry him! You couldn't have!" But in the days when she had thought of marrying him, he had no accent either and she remembered a time when, angry with his father for something else, he had burst out, "*Will* you, for God's sake, sound your final consonants?" The whole family had rocked with laughter and an aunt had cried, "Does he mean something like Gabriel tootin' on his final horn?"

Miss Duff, Hawthorne's unofficial and undisputed dragoman, was presenting to the St. Denises a lengthy dossier on the Widow Smithwick, on whose advice Katharine presumably did her gardening, and on the Smithwick boys. She dwelt at length upon a theory that she herself had arrived at, that Charles had sprue. ("Rampant in the Orient, I'm told, sprue. Funny name.") Katharine, having ascertained that her other guests were occupied—Miss Heminway with talking in an undertone to Harriet who had now to leave off casting sheep's eyes at Raoul, Mrs. Tyler deep in conversation with Brantley Wainright-Lowe on the subject of cesspools while his mother and Mr. Barker affirmed or emended Miss Duff's statements—busied herself in a needless shifting of pots and caddies on the tea table and retired into the state of mind in which she had stumbled and floundered since the evening before, finding in it, on reflection and now that the crisis was past (one crisis anyhow), a certain excitement and even an attractiveness like something romantically forbidden, like certain kinds of pain which one should not enjoy but did—opium-eating perhaps, that imperiled the spirit but quelled the pain. Though it had disturbed her deeply, John's letter was, in the end, no more than a letter and *sub specie aeternitatis* it was even less than that, only a sheet of paper hastily inscribed.

Protected by that thought and by her guests and by her duties to them, the last flickerings of her agitation had gone. There lingered only a vague dread of the possible return of her dislocation which resembled, she now decided, her conception of death. She was sure that no one saw or sensed any change in her and in this she took a healthy and mischievous pleasure and even bent her head to smile as she thought, "If only Mr. Barker could see my nightmare!" Such must be the needs and the dangers of addicts of alcohol and thievery and setting fires, cleverly hiding their macabre manias to relish them alone. She glanced from guest to guest and thought, "Not one of them guesses that I have had glimpses of a morbid world hidden beneath my reason and my senses."

But a gust of wind rippled over her white skirt and chilled her although it came from the south and was warmed with the sun: her eyes had fallen for the first time on Andrew who sat distant from the terrace, cross-legged on the lawn, his back to the party, presenting to her the long nape of his neck. His still, rejecting attitude alarmed her, and she realized now that earlier, when she had been talking about the party, he had not joined the discussion although, since he had been the first to hear of it, she would have expected him to aid and interrupt her. Had he really repudiated her? What else could explain the indifference of a boy of twelve to fireworks? As she stared at the small, heavy-headed boy, the wheel began, in the dark vault of her heart, slowly to revolve.

Terrorized and longing for the climax of her terror and knowing that her longing was obscene, she disciplined herself, she could stop the wheel; she took a deep breath and she held a whispered conference with Maureen, deflecting the nameless experience by concentrating on the tepidity of the water in the Guernsey pitcher, and telling the anxious girl for the fifth time that the sugar bowl she had broken was not of the slightest consequence. Surreptitiously looking at the watch pinned to the bosom of her dress, she saw that she must endure for the better part of an hour and as invisibly as she had departed from them, she returned to her guests. Miss Duff's discourse on sprue was long.

Dressed in umber from her trowel-shaped hat to her imported German walking shoes, Peg Duff graphically itemized the symptoms and the sequelae of the disease which she had read that morning in a medical encyclopedia. There was no possible reason for her to imagine that this was Charles Smithwick's complaint, but there was a general predilection in Hawthorne for the out-of-the-way or the archaic or the unlikely. Since no one specifically knew what he was suffering from (the doctor would not say through over-scrupulosity and Beulah did not say perhaps because she knew how much her patronesses enjoyed guessing) and the most obscure diseases had been proposed: yaws, fluke worms, psittacosis, dengue. Actually, they were all quite sure that it was only malaria but this they would not admit; they would have looked on that as too banal to discuss. And the ordinary was not Hawthorne's line.

They enjoyed discussing termite mounds in Africa, witchcraft, medieval *fin amour;* they could exchange receipts for sillibub and mead and directions for domesticating crows. And although they were staunchly Low Church and daily read *The Book of Common Prayer*, they also studied their horoscopes, took seriously Beulah Smithwick's Delphic screams, believed in ghosts and spirit rappings. Mr. Barker's house was haunted by the shades of seven aborigines who left their burying ground in the forest several nights a week to take turns sitting in a creaky Boston rocker in his upstairs hall. The Wainright-Lowes, who were not imaginative, often heard the clank of chains. It was not entirely unbelievable that Peg Duff was sometimes troubled out of sleep by the cry of a moose cow that she had shot out of season, a felony for which Yankee Doodle Lafontaine had been obliged to hale her into court, to the delectation of the whole country, three quarters of whose population had come to the trial.

It was Katharine's father who had started this vogue, peopling his house with an august body of ghosts to whom he had given names from the novels of Thomas Hardy which he much admired; and Katharine, continuing the mythology as an essential part of Congreve House, had early taught the Shipley children and her servants to distinguish them one from the other by the sounds they made as they shuffled and padded through the attics and promenaded up and down the stairs, troubling the country quiet with their sighs and their soliloquies. Michael Henchard came to pity himself, running his stick along the balustrade and to make a sound like the cracking of nuts. And the room where Maeve had used to sleep was occupied by Eustachia Vye who knew no rest at all and wept and beat her breast until the cocks began to crow. At lunch today Honor had said, "I heard Tess rummaging through the sea-chest where you keep the croquet set," and her twin, not to be outdone, said, "Jude had a frightful night."

Fondly Katharine watched her ancient playmates nibbling sandwiches. Their appetites were nearly as huge and simple as those of the village children who came in their Sunday best of linsey-woolsey knickerbockers and huckabuck shirts and of ruffled, rumpled organdy and tin barettes, to spill ice cream upon themselves and cry, not for the damage to their clothes, but for the loss of a single drop of food. And she thought how extremely pleasant her life of compromise among them all was and how extremely careless it would be to give it up and go to live in Mangareva; she knew herself sufficiently to know that she would never find in breadfruit trees a substitute for elms and she did not think that John could reproduce Merrion Square in palm thatch. She could not (it had been lunacy ever to imagine it) leave for naked Polynesians these vivacious creatures, brimming with gossip and personal style, loving to quote from Dr. Johnson's dictionary, perpetually happy because their work was finished and all the demands upon them had been withdrawn and they were married to their houses and their habits and their infirmities.

Miss Celia Heminway, for instance, a dry wisp lost in her wheel-chair, talking with such animation to Harriet, seemed, at this moment, to be absolutely indispensable to her. And because she knew that she was indispensable to Miss Heminway, she almost leaned forward to squeeze her crippled hand. Miss Heminway, who had read widely and was especially conversant in the novels of the nineteenth century and the memoirs of the court of Louis XV, depended upon Katharine's eyes, since her own had faded, to read passages of Saint-Simon, at which she would laugh so hard that she had to extract a handkerchief from her little beaded pocketbook to dry the pink corners of her eyes. "Trust Katharine to find that *mot* again for me!" she would cry. And Mrs. Wainright-Lowe trusted her to be an unfailing source of information on birds, and Mr. Barker relied on her to be, in his own words, "a bijou *par excellence*."

She could not leave any of them, certainly not this heavenly and preposterous Miss Duff who, having disposed of sprue, was now delivering Hawthorne's pronouncement on the St. Denis choice of summer resort. Bingham Bay was the sort of place that catered to tourists with tearooms upon whose walls hung studies in water color of the Bristol lighthouse and with antique shops that sold, as well as china broody hens, the bone and raffia produce of Japan. It was a false, expensive, loud-mouthed mecca for *arrivistes* and Miss Duff said, "Bingham Bay is unspeakable. Can't think why people in their right minds go there. Bar Harbor even worse, on a grander scale. Will fight day and night to keep hoi polloi out of Hawthorne. Can't have people mousing around in emeralds and not enough clothes." The two beagles that always attended her looked up lornly and she gave them each a piece of cake. "Went over to the Bay on my whizzer this afternoon to get booze—

don't use any of their shops except for martini mixings—and saw John Shipley's boat. Two big, half-naked blonde tarts for every one of those slinking Cuban men. It made me good and sore."

It would be out of the question to move out of the neighborhood where Peg Duff lived or where lived this beaming, baby-round and baby-bald old Mr. Barker who, having rejoiced in Peg's performance (no one had ever been able to determine whether or not she was a conscious comedienne) now returned to his earlier tribute to the gardens of Congreve House and asked her to let her friends in on the secret of her "horticultural sockdolagers."

"The secret isn't mine," she said. "It belongs to Maddox and he'll guard it with his life. My father used to claim that he was the son of a sorcerer and a sorceress and quite possibly he *is* and quite possibly he does say abracadabra by the light of the moon." She paused and wishing still to draw Andrew into the circle, she said, "Andrew, do you know what Maddox does on moonlight nights?"

He heard her and he shook his head but he would not turn around and Edmund St. Denis chuckled, "Man at work. Do not disturb."

"He bays the moon," said Honor, cheeky for the benefit of Raoul who looked at her and smiled faintly. "What does it mean, *to bay the moon?*"

"Merely to bark," said the literal Miss Duff. "Doubtless comes from the same root, only a transitive verb in this case."

"Well, then he doesn't bay the moon," said Honor. "He stews newts' eyes in brine."

Miss Heminway drolly shook her finger at Honor and to Katharine she said, "It shows the goodness of your heart, Katharine, that you let that cynical minx live with you. Do you know that last week, in this self-same spot, she told me—in a most defiant tone, I must say—that she doesn't believe in stars or ghosts. She says there's no such thing as levitation. To hear her talk, you'd think she thought her elders were insane."

"I do too believe in ghosts, Miss Heminway!" the girl protested. "Why do you think the croquet set is up? Because Tess made me think of it, rattling the balls in the sea-chest half the night last night so that I couldn't sleep. Do you play croquet, Raoul?"

Poor Harriet, minding her manners, continued to smile and nod at Miss Heminway who, after her badinage with Honor, resumed telling an amusing but interminable story about some prank in her distant girlhood. But Katharine could see that Harriet was glancing nervously and angrily out of the corner of her eye at her sister engaged in this unfair campaign.

Raoul shook his head and his father gave his shoulder a push. "Then go and learn. No time like the present." And he smiled a conniving, match-making smile at Katharine who, taking pity on Harriet, ordered all the young to go and play a round of croquet. The blond, long-limbed boy got up and ceremoniously bowed to everyone while Andrew, his back still to the company, went on ahead down the arching pergola.

Everyone turned to stare at the children as if youth were a curiosity not to be seen every day and Miss Heminway sighed, "Like something by Renoir. Those little girls, those lovely, lovely little girls." Their black hair lay free and long across their shoulders and as Edmund St. Denis followed their light and laughing retreat, there came to his rubicund face, in which the slovenly flesh sagged away from the bones, a look of hunger and regret, as if at last he had begun to remember the world of possibilities whose welcoming portals he had been too timorous to enter.

"What wouldn't I give to be that fellow's age!" cried Brantley Wainright-Lowe. "Smoking Egyptian Prettiests to impress the girls, what? I say that's the life."

"He's too young to smoke at all," said Raoul's mother. "But the young are not as young as we used to be."

"It's not really smoking when those fancy brands are involved," said Wainright-Lowe. "It's just living up to the ad, 'Be nonchalant: light a Murad.' And I repeat, I'd give my worldly goods and all my expectations to be a kid again."

"I wouldn't give a farthing," snorted Mr. Barker. "I like being old. Would you want to be sixteen again, Katharine? Sweet sixteen and never been kissed?"

She shook her head and gasped, as he expected her to do, and said, "Lord, no! What an appalling thought!"

Peg Duff said, "I was a tomboy then and I'm a tomboy now. Never wanted to be kissed, never have been kissed. Like things just the way they are."

"Oh, so do I!" agreed Katharine and she meant it;

she would like to have this peaceful hour go on and on, with the sound of the twins' carefree laughter and the cracking of the wooden balls coming to her, like a testimonial of security, across the sunny lawn and with these true friends around her offering her and each other their respect and their uninvolving love.

"This is the most beautiful house I have ever seen," said Madeleine St. Denis and she gazed upward reverently.

"It is also charmed," said Mrs. Wainright-Lowe. "Congreve House has always had a charmed life. The Congreves never have water trouble, to name but one of their divine rights. When the rest of us are buying Vichy water and bathing in the lake, these favored people are lolling in their tubs like Roman senators."

"Found a mouse swimming in my well this morning," said Miss Duff and patting the dog on her left, added, "Spotty killed the bad old mouse after I ladled it out, didn't the spotted doggie?"

"As the mistress is, so is the house," said Mr. Barker who was a little deaf and had not heard Miss Duff's unseemly revelation. He looked at Katharine, infatuated. "Could a queen live anywhere but in a palace?"

"She's got no servant problems," said Mrs. Tyler, a stout old widow famous for her inability to keep a cook longer than a month and equally famous for trying, always unsuccessfully, to steal the cooks of her friends. "Are you aware, Mrs. St. Denis, that this genius gardener of hers simply materialized one day twenty full years ago and has been here ever since? I'm lucky if I can get a high-school boy to come and cut my lawn."

It was true that Maddox had, as Mrs. Tyler said, simply materialized one day in the rose garden when Katharine's father was spraying his prize bushes. In the full tide of noon the strange boy had stood stock-still and breathing in the perfume of the profuse flowers he said, "I'll work here." No one ever knew where he came from nor what his antecedents were; he had a faintly Nova Scotian accent and his coloring was Scotch. Celibate and unsociable, he was interested in nothing but flowers and shrubs and trees whose Latin names fell unaffectedly from his lips although he could not read or write. She wondered again what he did so late at night in his room in the stable and she knew that unless she snooped and spied, she would never find out, for he was a private man, as private as a child.

"To say nothing of Mrs. Shea," said Brantley Wainright-Lowe, "and Maureen and that other little Irish smasher," and it was impossible to tell whether his leer, a constitutional property of his jerry-built face, was meant for Katharine or her blue-eyed maids.

"It's no virtue in me that Maddox and Mrs. Shea stand by. He is wedded to the gardens and she is wedded to the house. Where would they go if they left me?"

"I'd take them in a minute," said Mrs. Tyler who lived in one of the ugliest houses in the town, a sepia shingled warren beset by rank spirea and shaggy bangs of wisteria that blinded every window. "If you ever give up Congreve House, will you give them to me? Hear, everybody, bear witness, I'm first bidder."

"Give up Congreve House?" The indignant cry sprang simultaneously to the lips of the five other Hawthorne citizens and by their glares they set the greedy infidel beyond the pale.

"Give up Congreve House!" Miss Heminway's was a cry of pain. "What *can* you be proposing? If Katharine Congreve gave up the house, I'd have a warrant out for her arrest before you could say 'knife.' "

Shamed, Mrs. Tyler snickered unhappily and Katharine soothed them all. "Perhaps I can find another Mrs. Shea for you. But I shan't give up Congreve House. I shall be buried here 'under my own fig tree in my own backyard.' "

"That's the sort of thing we mean about Congreve House and Maddox and all the rest of it," said Mrs. Wainright-Lowe to the St. Denises, personally envious but publicly proud. "There really is a fig tree beside George Congreve's grave. It is put to bed in the winter in a contraption comfortable enough for a person to be buried in."

"Ceremony twice a year," said Peg Duff. "Bedding down of the Congreve fig tree in the fall, ascension of the fig tree in the spring. A movable feast, to be sure, depending on the frost."

Small silences fell as the western sky began to redden. The tea was tepid and the cake was gone and there was no reason for them all to stay except the reason for which they had partly come; not one of them had broached the subject of her lamp that had burned all night. And finally, as if she were rewarding good children, she said, "I could not sleep last night."

They clucked their tongues as if she had given them a piece of news. "I was planning my party," she said. "I was making lists."

"Oh, lists!" exclaimed Miss Heminway, to whom the making of lists was tantamount to a vocation; now, because her hands were stiffened with arthritis, it was a labor but it was still a labor of love. "I, too, would far rather make lists than sleep. But I so seldom have a legitimate one to make." Her voice was plaintive; she seemed to look back on halcyon times of inventories.

Now that the matter was out in the open, they all gave themselves away. Mr. Barker said he had thought she was reading *Gone with the Wind* and Mrs. Wainright-Lowe said she had accused Peg's crabmeat Mornay and humbly asked pardon and Peg herself said that she had concluded Kate imagined that she smelled fire, the notion having lodged in her mind earlier in the evening when they were all looking at the cactuses.

"Glad it was nothing worse than lists," said Mr. Barker and winking at Mrs. St. Denis he said, "I'm the lowbrow here. *I* read *Gone with the Wind*. In fact I ate it up." He signaled to his chauffeur at the foot of the drive, and now the prolonged adieux began and the exchange of invitations, the apologies for drinking so much tea and eating so much cake, the reiteration that this day was beautiful and that the rest of the world did not know what it was missing by not living in Hawthorne, the admonition to Katharine that she must not stay up again all night. Miss Duff was the first to go, striding down the drive like a soldier, loudly ordering her dogs to "March!" Presently only Edmund and Madeleine were left. Madeleine, disliking the thought of a boat trip to their island off the coast at Bingham Bay after dark, went around the house to take her son away from the croquet game and when she was gone, Edmund said, "You are a wonder, Kate. You haven't changed at all."

"Oh, no, I haven't changed," she answered. His wistful scrutiny broke her heart. His jowled face was mottled with the sort of colors, mauve and washed red and yellow, that appeared on picture postal cards from Venice. "*Not* changing is my only occupation."

"I think your fuddy-duddy old friends are grand. I think *you're* grand." He crossed the terrace to sit beside her and he said, "You ought to have married, Katharine."

"But if I had married, then I might have changed and changed in a way you wouldn't have liked."

"Maybe so. Still, I think . . . I'm going to speak freely, Kate, we're old enough friends for that, it seems to me. I'm going to say what's on my mind and tell you that you ought to have married me."

The impropriety was so unexpected that she could not reply but could only stare at his soft pink mouth, much smaller than she had remembered it to be. But he did not expect a reply and he went on in the same downhearted voice, "A man doesn't really know what he wants until he's forty, but why should the poor devil be penalized just because he was brought up wrong, too damned ignorant to know that nine times out of ten the woman he marries is never the woman he needs?" It was a gross and platitudinous burlesque of John Shipley's protestations, and the man was neither better nor worse than John in his effort to struggle out of his boredom and his disappointment in himself by pleading with her to build him a castle in Spain and take him on a magic carpet to the end of the rainbow.

"A man needs a woman to inspire him," he said. "A woman can make or break a man. I am not implying that Madeleine has 'broken' me. Madeleine wouldn't hurt a fly—maybe that's just the trouble, maybe if she had put up a fight on some issue or other, I wouldn't feel now that the starch was out of me."

The piteous, self-conceited jeremiad went on; he bent his head, staring at his hands that he kneaded steadily. "I think I could have been a painter. I might even be able to paint now." (John could have been a Bulfinch, could be one now.) He did not look at her as John had not looked at her when he declared that he was in love with her. "I'm a married man, I've got a son, and I swear I've fought against this feeling, but I can't win. I knew the minute I saw you again after all these years that I shouldn't have rested until I got you to say 'yes' to me. We could have had a wonderful life together, you and I."

A loon cried in the reeds of the marsh and a single whippoorwill prematurely began nearby in the meadow.

She heard the children's voices as they came back through the pergola and then Madeleine's as she urged Raoul to hurry, "Please, son, I'm leery of the water after dark."

"You think about what I've said, hear?" Edmund lifted his head and looked at her and wanly smiled.

"The first thing I'll do is forget what you've said."

"Don't be like that, Katharine. Don't sound so angry. I surely didn't take you by surprise. You surely must have seen that I'm crazy mad about you."

Fatigue after the long night and the long day had been gathering for the last hour in her muscles and in her brain and she had to think of each part of the process of standing up and of saying to him, "Won't you have a whiskey before you go back?" The improbable exchange between them was as remote and indistinct as, suddenly, Edmund's face was; it seemed to fade to a wavering ectoplasm. She said, "I'm terribly tired. I didn't sleep last night."

"It sometimes happens like that," he said, his normal voice practical and self-assured. "You go through the day and then it hits you all of a heap."

Andrew came running across the lawn. The game, which he and Harriet had won, had lightened his spirits and he devoured the remaining sandwiches, having refused to eat anything before. "Harriet said there was a letter from Daddy. Are they going to Germany because if they are . . . Cousin Katharine? Cousin Katharine? Are you sick?"

Green clouds rose, layer after layer, for the sun-like Catherine wheel, the absolute, unburying itself and edging up behind the dogs' backs of tremendous waves. The inseparable mind sang in its bone-cell and she was wheeled outward swiftly and the purblind mind nosed like a mole through splendid mansions of ice-white bone and luminous blood, singing with the music of the spheres.

CHAPTER V

A Dream of a Dove

No one in Hawthorne could remember a midsummer more comely than this. The genial rains fell in the night, spoiling no one's picnic plans or boating parties and keeping the wells and cisterns full. The elegant blue hydrangeas and the splendid lawns, sweeping downward to the river or to the lake, ripened coolly under the faithful sun. Everyone looked satisfied. People passing on the road in front of Congreve House whistled and sometimes sang and saluted Maddox in the rosary and Mrs. Shea pottering about the kitchen garden. The birds had never been more various nor voluble, fluting and trilling in the shrubs and thickets; on the lake, coots clucked deeply and two dapper cardinals came to live in the grape arbor. Cousin Katharine had to send away for another bird ledger because she used up the last page of the old one before July was half over. The bells, ringing for services and ringing for the hours, partook of this tranquil jubilation and their sound was woven into the fabric of the golden days. Even Mrs. Shea, a saturnine woman, was inoculated with the summer and in her singular good humour, she attended Beth in her childbed although heretofore she had never approved of cats, finding them wanton in their promiscuity with their own sons and grandsons; she accompanied the parturient purrs with "Lord Randal" and ordered Maureen to warm a bowl of milk for the brave mother who bore a litter of six.

For Andrew, though, the days lumbered on as slowly as they had done in June almost without incident. There had been one resplendent afternoon with Victor, but only one, so that afterward his loneliness was twice as great as it had been before. Cousin Katharine had got tickets to a circus for them and because Victor looked on an invitation from her as a command and also because Charles was on the mend and needed less attention now, he accepted enthusiastically; his spirits were obviously dampened when he discovered that Cousin Katharine was not going with them but he was mollified when she told Adam to drive them to the fairground in her carriage. All the way through town, Victor bowed and waved an imaginary hat and Billy Bartholomew looked up from his whittling and called, "You the personal representative of Lord Nelson?"

The circus was small and undistinguished but they saw a man eat a live rat and they had an instructive conversation with a hermaphrodite (Victor, though, was skeptical and quoting the everlasting Mr. Knowitall, Charles, said such people were fourflushers). They had seen a girl lion-tamer who was very skillful but who cared so little for her personal appearance that her dirty yellow hair was tied up with a shoe-lace and her bodice was held together at the back with a horse-blanket pin. They had ridden the Ferris wheel and had bought chameleons and Victor had won a swagger stick in the shooting gallery which he gave to Andrew to take to Cousin Katharine.

It had been exactly like old times, for after the circus they had gone to the smoke-house and, grimacing, had eaten their handouts until Victor remembered the rat the circus man had eaten and they had thrown what they had left into a can of gurry. They had gone to the store for tonic and had drunk it on the porch, watching and ridiculing the people who passed by, as much at home with each other as if nothing at all had happened and this afternoon had been preceded by others like it. Andrew tried to appear as casual as his friend but his laughter sometimes sounded hysterical, his praise was fulsome and he could not stop issuing further invitations to Victor who either refused or pretended that he did not hear. When Jasper Freeman had a fit beside the horse trough and the Black Maria came to take him home, Andrew laughed too loud though, in fact, he had never found the spectacle in the least funny and Victor told him frigidly to grow up. But Victor had been the one who had started it, long ago. Em Bugtown was on the loose, whining for Copenhagen from every passer-by, but Victor barely noticed her.

They went to call on Billy who, before he even said hello, read, "In Dumbarton, England, brides over twenty are married in sackcloth." An ugly stream of laughter jetted from his mouth and then he welcomed his visitors, pointed to a lard can full of cherries that they might eat and opening *The Northern Farmer,* read them a joke. It was a dialogue dealing with the taciturnity of New England farmers and Billy read it with lugubrious solemnity:

> "Morning, Si.
> "Morning, Josh.
> "What'd you feed your horse for bots?
> "Turpentine.
> "Morning, Si.
> "Morning, Josh."

Two days later:

> "Morning, Si.
> "Morning, Josh.
> "What'd you say you fed your horse for bots?
> "Turpentine.
> "Killed mine.
> "Mine too.
> "Morning, Si.
> "Morning, Josh."

Andrew had thought it an excellent joke but no one at Congreve House had even grinned when he repeated it. He seemed, even in such small matters as the telling of jokes, to be doomed this summer to failure.

They had been together, as formerly, till supper time. They had gone home by way of the lake, plunging through Billy's unkempt field, littered with scraps of machinery and the foundations of outbuildings that would never be finished; in his shiftless garden, the lettuce, gone to seed, was as tall as cosmos and the cabbages were striated with the black tunnels of worms. The whole place, in the fading light, had the look of ruin and the sight of it made Andrew heavy-hearted. At the lake, they bathed their faces and took off their shoes and socks and then, with their feet in the water, they lay down, their heads pillowed on mounds of moss. From far away they heard the chug and whistle of the evening train going its leisurely way to Portland and presently the first star came out; automatically, Andrew wished on it, but he had the feeling, uncomfortable and deep, that even if Charles Smithwick vanished, things still would not be the same between him and Victor. He tried to question Victor about his brother's adventures as if he were interested but Victor said, "Oh, you know, storms and stuff . . . I dunno. You'd have to get him to tell you himself."

"Would he, do you think? Could I come and see him?"

"I'd like to ask you, but Charles is funny that way. I mean he says when he's telling a story two's company and three's a crowd."

There was no doubt about it, the son of a bitch had

poisoned Victor against him. Three might be a crowd to some people but Andrew would bet dollars to doughnuts that Charles Smithwick liked big audiences for his boasting and his lies. He would bet anything that he invited every man and boy in Hawthorne except Andrew to lend him his ear.

Victor had nothing to say to him and all the way across the lake when Andrew was rowing him home, he yodeled. When he got out of the boat all he said was "See you in the funny papers."

Nothing had been recovered. The chameleon died soon and Mrs. Shea hardly reacted at all when he put its corpse on her missal; it was leglessness in creatures she objected to. Cousin Katharine had her picnic on Stork Island but Charles was sick again and he and Victor did not come, and so, instead of them, Raoul St. Denis came, bringing his house-guest, a brash seventeen-year-old dandy from Mobile named James Partridge, who had a mandolin and, inhaling, smoked Lucky Strikes, and who so swept Honor and Harriet off their feet that for days afterward they mooned and could not eat and when they were not writing in their diaries, stood looking at themselves in mirrors, stunned with foolishness. They wanted to fly a Confederate flag from the barn.

But while there had been no change in Andrew's life and the events of it had been little more than a way to pass the time, there was a profound and unnameable change in Congreve House that affected everyone and had begun, he thought, to take place on that remarkable day when Cousin Katharine, renowned for her stalwart health, had fainted on the lawn. Andrew knew why she had fainted; she had been overwhelmed by what her intuition had discovered to her about him; she had looked him in the eye and seen that he was a murderer. It was enough to make anyone pass out. There had been nothing he could do about it, for the die was cast and he could not silence the voice inside him that perpetually sentenced Charles to death.

From Cousin Katharine down to Adam, they all appeared, like Andrew, to be anticipating something; there was that sense of an impending storm which is a kind of taut quiescence or a sort of premonition of disclosure as if, at any moment, the firmament will be slashed open by the lances of lightning to reveal, if one's eyes are quick enough, the angels and the thrones of heaven. This mood was nothing like the stale blight of the winter past but had an invigorating element in it, so that while they waited, the members of the household were ceaselessly busy and even Adam, whose love of lounging was the principle of his life, stirred himself to build a doll house for a favored niece and to learn how to add and subtract on a Chinese abacus he had found in the barn. The twins were frequently fetched by Raoul and James in the latter's jazzy yellow roadster to go to rustic square-dancing parties or evening sails on the tourist steamers at Bingham Bay. And when she did not dine out, leaving the house in full and magnificent regalia at eight o'clock, Cousin Katharine entertained and though her guests were the same old ones and the evening's routine was the same—after dinner she played the virginals for a few minutes and then the company moved to the card tables except for Mr. Barker and Miss Duff who played a cutthroat game of chess—the air was gayer than it had ever been. One might have thought that Cousin Katharine, like Maureen and like the twins, was in love. But Andrew knew better. He knew that all this contagious gaiety was made up and what it was was really her fear of him. Often he woke in the middle of the night to hear her moving around in her room which was on the front of the house next to his and he knew that she was standing guard to see that he did not slip out of the house and down to the lake to row across and murder Charles in his sleep. Poor Cousin Katharine! It was a terrible secret for her to have to keep.

She talked continuously of the fireworks ball in August and the twins, who really did think she was in love (they always imposed their own state of mind on everyone around them), amused themselves by imagining that on that night a lover would appear and she would announce her engagement to him—that Ronnie Pryce, perhaps, back from Australia and less talkative now, or Max Pirsch who had had a dueling scar. However, she repeated whenever they asked, that the only thing special about this party was that it was to be unusually big and unusually elaborate but that it was to commemorate nothing more than another of Hawthorne's heavenly summers. She meant to establish it as a regular tradition, "an estival Thanksgiving," she said, "when we'll give our prayerful thanks for roses instead of pumpkins and phoebes instead of turkeys." The whole town talked of the party too and they assured one another that the fireworks show she would put on would be twice as sensational as any municipal display on the Fourth of July; Billy Bartholomew predicted that she would burn up the woods with her folderol but no one listened to him. There was an altogether groundless rumor that there was to be a set-piece of *Old Ironsides.*

Andrew, for his part, was not sure what she was planning unless she meant to send for the plainclothesmen to take him away that night. It was very clever if that was what she intended to do, for in all the confusion, no one would notice even if they handcuffed him.

The town talked also, rather less openly, of something else that had already happened at Congreve House, something that altogether baffled Andrew. For his unfathomable cousin had done the queerest thing of her whole life: she was having her tombstone made by a stonecutter in Thomas and once a week she drove over to see it as if she were going for a fitting for a dress. People of a sanguine cast of mind accepted her tossed-off explanation that there was nothing more morbid in ordering a tombstone than in making a will. Mr. Barker, in fact, thought it so excellent an idea that he considered having his own made and drafted several designs, but in the end he decided to be cremated and sent for illustrated brochures of urns which Cousin Katharine studied with him. "No one will make monkeys out of us when we are dead, eh, Kate?" the old man laughed. "We'll see to it that our houses are made in the style we are accustomed to."

But Mrs. Tyler, who was a pessimist, and Miss Duff, who was going straight through her medical encyclopedia this summer and whose thought, therefore, was largely dominated by disease (last year it had been the evolution of the automobile and Brantley Wainright-Lowe had said that if she used the word "carburetor" one more time, he would scream), connected Katharine's act with her fainting spell and a frequent absence of her mind. One day, Andrew, bearing a message from his cousin to her neighbor, had stopped under Miss Duff's open windows, drawn irresistibly to listen to the ladies' low-pitched voices, and he heard Miss Duff say, "Carcinoma of the breast or I'm a dead man, so it may be just as well she's getting ready. Must say I hate to think of Katharine pushing up the daisies, as they say, but when you're called, you're called and that's that and no two ways about it." Mrs. Tyler, who knew a thing or two herself, was inclined to suspect angina pectoris but, being shouted down by her friend, asked for evidence and was told, "Haven't got any, but have a distinct feeling. Usually right about these things. Knew about Dan Thornton's cirrhosis before the doctors did. Long before."

Honor and Harriet thought the tombstone a joke but it embarrassed them a little because they were growing more and more conventional. The maids and Mrs. Shea said she was tempting fate and Beulah Smithwick ghoulishly said, "If you ask me to run up your winding sheet, I'll refuse point blank."

Andrew did not know what to make of it and he was inclined to accept it as he had accepted all her other caprices (her manufacture of gunpowder, for example, and her passion, one year, for collecting swords), although, from time to time, he wondered if perhaps she did have some knowledge of her death, told her in a dream. (Miss Duff's theory was too ridiculous to consider for a minute.) Whatever her motive was, she had succeeded in doubling Andrew's interest in death, and he often went to stand beside his great-uncle's cedar-shaded grave, trying to imagine what the skeleton looked like and whether the shroud had rotted away; he roamed the churchyard at St. James's and he scrutinized the dead bodies of birds, slain by cats, of rabbits run over in the road and mice pinched to death in traps in the pantry.

He began to have dreams of Charles Smithwick from which he awoke in a guilty sweat and some of which propelled him into sleepwalking. He loved to think about these nightmares afterward although they terrified him at the time and one night when he woke to find himself downstairs in the library, he screamed, partly from shock and partly from astonishment at the phenomenal power of the dream that had physically carried him, sound asleep, all the way from his bed to this pitch-dark room. Cousin Katharine had heard him and she came downstairs to lead him back to bed. When she had asked him to tell her the dream, he could only babble incoherently but long after she had left his room, he reviewed its ominous details.

He had dreamed that he was in the picking garden hunting for Cousin Katharine's shears which she had dropped. The sun had set and the night was coming on; Congreve House was no longer white but was brown stone, domed like a museum. As he neared a great grille-work door, he saw Charles Smithwick, wearing a long beard, lying on the cement entry and when he tried to open the door to see if he were really dead, a black dog ran out from a shed and standing on his hind legs, bit at Andrew's neck. Then Charles, clean-shaven, loomed up over a little rise, carrying a gun and two dead birds. He called off the dog and came close to Andrew and he said, "We must not kill birds. I never kill birds," but he was carrying two and the gouts of their blood shone on his trousers. Andrew knew at once that Charles was both dead and mad, and in his wanderings through the house and grounds, he found the evidences of it everywhere, for it was the dead lunatic's whim to strew enigmas as he restlessly roamed, scattering them on the lawns, pinning them to trees, to walls or to the backs of chairs. In Minerva's temple, Andrew found one on the floor, its edges held down with stones, and it said, "I must have golden gold at once," and in the library he had pasted a banner over the front of the bird cage and this one read, "My coat of dove, my glove of deer." When Cousin Katharine had turned the light on, she had found him standing right there, beside the finches.

2

Not long before the fireworks party, Cousin Katharine and the twins went off one morning to the state prison where Cousin Katharine annually bought the handicraft of the convicts to give away as Christmas presents to maids and godchildren. Andrew, alone in the house, was glum and when the summer's record for fair days was broken by a black rain that began to fall at noon and he knew his cousin and sisters would not be home in time for lunch, he settled into a monotonous dark mood. He could not put his mind to anything and his dissatisfaction made every act an effort of the will. At his lonely lunch, he had to think each time he carried his fork to his mouth and if he had not been careful, his water glass would have slipped from his insentient hand. He ate the peas on his plate one by one, maddening Maureen.

Afterward, he tried to read and could not; he put together a few pieces of a jigsaw puzzle but it was much too easy. He stared at each object that entered his range of vision as if he had never seen it before, but there was no excitement in his discovery, only a kind of dull confusion. That is, there was no excitement until it occurred to him to become a detective for the course of the next hour or so and, like Victor in the shut-up houses, examine his cousin's history through her belongings. He pretended that he did not know her and that he had been sent as a spy to her house; sniffing and prying and listening, he wandered in and out of the crowded rooms, lingering occasionally in the long windows to gaze out at the roiled waters of the lake. Once, for no longer than a minute, the sun came out, but the rain went on. "The devil is beating his wife," he said and his voice seemed not to come from him at all. He moved toilsomely, pausing to wonder what vagary had caused Cousin Katharine to buy or to be given a cabbage rose carved of bone and having no other purpose than to lie alone on an austere marble mantelpiece in a back bedroom; he debated which of the objects in the house were gifts and which were purchases. The milk-glass cuspidor, he knew, had been used for its intended purpose until Cousin Katharine had wrested it from a quiet old gentleman in Bath by staking ten dollars against it in a local election. From a Japanese friend of her father's had come the Samurai sword she used to prune the Dutchman's-pipe that grew over her windows; lopping and brandishing, she sometimes sang "The Volga Boatmen" in a stylish contralto to the delight of Miss Duff who generally came right over and stood below, watching. When Cousin Katharine had finished, she called up, "I declare, Kate, you're more fun than a basket of chips."

He examined, in cabinets and miniature desks and lacquered boxes and in jewel cases, on hanging what-nots and in sewing drums the accumulation of four generations. There were banjo clocks and music boxes that played minuets; embroidered nightcap holders and stuffed owls; in nooks and turnings there were Chinese vases filled with petrified cat-tails and furry grasses as old as Mr. Barker. There were porcelain umbrella stands and trivets in the shape of ducks; there was a leather fire bucket and an artificial cedar tree of jade. In drawers, there were Japanese fans whose silk had rotted from the ivory stays, Spanish lace and Spanish combs, magnifying glasses mounted on bamboo. There were snuff boxes, camel bells, and scores of ornamental wooden boxes that contained the testimonials of moods and enthusiasms and friendships, ribbons and seashells and colored stones gathered for the sake of the gathering on beaches and along the banks of rivers; fragments of wedding cake in cheesecloth bags; scraps of Mechlin, of tribute silk, of tartan ribbon and tatted edging; sashes made of velvet, solitary chamois gloves, bald buckram waistbands. There were strawberry emeries and covered corks for bone bodkins and decorated darning eggs and cases for tapestry needles. There were marbles, jackstones, fish hooks, chessmen, golf tees, corks with silver tops in the likeness of Henry VIII and Theodore Roosevelt, water bowls from Chinese bird cages, a campaign button that pledged its wearer to vote for Grover Cleveland.

In the library, on a big round table, covered with gold-tasseled gray velvet, there were, behind the porringers and christening cups, a multitude of photographs of relatives and friends. Andrew and his sisters were there, immortalized in drooping bathing suits; each held a lobster by the tail and grimaced dreadfully although it was clear that the brutes were dead. His parents were present many times: on their wedding day they stood before the front windows of the drawing room in Congreve House and stiffly held up glasses of champagne; they posed on a beach before a dwindling Roman ruin with a company of men in collegiate-looking boaters and women in bucket-shaped hats. Several of the pictures showed them with Cousin Katharine, ankle-deep in shamrocks beside the River Boyne, drinking tea on a steamer crossing Loch Katrine, strolling through the Arboretum on Lilac Sunday. In one of them, the two girls sat on the lawn at Congreve House, plucking the petals from black-eyed Susans to learn if they were loved or not and John Shipley, a book closed over his thumb, lay in the hammock, looking fondly down at them. "Get out of my hammock, you drip," said Andrew and turned the picture face down on the table.

Here in this room an investigator saw that the lady of the house did needlepoint but not for long at any time because beside her easel there was a table piled with books and magazines: she was reading, at this time, *Henry Esmond*, Bulfinch's *Mythology*, an old cook book, *The Illustrated London News*. Even if he had not known her, he would have seen that she did not keep her mind on anything for long, for on the other side of the easel there was a second table on which she had half finished a game of Canfield.

He edged slowly up the stairs, and considered going into his room to work on a model of the State House that he was assembling but then he remembered that he had run out of mucilage. Besides, the box of parts was in the top drawer of his bureau and he felt like a criminal each time he opened it because he had never mailed the letters to his parents that Honor had given him weeks ago. He had not read them after all, for he had not dared know what Cousin Katharine had said about him, but he flinched each time he saw the neat, stamped pile.

The loud, toneless rain shut out all the sounds from downstairs and he felt as if this were the middle of the night and everyone was asleep except himself. All the bedroom doors were closed and the long corridor was full of shadows and the smell of dank. He thought of exploring the attic, he thought of going down to the kitchen to tell Mrs. Shea some perfectly awful lie such as that his father was a Hindu convert and slept on a bed of nails, but Mrs. Shea was in a bossy mood today and doubtless wouldn't listen. And for a moment he thought of paying a call on Maddox but he gave up the idea when he remembered how short-tempered Maddox was on days when he had to stay indoors. Adam was gone with the carriage and the maids made him shy.

Aimlessly he went into Harriet's room and examined her collection of ceramic pigs. What on earth she had them for he could not guess; incongruous garlands of dainty flowers girdled their necks and their round flanks were branded with arabesques and hearts and some of them had gilded ears. She had an equally worthless assortment of souvenir spoons, some with heart-shaped bowls, others with bowls like shovels and like arrowheads; one had a mosaic handle and all of them bore some legend that could not possibly have meant less to her: St. Louis World's Fair, From Colvin to Emma,

Niagara Falls. He looked at her closet full of dresses and her bureau drawers full of lace-edged underpants and all the scarves she never wore. A lanky French doll lay on a frilly baby-pillow on the bed. He picked up her Line-a-Day from her desk and finding that it was locked, he rummaged like a burglar through the jewel box and through the drawers again but he could not find the key. He did discover, to his mild titillation, a box of dark blue eyeshadow secreted in a handkerchief case. Finally he gave up and went into Honor's room, but her diary was also locked and the key was nowhere to be found. He wrinkled his nose with distaste when he found a piece of paper on top of her bookcase on which she had been canceling out the letters in her name and the name of the Alabama boy, James Partridge, to determine whether their relationship was to be one of friendship, courtship, love or marriage:

Jame̸s̸ Par̸tri̸dge (courtship)
Honor̸ S̸hi̸ple̸y (marriage)

With her small fountain pen he wrote beneath the names, "Honor Shipley is a moron."

Kneeling at his sister's window, he singsonged, "Rain, rain, go to Spain, never come back here again. Rain, rain, go away, come back on another day." He repeated the jingles until the words lost their meaning and became no more than syllables. Then, tired of that, he read a little in a book called *The Language of Flowers* which bore the name Katharine Congreve in a childish hand on the flyleaf. He learned that mistletoe signified

"I surmount difficulties" and that whortleberry, whatever that might be, meant "Treason."

Back in the spooky corridor, he mechanically opened every door on the west side—the huge linen closet smelling of pine soap; the bathroom with cold marble surfaces and the longest tub in the world and a mirror opposite so that while one bathed one could make faces at oneself, a far cry from Cousin Katharine's days in convent school when all the mirrors had been taken down from the walls on bath day and the girls had worn muslin shifts when they got into the water. How did the nuns themselves take baths, he wondered, thinking of his mother's cook's sisters whose habits looked to be a permanent integument like fur or feathers. Next to the bathroom was a storeroom filled with boxes neatly labeled "Kitchen Curtains," "Lamp Chimneys," "Coat Hangers & Shoe Trees." After that there was the sewing room where two ample-bosomed, wasp-waisted dummies, armless and legless and with a curved hook for a head, stood, sentry-like, on either side of the Singer; around the middle of one of them, he tied a girdle of bias tape; he filled a bobbin with green silk thread, wrote "Beware" with a piece of chalk on an old billiard table piled with bolts of cloth, and bifurcated the room with a tidy row of buttons, alternating black and white.

The last of the rooms on this side of the house was Eustachia Vye's. It was never used except once in a blue moon when an overnight visitor slept there. A long time ago, when he and the twins had still been very small and had needed the governess, it had been Miss Bowman's room and he remembered how, somewhat to Cousin Katharine's annoyance, she had converted it into a schoolish place, hanging up maps in place of Godey's ladies and substituting for the graceful little escritoire a sturdy golden oak office desk which she had had sent up from Boston, causing everyone trouble. There were no signs of Bowman here now. Indeed, there were no signs of anyone, for this was unlike any other room in the full house; it was swept and dead; its narrow, stripped-down bed had an air of final vacancy as if its occupant had been carried away to a coffin, as if it really were inhabited by a ghost beyond the need of any creature comforts.

And yet, by contrast, the open desk showed letter paper and a full inkwell, ready for a guest, and a vase of roses so fresh that they must have been cut that very day, stood on the top of a chest of drawers. Light books for summer reading were lined up between two square Chinese vases on the bedside table, Lear's *Nonsense Rhymes*, *The Memoirs of a Midget*, *The Green Hat.* Still in its wrapping, a cake of Pears lay in the soap dish on the commode and the towels on the rack were fresh. But the naked mattress and the frame of the bed, disrobed of its tester, were inhospitable; it was like a carcass picked by birds. He looked into the closet and found nothing there but an enormous empty hatbox from a shop in Paris. The drawers of the desk and the dressing table were empty; there was nothing in the sewing drum except a length of gray grosgrain ribbon, and on the shelves of a three-tiered what-not there was only a yellow pear made of wax with a hinged section in it, like a drop seat, which, when it was opened, revealed a minute crèche half lost in cotton.

And then his eye fell on a little box beside the vase of roses, a box that Cousin Katharine always carried with her, extracting from it lemon drops that she gave to children she encountered. She must have left it here, he reasoned, when she brought in the flowers, and though he found it peculiar that there should be flowers in this forsaken room, he found it even more peculiar that she had left the box behind. He had not imagined it had any existence except when she was making up to a child, just as umbrellas seemed to dematerialize between rainstorms. He opened the box to take a candy out and noticed, as he had not done before, that there was a photograph slipped into the inside of the lid.

It was a picture of his mother and Cousin Katharine as girls, examining the wares of a lace vendor before the doors of Chartres, and on the back of it was written, "Maeve and I buying scandalous lace gloves. M. in a black mood because of her eczema which is so severe that Sister Chrysostom thinks her skin may be permanently pitted." Eczema, how awful! Those horrid, pinky hummocks that often appeared on his own chin? He looked closely at the photograph again but he could see no mutilation of his mother's wide-eyed, lovely face. So tall that they dwarfed the lace vendor even in her high medieval headdress, the girls, hatless and wearing their dark hair in buns at their necks, gazed tranquilly into the camera, their arms entwined.

An arresting hypothesis came into his mind: if this Sister Chrysostom had been right, he doubted that his father would have married his mother, because he could not bear disfigurement of any kind (he could hardly endure the sight of Honor whenever she had hives and when the three of them had had chicken-pox, he talked with them through the closed doors of their rooms and never once came in). In that event, he probably would have married Cousin Katharine who, then, would have been Andrew's mother. But would Andrew have been the same person? Would he have been born to Katharine on the same day and at the same hour of the day that he had been born to Maeve? And would he be standing here now in this little room, and would the rain be coming down so madly at this very hour if his father had married the girl on the left instead of the one on the right?

A distant, uncompleted trumpeting of thunder startled him and he looked out the window. The stable was directly opposite this room and in the gardener's room, he saw a light-globe burning. Immediately, as if at a signal, Maddox's face appeared; he flattened his nose against the pane like a child and scowled. The rain was heavier than ever, lunging against the windows and lashing the tops of the maple trees and making a swift muddy river down the drive. The gardens would be a mess and Maddox would not be fit to live with for a week. For a moment Andrew watched Maddox, who did nothing but glower at the ruinous downpour but Andrew felt as if those angry eyes had caught him red-handed in some wickedness and he moved backward from the window, hearing the grandfather clock strike two in the endless afternoon.

Taking the lemon-drop box, he went across the hall to put it in his cousin's sitting room, partly out of thoughtfulness and partly as an excuse to lie on the chaise longue, an article of furniture he liked next best to a hammock. Beth and her family of six blind, naked kittens lay in a basket lined with flower-printed cotton flannel; the mother cat stretched her neck to be petted and purred loudly, narrowing her perspicacious eyes.

If Cousin Katharine were his mother . . . Taking up this speculation again as he lay on the chaise longue and stared up at the ceiling, he presented himself with questions and problems as if he were taking an examination. Would Cousin Maeve, in that case, be at the state prison today or would she be in Dublin, about to leave for France? Would it be Katharine who followed Paris styles and Maeve who wore what she wanted to regardless of fashion? He proposed a series of substitutions, imagined his mother in Cousin Katharine's little drawing room on Brimmer Street, serving tea to the boys from Harvard and, on other days, walking up to Mount Vernon Street to the Shipleys' house.

It was all unthinkable, really, because his mother would never *dare* to do the things his cousin did. It would never occur to her, for example, to take up Botany as Cousin Katharine had done for one semester at

Radcliffe. When she bought a microscope and announced her intention of watching the sex cells of slime-mold conjugate, Mrs. Shipley had put her hands over her ears and cried, "Slime mold? For pity's sake, don't tell me what it is!" To use one of Bowman's favourite expressions, his mother had no "intellectual curiosity."

He changed his tack, pretending now that Cousin Katharine, as his mother, was the person she had always been and that his mother, as Cousin Maeve, was that rather vague, somehow always slightly worried, rather humble, faintly discouraging woman to whom he returned on winter afternoons. How much nicer it would be to go *from* her house to Cousin Katharine's instead of the other way around! He remembered a typical day last February when it had seemed to him that all the careworn futility of being alive in the winter was crystallized in the person of his mother who, even while she accepted confidences and soothed tears and laughed at jokes, never gave herself up wholly but kept preoccupied with the mechanics of existence: her mind was always elsewhere—it was on the message that had come up from the kitchen that the alligator pear was bad, it was on the failure of the window-washers to appear, or the error in the address that Shreve, Crump and Low had printed on invitations to a party. If he came to her, bearing like a gift the intelligence that the word "hippocampine" meant "of or pertaining to seahorses," she did not ignore him and, in fact, she showed a considerable interest, but it was polite and after much too short an interval in which her questions were much too perfunctory, she was as likely as not to cry, "Oh, *dear!* I forgot to call the men about oiling the books," and to take up a pencil and write a note to herself; Cousin Katharine, on the other hand, would have written down *hippocampine.*

On that particular afternoon that came back to him today, he had gone to call on Cousin Katharine and had been wholly frustrated for she had to break her promise to show him a slide of tap water because, in the first place, an uninvited guest was announced, a doctor by the name of Codman who spent the time disrespectfully fingering the beard of a bust of Shakespeare and importunately telling Cousin Katharine that she ought to learn to drive a car.

And then, just after he left and they had adjusted the microscope, Andrew's father came. Failing to see his son at first, he said, "Well, thank the Lord, I find you alone," and then, "Oh, blast and damn—forgive me, Katharine—I left my briefcase in the hall. Would you get it for me, Andy, like a good chap?" He had drawn up a design for a guest house for Cousin Katharine, he said, and he wanted to go over it with her. When Andrew came back, his father commenced to shuffle through papers and to drum his fingers on the tea table and then he abruptly looked up and said irritably, "Do you mind if you cut your botanizing short today and go along home? I have only a few minutes to get through this business with your cousin." Cousin Katharine herself had let him out and winking at him just before she stooped to press her cool cheek against his, she said, "What a fusser he is! But since he's doing it for me free, I can't look a gift-horse in the mouth." He had been about to ask her where the guest house was to be and who were to be the guests who would sleep in it, but her manner hurried him and as he walked home through the cold, mean dusk, he felt cheated and scolded and he hated his father.

There was a dinner dress on his mother's bed and his mother was at her dressing table brushing her hair. "You're early. I thought you were having tea with Cousin Katharine and boning up on tobacco diseases. Wasn't it very gay there?"

"No, not very," he said. "Dr. Codman was there at first. And Daddy afterward. Just as we were starting to look at tap water."

"Tap water? What's botanical about that?"

"Bacteria," he said. "You probably wouldn't drink it if you knew what was in it. It's alive."

"Really? I never heard of that before. I wondered where Daddy was. Darling, you terribly need a haircut." She began to brush her hair again. "It doesn't matter that he didn't come home because there was no tea today anyhow. We're going out for dinner."

The purling of a pigeon on the roof came strangled down the chimney. The sound made him lonely the way the sound of a night train could do or the look of a dog staring through a window.

"I don't see why he can't let her come to his office at a regular time. Why does he have to spoil the slide she made?"

"But if it's only tap water, sweetheart, she can make dozens, can't she?"

"You wouldn't understand," he said but so softly that she did not hear.

He watched her in the soft and facile light that came from under the small pink silk shades that sat like parasols upon the crooks of two dead-white Dresden shepherd boys. From across the room he could smell her perfume; she smelled delicious, but she smelled like all her friends who bought their perfume on the Champs Elysées at the same shop and discussed the price of it, dispelling, thereby, half its magic. Cousin Katharine's, on the other hand, was brewed secretly by Maddox.

"Did she seem to like Dr. Codman?" asked his mother.

"I don't know. *I* didn't like him. He had a dead front tooth."

"I expect he could have that taken care of. Dentists are growing awfully clever. Did he do something offensive?"

He told his mother how the doctor, as he was leaving, ostentatiously reminded Cousin Katharine of the present of red roses he had brought to her and said, "An aspirin will help keep them. And be sure to cut the stems each day," to which Cousin Katharine replied with sincere thanks for his thoughtfulness. But when she came back after seeing him out she sharply fanned up the fire with the bellows as if she were attacking someone and said, "Cut the stems indeed! I know of nothing that annoys me more than to be instructed in matters I took in with my mother's milk. The curse of being female, Andrew, is that we must pretend to be quite incapable of grasping the self-evident."

His mother smiled to herself and said, "Kate would be bound to take exception to that. What a pity." Putting down her hairbrush she began to look at her eyebrows in a magnifying mirror. "I'm sorry you had a dull tea and I'm sorry you and Cousin Katharine don't like Dr. Codman. I, for one, wish she'd marry him. He's a very good doctor."

"Marry Dr. Codman?" His voice was a squeal. The pigeon moaned again like something sick.

"Dr. Codman or anyone!" exclaimed his mother. "Anyone at all! It has gone on too long. Her solitude has gone on far too long and year after year she has grown . . . she has grown more unpredictable."

He was indignant at the thought of Dr. Codman eating the pears at Congreve House with that blue tooth and running his hand over Minerva's helmet as he had fondled Shakespeare's beard, and he said, "If she does marry him, you can bet your boots I'll never go back to Hawthorne."

"Of course not. Cousin Katharine would have a family of her own then."

The possibility of never going back to Congreve House, of being supplanted by another boy (first of all it would be a baby and he loathed babies) so depressed him that he closed his eyes and behind them he saw small pictures of things he might very well not see again; the fruit room behind the kitchen where Mrs. Shea kept her jars of tomato preserves and grape catsup and chowchow, a room with a country coolness and a country smell where, on hot days, Beth lay at full length as limp and insensible as if she had been killed. He saw the lake and the river and the pond and the marriage elms; he smelled an early apple, freckled with pink, that he had picked up from the deep grass.

Suddenly he said, "She won't marry him, I promise you. He's a hootnanny and she knows it."

"What is he? A *hoot* what?"

There was a rapid double knock on the bedroom door and Andrew's father came in, bringing with him the chill of the street and, so Andrew thought, an echo of the smell of the room on Brimmer Street, of Cousin Katharine's unique perfume and Dr. Codman's roses and the fire on the hearth. He nodded to his son and to his wife he said, "Your match-making was a fiasco. She has sent Codman away with a flea in his ear."

Mrs. Shipley put her forefingers to her temples and closed her eyes and murmured, "It isn't natural."

"It isn't your business whether it's natural or not," her husband said brusquely. "If she marries, she'll marry."

"We shouldn't be talking this way before Andrew."

Andrew picked up his school bag and started for the door. "I'm not a child," he said. "Why did you say all that about the guest house when you were really there to make her get married?"

His father straightened up and looked in the mirror at Andrew's reflection. He smiled and winked though. Andrew was in no mood to accept such an intimacy. "I was killing two birds with one stone," he said, "catching two cods with one line." He laughed at his joke, but Andrew did not. He went on, "Sorry, old man, about that thingamajig you were going to look at. A frog's gall bladder, was it?"

Andrew clenched his fists and enunciating clearly, he said, "Botany is the study of plants. If frogs have gall bladders, which I doubt, you would look at them in zoology."

"They were going to look at tap water," said his mother.

"Jove!" said his father.

When he had closed the door, he outlined on it a skull and crossbones with his finger and for a moment he listened at the keyhole. His mother said, "What is it? Oh God, John, tell me what it is!" And his father answered, "Why, 'it,' I suppose, is nothing more than the inevitable changes that are taking place in you. And in me. Nothing to get stirred up about." And in a lighter voice he continued, "I meant to call you earlier but I got jammed up. I shan't be going to the Websters' tonight. My potentate from Indiana wants to see the sights." A silence followed and Andrew went upstairs, listening briefly at Harriet's door, but she was only conjugating *fero, ferre, tuli, latum.*

That story about the guest house had been a whopper. The only thing that had been built at Congreve

House this summer was Adam's doll house for his harelipped niece.

They were so flat and limp, both of them, and reconstructing that dispiriting scene, Andrew decided that while he wished Cousin Katharine were his mother, he wished someone altogether different were his father, someone he did not know, and he wondered what the drowned Mr. Smithwick had been like. If Cousin Katharine had married him, Victor would have been his brother. But would Charles also have been his brother? Now he was rattled and he pushed aside these philosophical experiments and gazed around the room, looking for something to do.

It was an excludingly feminine room. The painted furniture was French, thin-legged and daintily furbelowed; in the recesses of the windows there were two round tables on one of which stood a figure of Minerva, on the other, Venus. On the pearl-white walls, there hung six likenesses of Cousin Katharine, by six different painters; as a shepherdess, as a horsewoman, as a bird lover, a debutante, a bibliophile, as Marie Antoinette dressed for a masked ball. On the desk that had once been a spinet, there was a double inkwell made of Sèvres and silver and there was a mountainous supply of letter paper for her huge, incessant correspondence. Here was her black record of birds and here was her big diary. And here, as in the drawing room, there were the testimonials of her restlessness: another easel, smaller than the one downstairs, with needlepoint stretched on it and beside it, a low table over which spilled from the wide maw of her knitting bag the brilliant yarns of half a dozen unfinished sweaters. Her place in *Don Quixote* was marked with a letter from the Shelbourne Hotel in Dublin, addressed in his father's hand. He would have liked to read the letter, he would have liked even better to read her diary and he touched its plump covers and lifted it up to judge its weight. He took the two thin, closely written sheets of paper out of the envelope with its Irish stamp, but as he hesitated, he saw the cat out of the corner of his eye stand up in her basket and look at him alertly. His bad conscience made him shudder as it had done earlier when he had seen Maddox's face at the window and returning the letter to its place and putting the lemon-drop box neatly on the diary so that it was encircled by the signs of the zodiac embossed in gold, he left the room, feeling the vigilant cat's eyes burning into him.

The rain had begun at last to peter out, but it was still too sopping wet to go outdoors and the house was still dark and he felt like someone going crazy in a dungeon. He must keep busy or he might begin to scream, so he went up to the big attic that ran the length of the ell and resumed his examination of other people's property. A smell of squirrels and dust came from the old beams and hornets seethed sleepily in the rafters. His footsteps made the floorboards snap and a mouse sped through the maze of rounded trunks and wicker hampers, patched with the stickers, like heraldic emblems, of the half-mythical hotels of Florence, Athens, and Madrid.

Often in the past on just such stormy days as this, he had come up here with Honor and Harriet and had dressed up in the clothes left behind by people who had died or had left them to moulder because they were no longer in vogue. Against a trunk that had belonged to Great-Uncle George leaned a pair of snowshoes that probably belonged to Maddox; he put them on, skidding clumsily over the floor and rousing every small beast in the attic. Then he opened his uncle's trunk from which arose a smell of camphor balls and wool; under the withering tissue paper lay morning coats and dinner jackets and opera capes. Uncle George had been very particular about his clothes and he had gone annually to London to confer with his tailor for three weeks. Miss Duff said of him, "Best-dressed man on God's green earth." All the fabrics were old and soft to the touch; Andrew stroked a dark red smoking jacket with velvet lapels and heavily embroidered frogs. He took out a pair of white trousers and a blazer with broad blue stripes, a crimson foulard ascot and a canvas yachting cap and when he had put them on over his own clothes (he was swallowed up and he giggled idiotically to think how he must look) he began to look for a top or a pair of Indian clubs or something, anything, to distract him for the rest of the afternoon. He found a shuffleboard set that he deduced must once have belonged on the *Empress Katharine* and a box of lotto cards and a parchesi game. And then he did find a top in a carton that contained wooden curtain rings and the ends of birthday candles. It was a bright red one and when he spun it, it seemed to have a glad life of its own; it was bursting with energy and merriment and he hated to see it slow and begin to falter and finally to keel over and become again nothing but a shape in wood. He spun it over and over, endowing it with vitality, making it a being more substantial than his twin.

Andrew was in the entrance hall spinning the top when the ladies of the house came back. He saw them through the sidelights, his smiling sisters flanking his cousin who wore a white leghorn hat, tied down with an old-fashioned motoring veil; he slipped behind the bamboo screen, meaning to give them the surprise of their lives. But the top, unfortunately, was still spinning when Honor opened the door and he could see her, through the narrow slits of the wood, glance round, a little startled, "Fee, fie, fo, fum," she said. "I smell the blood of an Englishman." He waited, breathing shallowly.

"Ignore the Englishman," said Harriet and went into the library to put down her packages. "The Englishman has knocked over the trinity of Congreve House," she called out.

The top slowed, reeled and fell, the play gone out of it.

"Harriet!" cried Honor. "We'd better go see if the Englishman has been in our rooms. Did you take the key to your Line-a-Day?" And the two girls ran laughing up the stairs. He knew that in a moment when Honor found what he had written below her forecast of her love affair with James Partridge, rage would replace her lightheartedness and the infantile frolic would be over. So he stepped out of hiding to have, at least, the pleasure of fooling Cousin Katharine. She had her back to him, looking through a sheaf of letters in her hand, but she wheeled instantly when he said, "The Empress Katharine, I presume?" She seemed, she really did, not to know who he was. She stared into the dusky depths of the hall and the letters fell right out of her hand and lay at her feet in a perfect fan.

She was taken in to such an extent that she said "John?" and could not move. It was the most successful hoax he had ever perpetrated.

Honor ruined it as he had known she would do, flying downstairs in a tantrum, spluttering unintelligibly but doing it at the top of her voice. And then, to his astonishment, he saw that Cousin Katharine was angry with him too; she looked at him frigidly, freezing him solid, and without a word she turned and went upstairs. Skinned and smarting, at the dizzy peak of his restiveness and loneliness, he shouted at her retreating figure, "I hate you! I hate you all!" and savagely hurled down the top and while it spun he snarled at his raving sister, "You shut up or I'll kill you!"

CHAPTER VI

The Child in the House

Because her hands shook so, ostentatiously publishing to her mirror the dishevelment of her nerves, Katharine could not undo that knot of her veil and as if this failure were a catastrophe, she sank to the floor beside a window, still hatted, and tightly locked her fingers to stop their fidgets and tried, and failed, to cry. Even in extremity, she could not seduce a single tear from her eyes. She had misplaced her rose-colored glasses which until now had taken the place of the gift of tears, and because she was herself bedeviled without them, she saw in everyone the symptoms of decay.

Andrew, masquerading clownishly in her father's clothes, looming out of the palpitant light, had seemed instinct with crime, with an active immorality that transliterated his travesty into a threat. She had felt preyed upon. This time it had been necessary, such was the increasing delicacy of her inner balance, to show him, by refusing to take part in his harmless game, that she was angry with him. Just as she had been obliged, out of self-preservation, to berate him when his eye had fallen on Mangareva, so just now she had had to throw up a smoke screen of adult displeasure to conceal her staggered utterance of his father's name. It sickened her that she had cried it out but even more she was sickened by *his* tempestuous cry that he hated her. In the course of the punishment that must follow, and in his remorse, it was possible that he would forget her aberration and remember only his own misdeed.

But it was equally possible that he would not forget. One knew as much at twelve as one was ever going to know. Even more perhaps, since at that age one was still, philosophically if not practically, in a state of nature and could cleave through the toughest tissues to the heart of the matter. Certainly she had known, known even before she was twelve, how rickety was the scaffolding of her parents' marriage; she had proceeded from just such a slip of the tongue as she had made to Andrew a little while ago, to the knowledge that her father had a mistress. It had been through some process infinitely more direct than logic, something instantaneous and unquestionable, that she had perceived that the reason her father had often seemed to prefer Maeve was that Maeve was not the daughter of his wife whom he did not love. Later, when he grew accustomed to his guilt, he had begun to lavish on Katharine the fruits of his cool heart.

She remembered how in the beginning at school in France, when both she and her cousin were languid with homesickness, her greatest joy had lain in her letters from him in which he sent impersonal messages to Maeve; even though Maeve wrote to him every day and every day, finding no envelope addressed to herself, burst into tears. She was reluctant to admit it to herself, but she was afraid that she had never really forgiven Maeve for those two or three years when she had been her father's darling. The fact was that she had never really forgiven poor Maeve for anything though she had struggled to. Bending every effort of her will and her intelligence, she had tried to love Maeve and, failing, had come at last to this ultimate betrayal. In Katharine, a grown and apparently integrated woman, there bitterly rankled still the recollections of how all the young men in her girlhood had been taken first with her and every one of them had abandoned her the moment they met Maeve, who was not more beautiful, not more alert, danced no better. This imponderable in Maeve, even now, Katharine could not define, but clearly it had been there, immediately recognizable to men and immediately alluring.

She recalled that once the two of them had fallen in love with a German who lived there in the French town, and they quivered at the sight of his great height and his blond head, in the streets and the shops when they were allowed to leave the school to make small purchases and to drink chocolate in an approved café. One day they had separated and Katharine had gone alone to the stationer's shop where she had seen the man buying a quantity of foolscap and had heard the shopkeeper address him as "M. Faust." She had stood beside him at the counter, so agitated that her French left her, so giddy that she pointed to ink when she had come for envelopes. He had smelled richly of tobacco and pomade and out of courtesy to her, he had taken off his cap, showing a sculptured, intellectual forehead. When she left, he held the door open for her and she said boldly, "Vielen dank, Meinherr," and had been transported when he smiled and bowed and paid her baby-German a compliment, "Gut gesprechen, gnädiges Fräulein." She had kept the secret of his name from Maeve and yet, on the very next excursion to town, they had met Herr Faust in the road and Maeve had greeted him, calling him by name. Katharine asked her how she had come to know it and Maeve had replied, with her disarming candour, "He told it to me. He's a novelist, you know." Katharine had not known; she had been feverish with jealousy.

Afterward, a three-cornered friendship had sprung up and they had had meetings in teashops that the girls were forbidden to enter and had taken walks together in the woods, though this was not allowed. Though the young man had listened gravely to Katharine's observations on literature (she had begun, as soon as she had learned his name, to read Goethe) his eyes were forever on Maeve. It was Maeve's elbow that was cupped when they came to a log fallen across the path, it was Maeve who was asked if she were cold, it was Maeve who was invited first to choose her pastry. But Katharine had persevered; she *would* be noticed and, seeking to flatter him by imitating him, she began to write a novel. When she had finished twenty pages of it (it had dealt with a nun who had broken her vows) she had submitted it to Herr Faust to read, and at their next meeting, returning the manuscript to her, he had said only, "You should take up the harp. Or paint ring-around-a-rosy on saucers," and to Maeve, not to her, he had explained why women should never try to write. His heavy, arrogant, Teutonic waggishness had been unendurable. As soon as they got back to the school, Katharine had written to her mother that a certain man of the town had succeeded in converting Maeve to anarchy, a yarn that could not fail to arouse the law-abiding Alma Congreve. Until some weeks later, when Sister Chrysostom had a letter from her and both girls were reprimanded for breaking rules and their permission to leave the convent grounds was suspended, Katharine had had to put up with several more meetings with the man during which he teased her about the novel which had been called "The Bright Blight." Down the years of girlhood, she had suffered these small fractures of the heart while Maeve, infrangible and unbruised, had never been aware in her tranquillity that anything was wrong.

She felt, these days, that she was living in a void and that she would continue to for the rest of time with an occasional swift trip to chaos, changing the climate from despair to dementia. For in the evening after Edmund St. Denis had witlessly held up her relationship with John to such maudlin ridicule, after she had been attended by the little doctor and her frightened maids and finally had been left alone, she had written a letter to the Shipleys in which, embedded in gossip and bulletins on the welfare and occupations of the children, she had told John that the daydream, for her, was finished.

> Last winter I flirted with the notion of pulling up my stakes and leaving everything behind [she wrote], thought of going to live in Bermuda, perhaps, that blessed isle where the internal combustion machine does not intrude. If you can believe it of me, I thought of selling Congreve House or turning it over to the state for some good antiquarian cause. What possessed me, I cannot think, unless it was that usual slump that everyone falls into in February—I seem to recall that both of you were very low about that time this year—but in any case, I have come so fully to my senses that I intend to have my gravestone made in Thomas by the man who made Minerva and Papa's stone and when it's finished, to have it stored in the stable, until the solemn day when it is laid on top of me. It is a kind of insurance—however tenuous and symbolic—against my suddenly kicking over the traces and going off to a flamboyant island in my middle age. The stone will be superb, if Mr. Norman executes it as I plan. My neighbors have

formed two opposing camps, one horrified, the other benedictory, and if I have done no other act of generosity, I have provided Hawthorne with a meaty subject of discussion.

Maeve's reply had been, as she had expected, filled with anxious questions and it was evident, despite the shrouding tact, that she thought Katharine was either gravely ill or mildly mad. She suggested that they come home earlier this year than usual and she proposed that if the children were a strain they be sent down to Newport to Uncle Daniel. In a postscript she added, "Our difficulties, John's and mine, do not diminish. How on earth is it going to end?"

She had expected from John a storm of anger and had, to tell the truth, looked forward to it, had in her mind written back with equal indignation, sending the letter to the business address at which he had told her to write him. There had come instead a groaning petition that she reconsider, a plea to know if he had offended her in any way and it had ended, "You must ask yourself this question: Have you the moral right to destroy me? If you are thinking of Maeve or of the children, you are being ungenerous to everyone, for the divorce is a foregone conclusion. My life is in your hands."

But Katharine was certain that he would not divorce Maeve; he would not, that is, unless another woman appeared with her hands outstretched, delighted to take his life in them. No, he would go on living with Maeve Maxwell and after half a year or perhaps a year, the talk would die down (like Maeve, the gossips imagined that he kept a dancer) and his "bit of a fling" would be forgiven and even condoned as something perfectly natural in the life of any healthy, good-looking man of forty-two. And he himself, looking back, would probably think, "That was a narrow squeak." Eventually he would even be able to console himself for his want of accomplishment by imagining that he had sacrificed his career to his family and he could die praiseworthy in his own eyes.

But none of this would he foresee now. One time she had told him that if he botched this loop-the-loop, he would hate her with far more passion than he loved her now and he had chucked her under the chin (it was hard for her to believe, just as it had been hard to believe at the moment it happened) and had said, "There will be no botching. This isn't puppy-love, you know." And puppy love, of course, was exactly what it was, but how convey that to him? How tell him: what I wanted I have now achieved, *my* desire is consummated for I have supplanted Maeve, and we would have to be born again and to live our lives up to the night of the Catherine wheels for me to pull up from my earth my intricate, tenacious roots.

She had continued to write to the two of them and had not written privately to him, and knowing what pain it must cause him, had told them of the ball she meant to have, strewing the many creamy sheets of her letter with reminiscences of their first meeting ("It was I, the bystander, that knew the two of you were done for, not you the actors in that pretty pastoral play. 'The jig is up,' said I, looking at you, for you hadn't a ghost of a chance of getting your hearts back once you'd lost them to each other") and knowing how these ambiguities would make him wince and curse lost time and tell himself, as Edmund did, that until a man is forty he doesn't know where he is at. But she wrote with her blood, for all the while that she repudiated John Shipley as he was now, she was hungry to avidity for him as he had been then, as he might have been, as he had been this very afternoon, stepping softly around the wing of the bamboo screen.

A rainbow arched across the western sky, its nearer terminus behind the canting chimney of the Smithwick house and its yonder one lost in the trees that fringed the headtide. The stone curls of the Roman notables stationed along the boundaries of the rosary were roguishly plastered with leaves from the plane trees above. And the birds that had been driven to shelter in the storm were out again, singing in the arbors, undoubtedly nettling Maddox with their cheer since he, for days now, would be cheered by nothing, now that his belles had been decapitated and their tattered petals lay in the mud at the bases of Hadrian's and Caesar's fluted columns. Katharine could see him pacing the sticky paths of the garden, his hands slack at his sides, his head disconsolately hanging forward as he surveyed his slaughtered virgins. She sometimes felt that Maddox carried his personifications too far and one time she had been disturbed when, after a heavy wind, he had had a mass burial of the ravaged blossoms (some of them stabbed by their own thorns), interring the sodden, fragrant mass in a shallow grave beside the summerhouse. She had not found the ceremony sentimental—as her friends, on hearing of it, did: "Pathetic fallacy it's called, if I'm not mistaken," Peg Duff had said—but nearly psychopathic. Thinking back on it, she was reminded of a lemon tree she had seen today, growing in a solarium of the state prison; it had produced one fruit, still green but of titanic size, and its custodian, a short and hunchbacked parricide, referred to the tree as "he" and the lemon as "his fruit," and said that he "fertilized this boy with vetch." A foul effluvium had come from a stone crock of fertilizer; the whole scene had been one of hatred and scurrility and when she turned to go, the man had said, with sarcastic piety, "I took a life so now I make a life. You know the old saying, 'A lemon a day keeps the hangman away,'" and he had tittered shrilly, squeezing his eyes between dirty wrinkles, showing huge false teeth. She had no affinity for homespun wisdom but, even so, she was repelled by this perversion of it and so had pretended not to hear (Honor and Harriet laughed and one of them said, "Jimmy will love that!") and had gone to examine a rack of trays on which were painted teapots, windmills and love birds.

An incident like this was in itself too trivial to be more than noted in passing and at another time in her life, Katharine Congreve, who believed in sweetness and light and the superfluity of all else, would have refused to remember it; if the memory had gained access in spite of her, she would certainly never have drawn a parallel between the convict in his vengeful act of penance and her gardener, an honest man whose *idée fixe,* though it was often difficult to live with, implied no unseemly motive. But "at another time in her life" she had not yet opened up Pandora's box.

The boy must get his dressing down. She stroked the cat and touched the squirming kittens and steeled herself to call to Andrew and to deliver to him a lecture on the misuse of the word "hate." But as she started across the room, it struck her that there was something wrong at her desk and she stood for a moment looking down at it. Nothing was missing, nothing was in disarray. It was several minutes before she realized that the box she kept lemon drops in had been set squarely on her diary.

She remembered that she had left it in the small guest room that morning when she had gone in to see that Mary had begun to turn the room out (there were to be several overnight guests on the occasion of the ball). She had been carrying a vase of roses that she meant to put in the hall window and now she remembered that she had forgotten them, too, having been called to the telephone in the middle of her inspection. She had gone through the drawers to make sure that there was nothing in them to distract (or interest) a visitor and in the desk she had found a photograph of herself and Maeve. It was innocuous enough except for the inscription on the back which had been childishly unkind, bearing in it a reference to a skin disorder of Maeve's which Katharine had prayed would be incurable: actually had prayed, with humble Christian words and phrases, in the Lady Chapel at Chartres while, impatient in the aisle beside her, a subaltern of the sacristan had waited, sniffling and shuffling, to guide her and Maeve up the tower, the profanity of his avarice being less despicable by far than that of her appeals to heaven. How that day, as all shameful days, came back! When they had emerged from the murk of the cold, weird winding stairs onto the lowest of the church's roofs and had leaned over the parapet looking down upon the distant little houses and the puffs of budding April trees, her muscles had tightened against the desire to fling herself off and in her desperate fear of the height, which she had never experienced before, she had been frantic, certain that she could neither go farther up nor go back down the precipitous and slippery stairs. And yet, the moment she had seen this same terror in Maeve whose breath came spastically, who clutched the solid stone for dear life and tottered when she closed her eyes to the chasm of the narrow street below, Katharine, through an act of will, regained her equilibrium, unmercifully laughed at her cousin who, really sick with fright, began to cry. She had gone on with the guide, as far up as they could go, leaving the weeping girl crumpled in the sun. When they came back, she had not moved but her rigidity was gone and she quivered and her teeth chattered as if she had a chill. The swindling little Frenchman had been, if anything, more blatant in his taunts than Katharine; their conspiring giggles, on the slow trip down, had echoed in the malign twilight. The chaperone, waiting for them in the vestibule, having admitted freely to her own phobia for heights, had hectored Maeve with smelling salts though by this time she had fully recovered and wished only that her cowardice (for that was what Katharine and the batrachian cicerone had called it) be forgotten.

No one, she told herself rationally, could possibly read all of that into the casual photograph of schoolgirls on an educational tour. But, all the same, she felt invaded, for her desk was known as sacrosanct and no servant ever touched it, even to the extent of civilly putting on it something, like this box, that she had misplaced. And if a servant had committed this pardonable transgression, she would also have put the roses where they belonged and the table in the hall window, as she could see through her open door, was bare. So it must have been Andrew, alone in the house, idle and restless in the rain. What had he made of the inscription? And what else had he done? She turned to last night's entry in her diary and read:

> The boy's somnambulism has passed but his nightmares continue. He screamed in his sleep just before dawn this morning and when I went in to rescue him from his ogre, I found him already resting easily again and looking, in the half-light, so like John that I was too much drawn to him to touch him although the covering had fallen off and the wind was cool. I mean that I had no idea what form my gesture would take, for *he* has become the vor-

tex of these chimeral fancies that seek to undermine me and while I struggle to resurrect the past by any rapacious reading of his face, I wish at the same time to efface the face that in my own nightmares is omnipresently before me.

2

Himself again in linen trousers and a striped blue shirt, Andrew sat on the hassock at the foot of the chaise longue, the picture of contrition, his feet in sneakers pointing, pigeon-toed, at the tail of a golden dragon in the rug, his hands clasping and unclasping as he admitted that he had done everything he was accused of for no good reason except that he had had nothing else to do since he could not find any mucilage to go on putting together the façade of the State House, and had therefore occupied himself with whatever had come to hand. For no good reason, he had put the photograph of his parents and his cousin face downward and he denied his sisters' charge that this had been an act of disrespect to his elders; but he was sorry. And he had written on a piece of paper that Honor was a moron but if Cousin Katharine could see what she had written on it in the first place (he had promised, for a quarter, not to tell) she would agree with him; for this, too, he was sorry. Sighing, he went on with his list of misdemeanours: he *had* dressed up in Uncle George's boating clothes and was sorry for it, and had frightened her and was sorry and was sorry, above all, for having said what he did for it was not true, he did not hate them all. And he was sorry . . . but he stopped and lowered his head. In the quiet the clock's ticks crashed.

"Maddox says it will take more than him and Adam to set off the fireworks," Andrew said suddenly, invalidating his remorse with his exuberance and the smile that smoothed out the scowl on his forehead. "So can I help?"

"We'll talk about that later, but now I want to know what else you did this afternoon. *Did* you read your sisters' diaries?"

"They were locked," he said and lowered his head again.

"Then what else did you do? It couldn't have taken you all afternoon to turn over the picture and to write on Honor's slip of paper. I'm not really prying. I only want to know how you spent the afternoon." She tried to trap him with a friendly smile.

"Oh, you know! I walked around and looked at things. I hunted for that top. I thought."

He would admit no more; he could not or he would not say why it was that today, of all days, he had been urged to dress up in anachronistic clothes to match herself and he seemed wholly innocent when, shooting off at a tangent, he asked, "Honestly and truly, did you think I was Daddy? Just for a minute maybe?" and his disappointment seemed genuine when she told him that after her first surprise she had only played his game;

she had had to appear angry with him, she quickly explained, in order not to seem to be playing favorites in Honor's eyes: it had not been kind of him to write down what he had although, the Lord knew, she said, that one could stoop to almost anything on a confining afternoon like this. She paused, waiting for his confession that he had stooped to something base, but he said nothing and tired at last of the interrogation which proceeded nowhere, she dismissed him, telling him that for having said he hated everyone, he must not speak until after dinner. His jaw set stubbornly as he turned to go; facing the door, he said, "I don't hate you, but there are some people that I do."

"You mustn't be vehement. You don't *hate* anyone."

"Oh, but I do! There are certain people that I hate so much I wish they'd die. But I *don't hate you.*" He wheeled around again and said, "When is the tombstone coming?"

"Why? Why do you want to know?" she cried.

"I'll tell you why! Because I know that the day it comes something is going to happen." He stood with his fists clenched over his head, the tip of his tongue showing slyly at the corner of his mouth, his eyes rolled upward. In her alarm at this dreadful transformation, she looked away and heard him run from the room and scramble down the stairs, heard the front door open and bang loudly to and heard the maniacal child scream at the top of his voice, "I'll talk to myself if I want to! I can talk to the trees and the snakes and the road and the houses!" She saw him running down toward the lake, calling out his own name, "Andrew! Andrew Shipley!" and she turned weakly to her desk.

She remembered having read once, in a scornful, misanthropic book that the degeneration of a society was often marked by "graphomania" when verbiage streamed from the pens of the decadent and doomed. And from that she went on to think of a friend who had gone into a nervous collapse after the birth of her child and who had written letters unceasingly to everyone she knew, covering page after page with unrelated matter, quotations from poetry, diatribes against the nurses in her sanitarium, minutely described accounts of meals and quarrels; sometimes, in the middle of a paragraph she worked out a problem in algebra. The tragedy of the letters had been that here and there in the tenebrous purgatory of them, there had been light glades of sanity and Katharine thought now of the woman's picture of the institution's dining room, "It has a hush like Sunday and there is nothing to look at except our food and a fire extinguisher that hangs beside the door. I am too near-sighted to read the words on it from where I sit and so, instead, I count the little humps in the plaster that run like a frieze around the window near my chair, but I never remember from meal to meal how many there are. My life is so reduced now to the bare necessities that I do not know what will become of me if I ever do remember how many humps there are. Still, I suppose that if this happened, I might induce them to let me change my place so that I could read the words on the fire extinguisher." The irony had then caved in and the rest of the long letter was a wandering babble.

In six weeks, Katharine's loose-leaf diary had doubled in size. She had written more in this time than she had written in the sixteen years before, since this had been her only possible confessional and she had hoped, through the articulation of her fears, to quiet them and right herself. Heretofore, it had been her custom to make one daily entry after lunch, usually as impersonal as notations in a ship's log, but now, like the corrupt graphomaniacs, she wrote in it at all hours of the day and in the dead of night when she could not sleep, drawing her shutters and her curtains so that her light would not be seen by her cordial, inquisitive neighbors. Harassed by the whippoorwills, she would at last get up, shutting out the birds' lament with a pair of ivory earstopples. She seldom read over what she had written but she knew, without reviewing them, that these nocturnal outpourings, exaggerated as they were bound to be by the intensification of her loneliness in the dark and the silence, wholly revealed her. She should destroy the book, she thought, although, if the boy had read it, the damage was already done. (But he had said *I do not hate you* and he could not have said *those* words if he had read *these* words, "Is it not a sin crying to heaven for vengeance to be sometimes in love with a child and at other times, terrified of exposure, to wish him off the face of the earth?")

At times, the countless elements of her double life (it was more than double; it was a labyrinth of paths that turned back on themselves, crossing and recrossing) were as clear to her as a table of contents, and at those times the issues assumed their due proportion: she had burned no bridges and had not allowed John to burn his; she had returned from the only aberration of her life. But there were other times—and these were either in the night or when she was surprised by some fresh problem or snatched by some old misery—when she was consumed by the smallest of vexations.

One night, not long ago, she had not been able to turn her thoughts away from an absurd argument she had had with Brantley Wainright-Lowe on the subject of Cézanne. He, who "dabbled" in water colors and made dithyrambic studies of her swans and peacocks, had patronizingly patted her hand (his tactile need enraged her; he was forever touching her shoulder or her wrist as if without this physical accompaniment he could not speak), and had said of Cézanne, "There is a kind of simplicity about him that is rather charming, I admit, but he is really no great shakes. Of course I can understand how people who are in no way artistic would look on things differently from myself." Later, waking from her first light sleep, she had been beset by a hurricane of anger, no less turbulent than if the cause had been John or Maeve. Again, she had paced and fretted one whole night through over Maureen who, stupidly, was pregnant and who, trusting and devoted and naive, had put upon her mistress's shoulders the responsibility of solving her dilemma.

Her sleep could be extorted from her by word from her caretaker in Boston that a leak in the dining room had mildewed the wallpaper; or by the image of Edmund St. Denis at a picnic as he lay, rowdily spread-eagled on the sand in an unbecoming bathing suit, trying to catch her eye with a pleading, hangdog expression or to catch her ear with a cajoling whisper. Or she could spend the night calling off the roll of the men who had been in love with her as, in gentle lamplight, she gazed at herself in the mirror, drowning in her beauty; stripped of every amenity, enthroned upon her invincible self-love, she would fall forward on her arms without any warning, her realm sacked, her sovereignty dissolved and weep and weep and weep and with her wet lips pressed to the back of her hand, murmur, "They did not. Only the Humanist loved me."

She knew that it was only a question of time before the signature of her distress would be written on her face. The sleeplessness would show, staining the eyesockets, loosening the flesh from the cheekbones, and the headaches would assert themselves in lines, and the dragging weakness in her arms as if all the strata of her flesh were starving except the live, thrashing nerves. Tired to death, she could not stop the continuum of wounded-and-wounding, or of sinned-and-sinned-against (it could go on forever; if Maeve's parents had lived and Maeve had not, therefore, started it all by winning Katharine's father for those few but most important years, making it necessary from that time on for Katharine to compete with her; if Katharine's father's father had told him how to treat a daughter in that crucial situation and *his* father before him had been such-and-such—at last one came to Adam and the blame was spread out evenly upon the human race) and she could not remember when life had been anything but this, when it had been possible to enjoy, to look forward to, to want to own something or to meet someone. Now she could only take on blind faith the promise her reason made her, that there *had* to be an end to this sickness that alternated between coma and paroxysm, and that when that time came, her whole life might swing into a different course. She was not sure, she made no plans, but it occurred to her that perhaps she would no longer immolate herself to the distant August night. She, who had been constant, might change, but into what and through what means she could not yet imagine.

Her forefinger outlined the body of the gilded fish embossed on the red cover of her diary and a ceremonious plan came to mind; after the ball was over, she would assist herself in her release by burning this testimony of her years and years of frugal living upon wreckage. "After the ball was over." The tune of the song began to play and, afraid that it, like other minutiae, would go on and on like a stuck phonograph, she forcibly expelled it and turned level-headedly to making a further plan whereby to conceal her malady from everyone, for, above all, despite her outward eccentricities, she was conventional, and she did not want to have her melancholy anatomized by women at lunch and men in their clubs.

The children would stay, as always, until September and she, as always, would linger on as a denizen of

Hawthorne until election day. And only then would she close Congreve House. (How hard it was to leave the country in the autumn! When the leaves had turned, flaring in the steady sun, releasing their metallic leaves to the winds that riffled over the aging grass and the dying gardens. Dogs came to play in the dunes of fallen leaves and the geese came over across the faultless sky; in the river fog at dusk the deer drank at the lake, watched by the red foxes from their lairs in the meadow. The town began to close in on itself, snuggling its houses with banking boards and storm windows. The big summer houses were bleak and out of place and the summer gentry, no longer having the upper hand, began to leave in something like embarrassment. One thing was not gone from her, she thought as she thought of the autumn, and that was her abiding love of her dominion and all the natural enchantments that surrounded it.) So, she would close Congreve House and would go back to Boston and after she had seen John once, she thought she would go away, perhaps to make a retreat at some Roman Catholic convent of a silent order, not to pray, but simply, for a time, to drop appearances.

In time, all would be well. And if the boy already knew, there was no helping it. To every child there must come some wretched, sordid foreknowledge of what it's all about and if he hated her as a result of it (his statement that he did not could have been devious and deep) and hated his father (he was bound, finally, to hate him anyhow, for John was indifferent to his children and had only a vestigial memory of what it had been like to be a boy) and if his whole life was tinged by his secret knowledge—secret, for he could never admit to his sisters or his parents that he had read a private diary, this being, thank God, in their mores, an inadmissible and heinous crime—she would not take all the blame.

"Andrew! Andrew Shipley!" Now he was running back to the house and now down the length of the lawn. At the hammock, some sound or sight arrested him. The marine light of late afternoon after a rain, and the angle from which she regarded him, enlarged him and looking as tall as a man, as she watched, he clasped his hands over the back of his long neck.

"Mercy, mercy," she softly said, stepping back from the window, and from the foot of the lawn he mocked her, calling, "Honor! Honor! Your enemy is here."

CHAPTER VII

The Leaves of the Fig Tree

ADAM AND MADDOX AND ANDREW stood in the barn looking down at Katharine Congreve's tombstone that had come early that morning from Thomas by truck. It had taken five men, huffing and puffing and swearing, to get it into the barn. One of them had called the stone a bitch and another had called it a bastard and when they rested they marveled, using the same kind of language, at anyone who would anticipate death to such an extent in so calm a way. One of them had tapped his forehead and said, "Low tide, if you ask my opinion."

The stonecutter, Mr. Norman, an unprepossessing little old man in rimless spectacles and a square mustache, had sat on the terrace with Cousin Katharine watching the proceedings and drinking coffee with her as he accepted her compliments, bashfully denying them.

He wore gray suède gloves, only one of which he removed, that exactly matched his new fedora; with his sober black suit and his old-fashioned high stiff collar and his broad black tie, he looked like a pallbearer or an undertaker and he did nothing to dispel the illusion by his conversation. At one point he said, "If you know of anyone else who contemplates this move, would you be so kind as to put in a word on my behalf? Tombstones are my forte." Honor had burst into laughter and apologized immediately but said that the phrase "contemplate this move" had been the funniest thing she had ever heard and Mr. Norman, profoundly gratified, beamed at her, shuffled his spatted feet and allowed, "My wife tells me that I turn a neat phrase every once in a while."

It was hard to associate his masterpiece with Mr. Norman and his finicking ways (his little finger had stood out at a right angle when he picked up his coffee cup and he had pursed his lips into a rosebud before each speech) and the coachman and the gardener agreed that you could never judge a man's abilities by his appearance. For the stone was as impressive as the statue of Minerva and the figure of Cousin Katharine, in marble effigy, was as heroic and as handsome. It was a likeness awesomely accurate, though Mr. Norman had made only one sketch of her on the day she came to place her order. It showed, in the piebald stone, her protuberant pompadour arising from her wide forehead and her noble nose and chin and her broad, loving lips, but it showed, even more wonderfully, her pure and vestal air; the actual person seemed to lie beneath the folds of her full sleeves and her long skirt. Between her peaceful hands she held a full-blown rose and over her head there was an intricately carved circle; seven hooked spikes curved inward from the rim pointing toward the name engraved there and the date of her birth and the empty space below that would be filled in when she died.

"Katharine Congreve, born August 30, 1898," read Adam. "Is that supposed to be a halo? Is that what you make it out to be?"

But Maddox was examining the rose; his stained, heavy fingers palpitated over the petals and he smiled, glorying in the cleverness of the stonecutter. "That's an awful wonderful thing," he said.

"Could be a rowel," said Adam, still looking at the design at the top, "except the teeth go in, not out. Is it some kind of a family dohicus, Mr. Andrew, some kind of a coat of arms?"

"It's a Catherine wheel," said Miss Congreve from the doorway. She had brought out the maids to view the stone and they stood timidly in the sunlight, hanging back, not wanting to look at all but forcing themselves to express an admiration they did not feel.

"A Catherine wheel!" exclaimed Andrew. She *did* take the cake, as Adam had said earlier. A Fourth of July thing carved on her gravestone! Why not a Christmas wreath with bells on it or an Easter basket full of painted eggs? But then he learned, somewhat to his disappointment, from Mrs. Shea who was a fount of knowledge on matters ecclesiastical, that this was the symbol of the martyr Catherine. "They tied her to a thing like that and set it spinning, but it broke before it killed her and then they chopped off her head." The little maids were even more distressed and Maureen seemed about to cry and furtively she crossed herself while the cook went on to expatiate on St. Catherine's intrepid character. The men were puzzled but they said nothing; it was all over their heads as it was over Andrew's.

By now there was a huddle of spectators in the doorway, for Miss Duff, who had seen the truck drive up, had spread the word around and all of Cousin Katharine's friends had dropped what they were doing and had come straight to Congreve House in order to be among the first to see what Brantley Wainright-Lowe called "Katy's hick-jacket." Unlike the servants, all of them at the sight of the *memento mori* were infected with an inexplicable delight and while they praised the workmanship ("an estimable performance!" said Mr. Barker and clapped his hands) and the way Mr. Norman had uncannily caught Katharine's singular look ("Damfino," said Miss Duff and slapped her jodhpurs with her riding whip, "the very spit of you"), they all agreed with old Miss Heminway that "our Katharine" was a humourist. Miss Duff and Mrs. Tyler were as gay as the others but Andrew saw them exchange a wink.

"What's that thing there?" said Mrs. Wainright-Lowe, pointing to the Catherine wheel with the handle of her butterfly net, and after Cousin Katharine had explained, in the absence of the expert, Mrs. Shea, who had returned to the house and her baking, the grass widow, whose cross she was fond of telling friends was heavier than most, chided, "Oh, now, Katharine, that's too far-fetched for words. Whoever in the world scourged you?"

"Whips tipped with metal," said Miss Duff to herself. "Interesting." The whole of Miss Duff's mind was seldom in attendance when there was a gathering of more than three.

"Far-fetched or not," said Mr. Barker defensively, "I call it a crackerjack idea. Her name's Katharine, isn't it?"

Mrs. Wainright-Lowe wagged her finger at him, made sure that the maids had gone and said, "You're going into your dotage, Rodney, if you imagine that Alma and George Congreve would ever have named her for a Popish person."

There was some discussion then over whether or not Catherine of Alexandria was included in the hierarchy of the Anglo-Catholic saints and Mrs. Wainright-Lowe, the only Presbyterian that Mrs. Tyler admitted knowing socially, was ignored. Seeking then to make amends for her blunder, she sadly said, "It's true, it's true, everyone does have a cross to bear."

Cousin Katharine smiled and said, "I'm only giving myself airs, Aunt Lowe. I fixed on this only because I thought the design was handsome. I do not really claim to have a cross." And herding them all out she asked her friends if they did not think that this was an occasion for brown sherry, the drink she said she always associated with funerals. "The most delicious sherry I ever drank was after we buried Uncle Tim who was so extraordinarily glad to die. You know he was sensitive to noise to a degree and from the time he was fifty, prayed that in his old age he would go deaf. But he never did and, in fact, his hearing seemed to get sharper. The very last words he said were 'If there is whistling in the great beyond, I'll kill myself.' "

They laughed, accepted the invitation to drink brown sherry in the library and started toward the house. "Good old Tim," said Miss Duff. "Haven't thought of him in years. We'll drink to silence in the great beyond."

Andrew lingered for a few minutes in the cool of the stable. The arrival of the gravestone had been a disappointment, for ever since he had told Cousin Katharine that it would be a sign, he had believed it. He had expected, for no reason now that he could think of, that the men who brought it would be dressed like executioners in black robes and peaked hoods and possibly even half-masks. And they had come, in harmless daylight, nothing more than ordinary workmen in dirty pants and blue shirts. He had been convinced that on this day they would learn of the end of Charles Smithwick and then all the waiting would be over, the nightmare would be done and whatever it was that had been boiling in him all summer long would quiet down. He wanted to give up his obsession, but the obsession had resolutely stayed of its own accord.

With his announcement to Cousin Katharine, it had reached a fever pitch, hotter and hotter until there was in his very heartbeat a voice that constantly said, "Charles Smithwick, die." And the worst of it was that he did not care any longer whether Charles Smithwick lived or died or became the President; he wanted only to be free, to be able to read Mark Twain and play poker with Honor and Harriet and have a little fun, for pete's sake, but the voice would not let him be. It was an undertone when he was with other people, but when he was alone, it was a roar and he had come to think that if Charles didn't die, this would go on for the rest of his life. He would never be able to study at school, he would flunk and be sent back or be subjected again to Bowman who would tutor him in that mausoleum house where his parents . . . Oh, his parents! They would be home so soon, the summer was so nearly over! At the thought of them, he turned and slapped Derek's flank; the horse disdainfully lifted his lip to show a row of grass-green teeth.

He had definitely appointed this day as the day on which Charles would die not because there was any connection between his death and Cousin Katharine's tombstone but because the fact was that he, Andrew Shipley, could stand the voice no longer. And this morning, just as the truck was coming up the drive and just as Andrew was getting out of bed, what had he seen through his window but the lanky towheaded sailor himself sauntering down the road, looking as if he had never had an ache or a pain in his life? At breakfast, which he could not eat, Cousin Katharine had come into the dining room to tell them that Charles was coming to help Maddox and Adam set off the fireworks on the next night.

It was really amazing that no one could hear the voice that made as much din in his blood and his brain as Victor's yodeling ever did; he sympathized with Uncle Tim. It was extremely loud and shrill just now and in order to modulate it, he crossed the lawn to watch the men who were putting up the stand for the orchestra beside the dancing platform. Below this, there had been pitched a red and white striped marquee for the buffet supper and some of the workmen were sitting under it, eating their lunch out of black boxes, their heads bent down in an attitude of diligence as if their very lives depended on the wedges of apple pie and the cold pork chops. When Andrew's shadow fell across their picnic ground, one of them, Congreve Smithwick, looked up. He stopped in the act of cracking a hard-boiled egg on his knee and stood up, brushing off his fingers on the seat of his pants, and came across to shake Andrew's hand in both of his. He wore Victor's knife at his belt.

"I have been meaning to write you a thank-you-kindly-ma'am letter for that knife," he said, "and partly I took this odd-time job so I could tell you in person. I said at the time it was like manna from heaven because I sorely needed that knife."

"Connie treats that knife of his like it was a baby," said another of the men through a mouthful of pie.

"It's all right," murmured Andrew. Connie unsheathed the knife and flicked his forefinger lightly over the blade and from a pocket, he brought out a small whetstone; he said that when he had nothing else to do, he spent his time sharpening it until now it was keen enough to shave with.

"There'll be no knife left when Connie gets through with it," said the man who had spoken before.

"Do you mind my asking one thing?" said Connie. Even here, miles inland, he smelled as strongly of fish as the smoke-house. "What does V.S. stand for?"

"Very Simple," said one of the men.

"Virtue and Sin," said another.

"Go on!" cried Smithwick. "My wife maintains you bought it for somebody else and those were their initials. But I maintain that you knew I needed a knife and you bought it for me."

He was in dead earnest, this credulous yokel, and Andrew thought what a simpleton he himself had been to imagine that he could ever in a million years get the knife back to give to Victor. Not that Victor deserved it or anything else except, perhaps, a swift kick.

"V.S. stands for," he began and paused, trying to hit upon a hoodwink to while away the time till lunch. He thought of the Latin words *veritas* and *semper* which together sounded like a motto, but he did not want to sound snobby and so, instead, he invented a name and told Congreve Smithwick that the man who had made the knife was called Vernon Saltonstall.

As long as he was talking, the voice was no louder than a whisper, rather like a purr, and so, sitting down among the men, he began to tell a long lie about the mythical cutler and how he had come to buy the knife, through mental telepathy, for Congreve Smithwick.

Realizing that no one believed him except Connie who listened, rapt, forgetting his lunch, he gave the other men a knowing, sidelong look from time to time and imperceptibly they winked. It was a snug, club-like atmosphere there beneath the festive canvas and Andrew felt proudly popular with his audience whose connivance and buried mirth spurred him on to higher and higher flights. He said that one afternoon after school as he was going through the Common, a man had given him a leaflet about Christian Science ("C.S., you see," he said and Congreve Smithwick gaped and his companions hid their smiles with apples) and just as he sat down to read it he thought he heard a voice that spoke to him, "Do you happen to know where I can get a knife? I am a stranger here." He had turned on the bench but there was no one nearby except a fat squirrel eating peanuts on the path; this was in about January. Did that mean anything to Connie?

It certainly did! The loony flushed and fidgeted and stammered that it had been January that he had lost his old knife which, anyhow, had never been much good. The fabrication rolled on and Congreve Smithwick believed every word. The more the men showed, by nods and bogus coughs, that Andrew was a success, the softer grew the voice inside him until finally, when he hesitated once in search of some fresh improbability, he realized that it was altogether gone. He was extremely happy being the center of attention, and all the time he was spinning out his yarn, he was thinking that Victor, after all, was not the only pebble on the beach and that he was going to ask permission to join this band of workmen as an apprentice or, if they did not need one, as a jester to amuse them during lunch. He imagined himself traveling with them throughout the county, becoming famous as an entertainer, Andrew Shipley, the One-Man Show.

But before he had finished his account of Vernon Saltonstall, Honor burst out the front door crying, "Andrew! Something awful's happened!"

The men rose as a body and followed him like a herd of animals, muttering, "House on fire?" "Somebody got hurt?" Connie Smithwick said, "Lucky I got my knife along in case it's needed."

But besides the workmen, there came with Andrew the voice, more insistent than it had ever been before and it was to it and not to his sister that he shouted, "I hear you! Stop yelling at me!" When he was at the columns he panted, "How did it happen?"

"How did it happen?" she said. "How did *what* happen? Did you do it? Andrew Shipley, if you did it, I will never speak to you again in all my life and neither will Harriet or anyone else."

Harriet, the cool one, was in the hall. "Don't be ridiculous," she said. "Beth did it herself."

"Oh. The cat." He turned to face the men; he felt rather as if he were dismissing troops. "It's just about a cat," he told them and as they started back, disappointed, having hoped for an excitement, one of them said, "I'd mighty like to hear the rest of that story about Mr. Saltonstall."

"Mr. Saltonstall!" whispered Harriet harshly. "You weren't telling them about the Saltonstalls' divorce!"

"Ask me no questions and I'll tell you no lies." He had not known, until now, that the Saltonstalls were getting or had got a divorce. "What's the big idea of yelling all over the place about a cat?"

Honor was crying and it was Harriet who had to tell him what had happened. It was awful, though awful in a way so different from what he had expected, dreaded and longed for that he was not nearly as horrified as he might have been at another time. Cousin Katharine had gone upstairs to get the key to the wine closet in the library and the ancients had waited and waited and finally Mrs. Wainright-Lowe had come into the drawing room where the twins were sewing and asked them to go see if something was wrong. Honor had been the one to go and she had found Cousin Katharine in a faint again, lying on the floor of her bedroom and when Honor saw what had made her faint, she had almost fainted herself. Or died. For right in the middle of Cousin Katharine's bed, right on the lace counterpane, lay one of Beth's kittens with its head chewed off.

Cousin Katharine had been brought around with aromatic spirits of ammonia administered by Mrs. Shea but had refused to have the doctor and in spite of their protests would not hear of her friends' leaving without the sherry she had promised them. They were all in the library now and as the children entered, Miss Duff as coroner, in a visored cap, was conducting the inquest and helping herself liberally to the wine in the decanter. She looked a little tipsy or else a little thrilled. Certainly she was flinging herself wholeheartedly into what she called, from time to time, "a phenomenon of the first water." No, said Cousin Katharine, Beth had not had an abnormal labor and Mrs. Shea, who had been with her, would bear her out. The decapitated kitten, to be sure, had been the runt of the litter but he had been well-formed and as healthy as the others; Cousin Katharine had promised him to Beulah Smithwick who for some time had wanted a black cat.

"Fitting," said Mr. Barker. "I have always said that woman was a witch."

Enthralled, they probed the possible solutions to the mystery. Why had a cat, by nature secretive, left the body of her murdered kitten in a place so public? And were the others now in danger of their lives? Had Beth gone berserk like a human being, like those mothers and fathers one was always reading about who suddenly could not put up with the crying of their infants another minute and strangled them or fractured their skulls with the first object that came to hand? Brantley Wainright-Lowe suggested that the cat's mind "had lightly turned to thoughts of death" on this particular day because the tombstone had arrived and his mother, on wondering why the creature had chosen that particular method, was told severely by Miss Duff to use her "bean," for how else could she have done it? They discussed whether or not Beth should be punished and Mr. Barker who knew a smattering of law said, parenthetically, that in ancient Greece, rocks that had fallen on people's heads and killed them had been tried and sentenced and executed although he was not just sure how.

"Pulverized," asserted the omniscient Duff who had probably never heard of the practice until now. Obviously, she said, it was impossible to punish a cat (except by putting it into a weighted gunny sack and dropping it into the lake from a boat) and this was the reason why she, personally, would never own one. "Beat a dog once or twice and he knows who's in charge but a cat, to my way of thinking, is devoid of any moral sense whatsoever."

Beth, the tribunal decided, would have to go scot-free. They clucked their tongues over the damage done to the counterpane ("which must have cost a fortune," said Mrs. Tyler who, it was rumored, had recently suffered serious losses on the stock market which she could ill afford) but said it was surprising how little blood there had been, leading them to believe that the deed had been done elsewhere and that the placing of the body on the bed had been an afterthought. They remarked, offended, the complacency of the animal when they had all gone up, the very picture of motherly love and pride, lying there in the pretty basket with her remaining kittens suckling her, purring and holding up her pansy face to have her cheeks stroked as if she had just done something bright. They talked of other cases in the lower orders in which the maternal instinct went amiss, of ewes that abandoned their ailing lambs and neurasthenic turkeys that would not take care of their eggs; but no one had ever heard of anything so gross as this, even in the order *homo sapiens,* and they did not wonder that Katharine had fainted dead away.

But it was evident that Mrs. Tyler and Miss Duff thought there was more to her fainting than met the eye, for Andrew saw how they looked alternately at her and at each other, ever so slightly inclining their heads or elevating one shoulder and Mrs. Tyler began presently to make an attempt to get the others to leave. Hadn't Mrs. Wainright-Lowe planned to catch butterflies before lunch? Didn't Mr. Barker always work up his appetite with a brisk walk? Was she wrong in her belief that Celia Heminway was under strict doctor's orders to rest, rest and rest some more and especially before meals? How well trained the Shipley children were to listen so patiently to grown-up conversation when they must be wild to be outdoors! Just a few minutes before, she had seen Andrew down with the men . . . boys did have such a jolly time around men who were working with hammers and saws.

But no one made any move at all to go and, inspired with the unusual events of the morning, they allowed their sherry glasses to be refilled and didn't mind saying that they were rather shaken, juvenile as it might be when the victim involved had only been a cat and so young a cat that it had not even developed any personality. Foiled, the diagnosticians were obliged to content themselves with a close surveillance of Cousin Katharine.

She had not touched the little green-stemmed glass of wine on the table beside her; earlier, Andrew had seen her start to pick it up but her hand was so unsteady that she could not have carried it to her lips and she put it back again. She entered into the conversation only to the extent that her role as hostess required her and did not add to the fund of parallel cases nor offer any theories. She sat in the midst of her friends, gamboling in their second childhood, as pale and unblemished as the filmy pink dimity she wore and she seemed, by her straight back and her tightly clasped hands and by the way she held her head at a slightly backward angle, to be listening for something. She was not listening to the voices of her friends but to some sound beyond the room or even beyond the house and Andrew, leaning against the door, tried to hear it too.

He could hear the drone of the lawn mowers and the erratic pounding of the hammers; he heard a motorboat's rapid snore diminishing. Nearer, he could hear someone moving about upstairs and he heard the sound of Honor's ballet slipper as she traced a parabola with her left toe on the newly waxed floor. And then his interior voice, which had been silent for some time, began clamoring. Was that what she was listening to? Could she hear it all the way across the room? His heart banged brassily and he edged backward out of the door. Just as he was about to turn, Cousin Katharine seemed to rouse herself, shaking her head a little as if she had dropped off to sleep and as he watched, the color came back to her face and she smiled and her quiet hand picked up her wineglass and said, "This is no time to be *triste* on the eve of my party!" They toasted the party and Harriet said, "Oh, yes, for heaven's sake, let's think about the party and not about that cat."

"I should have expected something of the kind," said Cousin Katharine. "It was days and days ago that Andrew told me on the day my stone arrived something awful was going to happen."

"He didn't!" cried Honor and reached out to seize him by the arm, but he flung away from her and stood just for a moment in the doorway before he ran. "You *did* do it!" she whispered but Harriet again defended him. "You are *insane*. Do you think anybody in the world would *chew* the head off a kitten? It was *gnawed*, Honor. It must have taken her hours."

"Lucky guess," said Wainright-Lowe, leering at Andrew. "If it hadn't been pussy I suppose there would have been some other little old carnage." He laughed indulgently. "Boys will be boys. I was a boy myself once, believe it or not."

They all gave Andrew a kindly, condescending look of appraisal and Mrs. Tyler, as if he were five years old, said, "He didn't want his cousin to get a tombstone, did he? Nobody wants to think that anyone close and dear is going to pass away, does he? Between you and me and the gatepost, Andy," she cupped her hand around her mouth and whispered loudly and he hated her for using a nickname that only strangers ever used and sometimes his father when he was in a falsely jocose humour, "this lady is going to live to be a hundred."

"Andrew doesn't care," said Honor but softly so that the others did not hear. "Andrew has no heart. You willed that little helpless baby cat to die."

"Honor, be quiet," said Harriet sharply. "You'll make him have a mood. Besides, he didn't do it."

Now Cousin Katharine, released from her strain, was really laughing and she said, "Will it make you all feel better if I cover it up and put a billiard table on top of it? Does that seem too bizarre or wouldn't it be rather a lark to let people play on it tomorrow night? The ones who are coming from a distance won't know what's underneath the baize."

"Kate, you're the limit!" cried Mr. Barker and laughed so hard that he had to wipe his eyes with the neatly folded ornamental handkerchief in his coat pocket. "And then you would unveil it afterward, I suppose?"

"Most gruesome thing I ever heard of," said Miss Duff, "but knowing you, I'm not going to be surprised if you do it."

"Listen!" said Cousin Katharine suddenly. Her smile was gone again and again she sat up straight. "Listen! Is that the wind? That sound?"

He ran then through the corridor and out of the house and down to the dancing platform and stood in the middle of it with all the men around him.

"Do us a jig," said one of them.

"I want to get something straight in my head about this Vernon Saltonstall," said another. "Did he know about Connie needing the knife too or did you pass that along to him?"

He had to shout over the voice to make them hear. Dizzied, he could only dimly see their faces, swimming in the hot sunlight. He shrieked that this was the last knife that Vernon Saltonstall had ever made because, with it, he had stabbed a man to death and he had given it to Andrew just before he went to the electric chair. The waving faces that had been split apart in grins began to seal themselves together and he heard someone say, "Take it easy, son." Finally, pausing for breath, his eyes focused on Congreve Smithwick whose stupid mouth was open wide and who was staring at the knife in his hands. Momentarily the men had all stopped working; an enormously tall one with a pock-marked face went over to Connie and put his arm around his shoulders, "Don't you worry about your knife, it ain't bad luck. The boy is only poetizing." The hammer began again and he knew that they had had enough of him.

"You ought to be a story writer," said the man who was consoling Connie. "Good luck, boy." With this he was dismissed and he drifted down the lawn toward the hammock. The voice, mercifully, seemed to be as tired as he was and though it was still there it was slow, like the pendulum of the grandfather clock.

As he lay down, he saw Victor and Charles meandering down the road, carrying pails and diggers. He covered his eyes with the pillow and put his fingers in his ears and he counted by fives to a hundred and fifty until he was sure they were out of sight. Out of sight and out of mind. He flopped over then and aloud he said, "You get out of my sight and out of my mind, you Smithwicks."

He began to think of the harvest of worthless mussel-pearls he had gathered once with Victor, and of a still moonlight midnight when they had stolen out of their houses and had met in the graveyard of St. James's to tell each other ghost stories; he thought of the solemn rite of the alewives and the raspberry tonic, of the parrot, and the pet vixen and Billy Bartholomew's battery radio, and the seals, and the eels, and when Maureen came down to tell him that lunch was ready, he was crying so hard that she had to call him twice before he heard her.

CHAPTER VIII

On the Final Night of Summer

"BEEN DOWN in the garden when Maddox, the Dragon, wasn't there," boomed Peg Duff from the lawn. "Your Ulrich Brunners are gorgeous."

Katharine stroked the coon-cat who was dozing in the last of the sun on the windowsill. "They're his especial pride," she said, "those and his Dr. Hueys." She had often wondered why he chose to call his roses by variations on her name when their own were so sonorous: Baroness Rothschild, Marie Pavic, Condesa de Sastago, General Jacqueminot. But it was a tribute, and she would not have liked it if he had changed.

"Any signs of remorse in the creature?" Peg pointed at the cat.

"None that I've seen. Her appetite is excellent."

"You have a forgiving nature, I must say," said

Peg. "If I were you, I wouldn't touch the little bitch with a ten-foot pole. You did say buffet, didn't you? I told Maxine I wouldn't fool with dinner."

"I did. How do you like the looks of things, Peg? Doesn't it all seem like old times?"

Miss Duff looked around the lawn at the dancing platform where crepe-paper lanterns hung and the candy-cane marquee and the moon, as big as an archery target, hanging between the elm trees with a man in it looking like Theodore Roosevelt disguised as the man in the moon, and the round raised dais for the orchestra like a bandstand in a village park.

Her voice softened with nostalgia as she looked up at Katharine again. "It does seem only yesterday. I can see George Congreve as clearly as if he were standing at my elbow. He would dance the first dance and the last if you recall and in between times he would be in that everlasting library of his with a crony, holding a gab-fest in Greek. What was it he called the writing room?"

"He called it his 'microcosmal Athenaeum.' Papa was a bit of a pedant."

"But a lamb," said Miss Duff and then, embarrassed by her sentimentality, she resumed her gruffness. "Got to get ready for your shindig. Forgot to tell Maxine to press my best bib and tucker." Touching her khaki cap, she strode off across the lawn.

There had been much life within this house, thought Katharine, when the guest rooms had been occupied by long-term visitors, agreeable scholars with whom her father had all *but* talked in Greek, and feminist friends of her mother whom the men had controlled by turning upon them a bland, deaf ear. She remembered a pugnacious Mrs. Rowe who had once inquired of an English Latinist his opinion of Mary Wollstonecraft and the man had answered, "Do you mean the lady who felt it was right to expose the limbs so long as they were clad in blue stockings?" Worlds apart, the visitors, nevertheless, had not encroached upon each other's provinces; the Amazons went out to war for principles and rights while the men stayed indoors in their ivory tower. The sense of ease and holiday had made them tolerant and there were even times when they met on the common ground of play. (Was tennis not the same game it had been then? Why did it seem, today, so much faster?)

She grappled for the lost time, for the interplay of learned wit, for music as music had sounded then. She hunted, in the hollow of the present time, for the sensations that had once enlivened her on such an evening as this before a party, for those sensations that now were flittering over the skin and fevering the blood stream of the twins who were ready to cry, ready to laugh hysterically, equally ready to fall in love and to spoil all their chances by gabbling nonsense. She had seen them a little while ago in Honor's room, fresh and pink and fragrant from their baths, wearing lacy slips, pinning up their hair; breathless and intent, they had been sitting side by side before the dressing table, making braids with which to crown and age themselves and they had not known that she was watching them. Honor's blue dress lay on the bed with its morning-glory skirt spread out and beside it was a pair of brand-new silver dancing slippers. The party, after all, thought Katharine, was not for her and the cremation of her regrets, but it was for these flower-like, simple, punctiliously feminine girls, devoutly putting all their eggs in one basket. Their pantomime was as graceful and as fundamental and as revealing as the dances of birds, and Katharine tiptoed away.

For the point of the ball, except for Honor and Harriet, was gone. While she intended still to burn her diary after the guests were gone and the lanterns had been extinguished, she did not expect to arise from the ashes of it; the act was far more expedient than symbolic (but because she died hard and gave up her habits of thought grudgingly, she could not relinquish the two small rituals of time and place; she would destroy it after the commemorative ball and in her father's study). And the act necessary rather than elective. It was an act and not a gesture for, uncertain of the course her life was now to take, she did not want to leave behind these lares to be rummaged through. If they had not been already rummaged through!

Her fear of Andrew was inescapable. What he knew, she could not guess, nor could she guess the terms by which he scrutinized his knowledge, but yesterday in the library when she had asked the others if they heard a sound and they had not, he had turned at once and run from the house; in the split second before he took to his heels, he had given her a look that she had construed as unspeakable hatred. He had looked at her through half-closed eyes and his lips parted in contempt.

It had been the fear of him that had made her faint earlier when she found the mangled kitten. Before she lost consciousness, she had attributed to Andrew the sophisticated blackmail of this desecration of her bed, and she remembered that as she began to fall, she had vainly tried to call him in the intention, as she now supposed, of finally ferreting out of him the reason for his preoccupation, unbroken since the day he had arrived. She had been alarmed when Maureen had found him crying in the hammock, so passionately and convulsively that the maid had had to take him by the hand and lead him, stumbling, blind with his tears.

And still, he had allowed himself, like a much younger and much more pliant child, to be consoled with promises. He was to help set off the fireworks and if the carpenters agreed, he was to watch them move a house from Thomas to Hawthorne; his requests had been so normal and so boyish that for a while she had been reassured. He had even nestled against her for a pitiful moment and the shudder of his final sobs, running the length of his body, had been copied in her own nerves and muscles. But she had not been convinced that the freshet of his tears had been released, as he said it had, by a bee sting, for he was a Spartan child (all Congreves, Shipleys, Maxwells were physically courageous if that was any virtue) who would never admit to fatigue or aches.

"It's the excitement of the party," said Maureen to her privately and, having no wish to analyze her cousin with anyone, she agreed. "It's the gravestone that makes him sad if you'll pardon me for saying so, Miss Congreve," said Mrs. Shea and Katharine nodded her head. Mary said he had had too little breakfast and too much sun and Harriet accused Honor of badgering him into this collapse. But the proud boy stuck to his story of the bee and even asked for baking soda which he took up to his room, saying, with an attempt at a smirk, that he would have to make the application himself because the "scurvy bee" had stung him in the belly button.

All afternoon he had mooned in the hammock, and all of this day he had been invisible except at breakfast and lunch. It was almost four o'clock when he had come up from the direction of the lake with a string of fish, the very last thing on earth anyone wanted today, and when Mrs. Shea, who was on the verge of tears with worry over the success of her meringues, ordered him to take his reptiles back where they came from, he had savagely flung them into the garbage pail beside the door, thrown his rod into the lettuce bed and thudded upstairs to his room from which presently there came to the ears of the edgy household the sound of his jew's-harp squeaking through the opening bars of "Jerusalem, the Golden." But then, a little later, he had knocked on her door and had asked to see Beth and had shown only a natural curiosity to know, as Peg Duff had wanted to know, if Beth was sorry for what she had done. Thoughtfully, using the terms of the newspapers as glibly as if this were his ordinary speech, he said, "I think it was a mercy killing. I think there was something wrong with the kitten that the cat would know and we wouldn't. It may have fallen down and sustained injuries, in which case she ought to be shown clemency."

Katharine dressed slowly, taking a long time before her mirror to brush her hair into a Psyche knot and plait it with a string of baroque pearls; with silver hairpins she arranged in it two rosebuds, doled out grudgingly by Maddox who hated parties because they meant that his gardens were stripped to fill the vases; he had once, in all seriousness, suggested that she keep artificial flowers in the house.

Her dress was a masterpiece. Beulah had outdone herself. The yards and yards of *mousseline de soie*, cloud-white and gossamer, cascaded over a ridge of crinoline at the waist and fell to the floor, showing through its mobile folds a full and pale blue rustling petticoat; the dead-white satin bodice was cut low at the shoulders, smooth and unornamented, for she had refused Beulah's suggestion of a frill of starched lace at the neck. No matter how gifted they were, these diamonds-in-the-rough, they could not leave well enough alone but wanted always to add extras to their work. It had required consummate diplomacy to keep Mr. Norman from carving a bed of roses for her to lie on, and one year she had disputed a full afternoon with a carpenter who had come to repair the capital of one of the columns and who had implored her to let him make a connecting molding across the front of the house, looping a wooden ribbon from pillar to pillar. Or let him, even better, take down these useless "fence posts" and build for her a porch on which, protected from the bugs and damp, she could far more comfortably watch the world go by than she could on her terrace. He had advocated, she shuddered to remember, screens. She had withstood Beulah Smithwick's further suggestion that she wear a high Spanish comb like a battlement upon her castled hair.

It was dusk. Maddox was lighting the candles in the lanterns with a taper longer than himself and the small orchestra were tuning their fiddles and a cello. They were five old German brothers with faded brown faces like withered apples who had arrived that afternoon from Boston, overwhelmed with happiness to leave the city's heat and to find a landscape that reminded them of the Tauber valley. The sweet and sour scraping of the violins and the swaying of the lanterns at the touch of the taper and the smell of the coffee that was being brewed in the dining room in the immense urn made her tremble with expectation and suddenly she wished she had invited an escort for herself; even Jack Codman, who was a simpleton, could have been metamorphosed through her party eyes.

She envied the twins who came in to ask her if they

"looked all right" perfectly knowing and preening themselves on the knowledge that nothing could have improved upon their looks. They pirouetted before her long glass and boldly sprayed themselves with her perfume and exclaimed rhapsodically as they leaned out the windows to look at the lanterns and at all the other finery of the lawn.

A regiment of servants recruited from the kitchens of her friends were stationing the punch bowls on the long tables under the marquee and covered platters of salmon mousse and lobster salad and partridge in aspic and *daube glacé*.

From Honor's windows, they had earlier seen wine coolers and bottles of burgundy and magnums of champagne being taken to the summerhouse. Could they have champagne? They knew they would be too excited to eat a bite, would Cousin Katharine be able to? Was she *sure* that this way of doing their hair was becoming? Their skirts were not too long? Were the seams of their stockings straight? Would she not grant that their shoes were absolutely the last word in chic? They were not interested in the answers to any of their questions, for the ecstasy of their anticipation was their sole concern. They did not even notice Katharine's dress and she was shocked to realize that their failure to do so wounded her; she was cast into a shadow by their conflagration, for they were so very young! And their hearts were so very simple and their minds were so clear and shallow, their ambitions so modest and direct that she was certain they would never come to grief.

Theirs, in the end, was the supreme talent: they had the talent for happiness and it radiated from them even in their perpetration of these addled, adolescent idiocies; it was their one depth and it amazed her for they had had neither the help of heredity or environment to bring about its cultivation.

The first car to come up the drive was James Partridge's yellow roadster and, beside themselves, the girls froze at their post and in the end had to be urged and all but pushed downstairs to receive the boys. Katharine heard them, refusing to acknowledge the ague of their lovesickness, talking matter-of-factly about the headmistress of their school as if she were a subject of pressing interest.

Now Edmund's car came in between the maple trees and when she saw him get out, his plumpness seeming everywhere to push at his clothes, a momentary disenchantment chilled her; the evening lost its dimension of romance and the violins grated and the lanterns appeared sleazy and absurd. Edmund's temerity had been put to flight at once as soon as she had fainted and he kept a nervous distance from her now even while he continued, out of habit, to cast lovelorn glances at her and endeavoured at large gatherings to be alone with her to pay her some proprietary compliment. She had awakened that day in the drawing room to hear him say, "I'm staggered. I thought Katharine was made of iron." The violence of her reaction to his profession—for he would have no way of knowing that a far greater weight had crushed her down—had flattered him a little but far more had dismayed him and he had sent her an apologetic note, typewritten and noncommittal and signed only with the letter "E" in which he implied that he had thought she knew all along that he had only been joking. His need for her, now that he saw she was in need, was gone.

The house was lighted tonight only with candles and, by accident, with the green flashing of fireflies, and as she went down the stairs, hearing her sibilant petticoat, she thought it had never been more magnificent. Always immaculate, it had been washed and polished and burnished from the cellars to the attics for this occasion so that glass glittered and metal burned and wood gleamed like hide. Perfect and plenteous, Congreve House was the locus but was also the extension of herself; not the events that had taken place in it which she had clung to out of her stubborn self-destruction, but the very paneled walls themselves and the wide random boards of the floors and the marble mantels and, above all, the ironic spirit of the house, mature (as she must learn to be) and indestructible (as she was despite all her efforts to destroy herself).

It was her father who had imbued the house with its spirit of acceptance; she looked back up the stairs at his portrait and was ashamed, meeting the face in which judgement and resignation were balanced equally. As if he were there and had held her up to friendly ridicule, had said all this emotion was infantile and unattractive, she felt her broken structure begin to mend, begin to move articulately, and whole, mistress of Congreve House, she emerged from the embrace of it into the summer evening.

2

For the first time, Andrew had a close look at Charles Smithwick. He had come into the stable where Adam was teaching Andrew to play pool on Cousin Katharine's tombstone (she really had done it and Adam had told him what Billy Bartholomew had said when he had heard of it. He had said, "She has bats in her belfry as big as my old white horse") and began at once to correct Adam, saying, "Your form's all haywire. Here, lemme show you how." He wore a pin-striped business suit, much too small, so that his knobby wrists hung long below the sleeves and the tops of his white socks were visible below his trouser cuffs; he wore a proper white, starched shirt, a red bow tie and squeaky ox-blood shoes. He looked dressed for a business interview, and he was so brash and toplofty that Andrew wanted to ask him if that suit was left over from high-school graduation or if it belonged to Victor. Popping his gum loudly, he said. "Who's getting the twenty-one gun salute?" And when Adam asked him what he meant by that, he said, "Who's the blow-out for? The king of Canada? Or the Jewish postmaster general?"

He sneered at everything though Adam tried to shush him because of Andrew. He said, "Oh, stow it. It's a free country, ain't it?" He said he had never seen anything on land or sea to beat the paper moon and he would like to know just who she thought she was kidding, the kindergarten? Was *that* the band? That bunch of dried-up hardware salesmen-looking shrimps? He had bright tumid lips and stupid, glassy eyes, and the smell of his Juicy Fruit gum was sickening.

"How come the pool hall's here?" he asked, and immediately leaped back, sending the cue ball lolloping down the felt. "Oh, hey, Billy told me. Jesus, that gives me the creeps!" Serious for a moment, he looked around uneasily and started when Pegasus gave forth a muted whinny. But seeing Adam start to make a shot, his egotism overrode his uneasiness and he came back to the table to offer advice.

"When are you going back to your ship?" asked Andrew and Charles, intent on pocketing the red ball said, "One of these days if I feel like it."

"How *do* you feel?" Andrew watched him from the foot of the table and hoped he would miss the shot, but he did not. The ball rolled smoothly and surely into the pocket and Charles gave himself a warm handshake.

"How do I feel? Well, I'll tell you. Some days I feel like a million and some days I feel as good for nothing as one red cent. I'm up and then I'm down, if you follow my meaning."

"On the days you're 'up' do you do things with Victor? You know, like fishing? I mean do you dig clams and things like that?"

"Oh, sure," he said. "Yeah, I play nursemaid to the kid brother."

"Missed!" crowed Adam for Charles's ball had sailed past the pocket. The sailor snapped his fingers. "You joggled my elbow, dammit," he said. It was not true; Adam had not been anywhere near him. Andrew was delighted to find that besides being a braggart Charles was a liar and a bad loser.

"Well, on the days you're 'down,'" he pursued, "what do you do?"

"Lie around the house and wish I was dead."

"Do you really wish you were dead?"

"You betcha I do. And you would too if you felt like you had a buzz saw in your bread-basket." He stopped in the act of taking his stance for another shot and addressing Adam he mused, "You know about that wishing you were dead, it's a funny thing. Once or twice, I've gotten to feel so god-awful that if somebody came along and offered to shoot me, I swear I think I'd take them up on it. I never would go and do it myself because in my opinion people that commit suicide are cowards and I don't care what reasons they give or how they try to whitewash it. But if some one of these traveling nomad gypsies came up in the yard and offered to kill me I swear I think I'd say 'hop to it' if I was feeling the way I sometimes do."

The voice began again and Andrew lurched backward into a shadow.

"What's that?" said Charles Smithwick. "Is that a musical saw?"

Andrew's throat constricted suddenly. The air seemed shut off by a thin membrane.

"That's one of the twin girls singing," said Adam. "Miss Honor or Miss Harriet, I can't tell them apart unless they're standing side by side and then I know that one of them is on the east and the other is on the west."

Through the roars of his own voice, Andrew could hear Harriet, somewhere close by, singing James Partridge's favorite song, his favorite because his name was in it, "On the first day of Christmas, my true love brought to me a partridge in a pear tree."

"No kidding, I mean it," said Charles reverently. "It's like a lady I heard playing the musical saw in Tokyo."

Her voice diminished with distance and then it stopped as the orchestra began to play the first waltz. Charles Smithwick, reminded of Japan, began to talk in man-to-man innuendoes of geisha girls. Andrew left the barn, driven by the voice that clashed and clanged like a brass band and boomed like kettledrums, although he did not *care*. Charles was stuck on himself and rude and unlikeable, but Andrew did not *care*. Between clenched teeth, he said furiously to the voice, "Shut *up*. I say, *shut up*."

He felt no part of this festival gathering. He watched the dancers on the platform, circling and dipping in the waltz, his sisters' blue skirts whirling out as round and round the outer edges they danced with Raoul and James. Cousin Katharine was dancing with Mr. St.

Denis who looked like a porpoise and wore the kind of mess-jacket Mr. Barker's butler wore. If Andrew had to dance, he thought, that would be the very end. He moved down toward the pond where a group of older people were sitting, hoping that their conversation would be interesting enough to drown out the voice, but they were only telling each other, as if it were news, that the face of the man in the moon was accounted for by craters. He wondered contemptuously if anyone had told them about the Easter rabbit. There followed some dispute over the identity of the man in Katharine's artificial moon but it was agreed, at length, that it looked the most like Theodore Roosevelt.

"The Rough Rider," explained Miss Duff, who had also posited the original statement about the craters of the moon. "Invented the word *mollycoddle.*"

She was ignored though several people smiled politely at her. "The only things left out of this picture," said a dreamy-eyed old lady Andrew had never seen before, "are John Shipley and Maeve. Do they never come to Hawthorne now?"

"Sometimes they come to take the young fry back, that's all," said Miss Duff. "They're city people. City people don't know what they're missing by not getting on the land."

"Is Katharine quite well again?" asked the same woman. "We heard in some very roundabout way that she hadn't been well this summer."

The talk was diverted then to the fainting fit of yesterday and what had brought it on and Miss Duff went through the whole post-mortem again while Mr. Barker implored her not to go on, seeming to feel that she was somehow blackening the name of Hawthorne and of Congreve House.

"I don't see how she can stand to have the cat in the house after what happened," she concluded. "I'd be reminded of that mess every time I looked at a cat."

Mr. Barker said, "That's nonsense, Peg. One must rise above such things. Else would we not quail at the sight of the Atlantic because the *Lusitania* went down? At oil lamps because Mrs. O'Leary's cow kicked one over?"

"Always wanted to see Chicago," said Miss Duff. This message was followed immediately by another, "First dance over. Katharine coming this way, no more talk of you-know-what."

She spoke in telegrams but Mr. Barker, Cousin Katharine said, sounded frequently like a greeting card. He got up and said, "Hail to the mistress of ceremonies! Methought I had wandered into Arcadia."

"You all must go and dance," cried Cousin Katharine.

"Too old to dance," said Miss Duff, but Mr. St. Denis bullied her to her feet, laughing noisily, and in her surprise she permitted herself to be propelled across the lawn and up to the platform; she danced like a bundle of sticks.

"The very picture of carefree youth," said Mrs. Tyler peevishly. "I mean, of course, the Shipley girls and their swains."

"Oh, surely you don't think that youth is carefree,"

said the woman who missed John and Maeve. "At their age—perhaps a bit older, I was wretched. Growing up for me was like coming out of purdah. To be relieved at last of those awful jealousies! Those dashed hopes!"

Except for Mrs. Tyler who held out a little longer for the reality of joy she was sure lay within the girls' appearance of it, the elders on the terrace agreed that they would not for anything be under thirty-five again.

They complimented Cousin Katharine on the music and though they would not agree to dance, for all her urging, they would agree to eat and drink. In pairs and threes they drifted away from the terrace in the direction of the buffet and of Minerva's temple. When they had gone, Cousin Katharine loitered, picking up the petals of a shattered flower that lay on the stones. She came to the edge of the pond, so close to Andrew that he could have reached out from the shadow that hid him and touched her dress. He saw her toss the petals onto the black water and watch the swans move slowly toward them. She seemed, again, to be listening. He looked at her and then looked up at the stable where Charles Smithwick was standing to one side of the door to let two of the men guests by.

"Can you hear it, Cousin Katharine?" Andrew said softly.

She put both her hands over her heart but she turned her head very slowly and when she spoke, her voice was even. "Do you mean the pump, dear? Or do you mean the music?"

Picking up her skirts so that the grass would not stain

them, she went back to her party to mingle with her fifty happy guests, pretending that she had not heard the voice. Always pretending! He would have to go somewhere to drown it out by screaming; sometimes it stopped for a while if he ran fast. He ran now across the meadow and when he was deep in the pine-woods, near the Indian burying ground, he hallooed to himself, "Androoo! Yoo-hooooo! Androoooo Shiii-pley!"

It was the longest party Andrew had ever been to or ever heard of. The first people had come before six o'clock and at midnight they behaved as if they had just arrived. There was a steady parade of servants bringing fresh platters of food down from the kitchen and stacks of clean plates and pitchers of punch to fill up the bowls. In the summerhouse the grownups were drinking wine from George Congreve's cellar and champagne that Mr. Barker had brought. The orchestra, barely pausing between waltzes, went on like a perpetual motion machine without a sign of fatigue.

Down in the meadow, Andrew waited with Adam and Maddox and Charles for the signal to begin shooting off the fireworks. They stood at the four corners of the square they had sickled down that afternoon and all of their hands itched to get at the flares and skyrockets in their bright Chinese wrappings.

The road in front of Congreve House was crowded with the townspeople standing on the running boards of cars and even, in the case of children, sitting on the tops of them. "The rabble waits without," Andrew had heard Mr. Barker say to Cousin Katharine and Miss Duff had growled, "Typical. Always after something free gratis for nothing." But Cousin Katharine defended them, said she had let it be known that everyone was welcome and that, in fact, she would have been offended if they had not come.

She was flushed with high spirits and to three different people, he had heard her say, "I have never been happier in my whole life!" and Edmund St. Denis, quite drunk and trouty, remarked to no one in particular, "She doesn't look a day over sixteen. I say Katharine Congreve is nonpareil," and as if someone were about to deny it, he tentatively put up his hands for a fist-fight.

Everyone was there except Em Bugtown who was down with summer complaint. Billy Bartholomew was there on Carrie Nation who wore an old Western saddle with the pommel broken off; he sat in it as if he were sitting in a chair and tilting it back on two legs. "First we'll see her ladyship's pyrotechnical to-do and then every able-bodied man in the county will spend the rest of the mortal night in a bucket brigade putting out the forest fire," he declared in a voice of doom and his wife, a safe distance from him and from his horse, told him to dry up. Poor Hollis was there and so was his mother; she was very small and withered but she had her arm around her son as if he were an infant. They were near the gate and Andrew had seen how, when Billy's angry voice frightened Poor Hollis, his mother tugged him closer to her and he heard her say, "There, now, let me hear you ring your pretty bell." Jasper, the epileptic, was treading an erratic path up and down the road and Billy said, "He'll be going in circles, sure as shooting. Somebody'd better go get the paddywagon for the inevitable event of our fair city."

They had been waiting an eternity when Andrew saw someone coming up from the lower edge of the meadow. In a moment, as the figure came closer, he recognized Victor Smithwick's lope, a wasteful gait in which the arms and the head participated far more than necessary. He went directly to his brother without so much as nodding to Andrew. "Do you know what the five-letter word for 'legal excuse' was? Alibi!"

"I'll be damned," said Charles. "I didn't know alibi was a *legal* excuse. I thought it was just the opposite. I mean I thought an alibi was an *illegal* excuse."

"Hello, Victor," said Andrew.

Victor peered across at him. "Oh, hello, there, Shipshape. I didn't recognize you with your hat on," and the brothers burst into laughter.

"Did you shoot pool? You know where I mean?" Victor's voice shook with giggles. They held a conversation, Victor and Charles, showing off the security of their brotherhood as Honor and Harriet often did, laughing madly at allusions no one could understand except themselves, speaking in a kind of code so that a listener felt himself to be the butt of jokes, pilloried and hooted at. What had happened to Victor's admiration of Cousin Katharine that he would make fun of her tombstone, not kindly as he used to do of her horse-drawn whatsis but meanly, like Billy Bartholomew? What was the matter with him that he had spent this whole evening at home doing a crossword puzzle when he might have been here where everyone else was? Everyone including his brother? There was only one possible answer, that he could not bear the sight of Andrew.

"Anchors aweigh!" cried Charles, breaking off in the middle of an exposition on the differences between billiards and pool and those between real pool and the kind of pool that Adam played.

"We're off," said Maddox, for the signal had been given. The orchestra had stopped playing and through a megaphone, James Partridge, elected because both the twins were in love with him and were under the impression, therefore, that the party was in his honor, announced that the fireworks display was now to take place and that his "gracious hostess" had asked him to say that the dancing would continue when it was over.

Adam and Andrew set off the first two girandoles. They went in opposite directions, one toward the lake and one toward the river, bursting five times. From the dying shower of scarlet, there shot a higher spray of violet from which sprang blue, then green and the far, last opening cone was brilliant gold. When the last of the sparks had perished, applause came gustily from the road and the lawn and then everyone fell silent, waiting as if for the curtain to rise in the theater on the next act.

In the south sky they saw a blood-red waterfall and in the north a silver rain. An ephemeral sun, hissed into existence, hung in the summer firmament, blotting out the Pleiades. They saw serpents coiling upward to dissolve at the highest point of their path into radiant green stars. The tourbillion fires ascended, spiraling straight into the sky and beneath them, like a ballet chorus, the small pastilles spun themselves quickly to nothing. Two of the skyrockets were delinquent and ploughed through the timothy to fizzle out, but all the others, the blazing, blasting garnitures and galaxies, rose triumphantly to the sky.

The finale was to be five Catherine wheels, set in the clearing, four of them revolving simultaneously and the fifth coming a little later as the *premiere danseuse.* Andrew was watching a curving rain of gold falling, gently like snow and dying in the air above the pine trees by the lake when he heard Cousin Katharine's voice behind him. "I have come to superintend the final outburst," she was saying to Maddox. "It has been stupendous."

Respectful of the men, she stood aside and Andrew saw Victor move toward her and heard her say, "Victor Smithwick! You're a total stranger these days. Why didn't you come earlier to stand on your head? Your mother tells me you have got a whole book of crossword puzzles. I'll tell you one thing, 'slave' is always 'esne.' " Victor started to reply but she silenced him, "We'll talk about ers and ems another day. The Catherine wheels are going off."

Andrew and Maddox and Charles and Adam, at Victor's count of three, struck their matches to set off the fuses and leaped back into the tall grass. In a moment, Charles ran forward again to light the fifth. There was a flare too low and everyone at the same time realized that the Catherine wheel was a dud.

He heard Adam say, "Too bad to spoil the grand march," and then he saw fire illumine Charles's face as he knelt, still trying to make the wheel go off. His high white hair was on fire! Charles Smithwick's head was blazing like a torch! It had been bending over, the head with its shock of coarse hay-hair, and the gunpowder had set it on fire! It was a Catherine wheel that was killing Victor's brother, it was beloved Cousin Katharine's quick, ravishing wheel that would burn him up as it burned itself up, while in the stable her other one, motionless in stone, was as cool and as permanent as the sky. Andrew had been right, after all: her tombstone was a sign.

He stood where he was, assailed by the voice, bending with it and resisting it. He was a tree and this was the wind and he could not move a step forward because his obstinate roots were in the ground. He saw the other four of them, his cousin first, rush to pound and stamp Charles with their hands. The fire eddied like a thin, roiled liquid at their feet, burning the bodies of the used matches and the seepings from the rocket cases, and the sailor, turned into a candle, squawled.

"*Now* do you hear it, Cousin Katharine? You hear the voice inside my head, don't you?" roared Andrew above all the other cries from the startled bystanders in the road and on the lawn.

But she was busy. She was beating the sailor's head to save his life and her white skirt was on fire at the hem. He watched, fascinated, as it ate scallops into the filmy cloth.

"Katharine!" Mr. St. Denis came scrambling down the lawn and into the field and after him came a phalanx of men and behind them came Honor and Harriet. The gardener was the first of the men below to see that her skirt was burning and, leaving Charles, he seized her by the arm and pulled her down into the higher grass, but then, insane with terror and confusion, she evaded him and ran by herself in a widening circle, fanning the fire until it reached her waist; she screamed unceasingly.

A battalion of her guests closed in upon her, like dogs on a fox, and someone managed at last to fling her to the ground and roll her, as if she were inanimate, until the ravenous flames stopped eating her. For a minute, there was a vast, unnatural silence and in it, as soft as an insect sound, Andrew heard the tinkle of Poor Hollis's bell. He turned a little in the direction of that soft, affectionate noise and as he did so he saw Charles Smithwick standing where his rescuers had abandoned him for Cousin Katharine. He was holding his hands on top of his head but he was already beginning to relax from his surprise; in a moment, unhurt, he went to join the others.

✦

After they had taken her up to the house and after all had been done that could be done, it was Andrew that she asked to see. At the sight of her hideous black face and the intolerable, sickening suffering in her eyes, his misery pushed before it a tide of tears. Her arms were swathed in bandages and there was a turban of gauze wound round and round her head. But her voice, though it was weak and hesitant, was almost her own when she said, "I heard it, Andrew. I heard it when you heard it."

He swayed against the bedpost, sightless with his tears; it seemed a sacrilege to make these gulping, baby sounds but he could not stop. The pain must have driven her out of her head for when she spoke again she said, "I heard the Catherine wheel swinging low to get me . . . only it swung high, it swung, it swung, it swung . . ." She tried to move her hands to imitate the revolving lights, but the least motion was agony and she moaned. Across the bed from him the doctor nodded his head in some signal that Andrew could not understand at first and then he indicated that the boy should move closer to his cousin. Reluctantly, he edged along the bed until he was looking directly down on her dying, unrecognizable face.

"Is that boy all right? Charles Smithwick?"

Before Andrew was obliged to answer, the doctor said, "Don't trouble yourself on that score. His hair was singed, that's all. He's home asleep by now, resting up to go back to his ship next week."

Her voice grew slower and slower as if she were going to sleep and long pauses came after each word. "Andrew," she said, "do this for me. Take my big red diary and burn it. And forgive me my trespasses if you love me."

The last thing she said, she said to herself. "He was not worth it."

Oh, no, no, he had not been worth it! Victor Smithwick's friendship had not been worth the shortest moment of Cousin Katharine's love. When at last he found it and could use it again, his voice came out in a questioning plea, "Cousin Katharine? You're the only person I ever loved, ever, ever, ever!"

He could tell that she was trying to smile but her lips barely moved and her eyes seemed not to focus. The doctor, bringing the diary to Andrew, put it into his hands and told him to leave. He took the heavy book down to the kitchen where the fire was banked in the coal stove and leaf by leaf, without reading a word of them, he fed the pages to it, his big tears hissing and skittering away in minute bubbles on the iron lids.

The thin leaves curled and disintegrated into cracking char. The voice in Andrew was silenced now but in its place there was a swishing, sibilant swirl and the eyes in his mind saw four bright Catherine wheels perishing in glory. Wheels wheeled within the wheels and Cousin Katharine wheeled with them until the last page of her history was black ash. He put the stove lid back and after that he heard nothing but the sound of her faithful servants weeping.

Printed in the USA
CPSIA information can be obtained
at www.ICGtesting.com
LVHW091139150724
785511LV00005B/426